THE DEATH OF THE UNIVERSE

Hard Science Fiction

BRANDON Q. MORRIS

BRANDON Q.
MORRIS
HARD SCIENCE FICTION

Contents

The Death of the Universe

Cycle YA7.3, K2-288Bb

"Breakfast, John!"

Kepler lifted his head. This butler annoyed him.

"Johannes! How many times do I have to tell you?"

"Excuse me, Jo... hannes." The butler pronounced the name with an English 'J.' Incorrectly.

Kepler sighed. "Think of it as a 'Y.' Yohannes."

"Wy-o-hannes."

"Never mind. Just call me Kepler."

He got up from the seat in which he had spent the night in sleep mode. He imagined fresh coffee and croissants.

"Very well," said the butler, "I'll call you Kepler."

The butler bowed flawlessly, as far as Kepler could tell, and led him into the neighboring room. Where did Zhenyi ever get this antiquated model? He estimated its age to be at least two kilocycles. Old-world butlers had come into fashion again then for a short time. He had externalized his memories of that year on Terra, so he couldn't remember any other details. But this butler could be several mega-years old. Who knew these days? Kepler wondered whether he should ask him, but that seemed somehow improper. The butler was a machine, but he played his role so believably that Kepler felt a certain respect for him.

"Please excuse me, venerable Kepler," said the butler, "for

not meeting your language requirements. My vocalization memory is no longer as flexible since the last mega-flare from K2-288B."

"Why haven't you repaired it?"

"It wasn't a priority."

Of course, Kepler thought. *How long had Zhenyi been underway?* The butler hadn't had anything to do for a few cycles, until Kepler's arrival on K2-288Bb.

"Your breakfast," said the butler, pointing at the table.

The table looked like it was made of wood. It was an exceptional imitation. You could almost smell the scent of the hardwood. The room was bathed in atmospheric light. The walls glowed a warm yellow. On the far side a fire blazed in a fireplace. Kepler went around the table. The fire radiated heat. Flames licked around the logs. Such excellent work! Zhenyi had always had a penchant for luxury. These weren't algorithms at work. The hologram had to have been designed by a human. There were only two holographic masters capable of something like this.

Kepler knelt in front of the fireplace. The master must have left his signature behind somewhere. Maybe he'd recognize it. He stretched out his hand to lift up the uppermost log. "Ouch!" Kepler cried out in shock, pulling back his hand. Either the hologram had no safety circuit or... "Butler, what's wrong with this hologram?"

Kepler looked at the hand he had held in the flames. Two large blisters were forming on the skin, white in the middle and pink around the edges. He activated the pain sensors that had automatically switched themselves off, appreciating the pain. The wounds burned like hell. He concentrated his perception on them. This was life. It wasn't so easy to be in touch with it anymore.

"The fireplace is not a hologram," said the butler. "The wood comes from Terra."

Was that something resembling pride in his voice? If he hadn't misheard, then this butler couldn't be a level 1 AI, as prescribed for ordinary servants. That would fit with Zhenyi.

She liked pushing boundaries. But what had the butler just said? Kepler swung around to face the flames again.

Real wood was burning in this fireplace! Kepler couldn't believe it. Doubtless Zhenyi knew what she was doing. She was burning biomass, organically grown! There had been no forests on Terra for a long time now. The last tree had been incinerated when the sun had expanded into a red giant, mega-cycles ago. Or was the butler lying to him? Level 1 AIs couldn't lie, and neither could a level 2, if Zhenyi had upgraded him illegally.

Kepler stood up. He breathed deeply, then turned back to the table. Was the food also biologically generated? Nothing here would surprise him now.

"Please have a seat," said the butler, pulling out the only chair.

Kepler walked around the table and accepted the invitation. The butler pushed the chair in. The wood creaked as he sat down.

In front of him stood a large plate and a glass. It was a simple drinking glass, transparent, a narrow cylindrical shape holding a colorless liquid. He picked it up and took a sip. It contained cool, clear water with almost no taste. On the plate were mixed vegetables and half a roasted fowl, probably a chicken, but Kepler wasn't sure. In the last few kilocycles he had nourished himself bio-optimally. The chicken could also be a pigeon or a duck. He could no longer remember the actual size of these terrestrial animals. This knowledge was most likely among the memories he had externalized. It was the only way to stop the memory load over so many megacycles from gradually poisoning his brain.

He reached for the cutlery. A fork and knife lay on either side of his plate. He carefully sliced off a piece of the animal flesh, pushed it into his mouth, and closed his eyes. It was chicken, there was no mistaking it. He hadn't forgotten that flavor. He chewed thoroughly and swallowed, then opened his eyes again.

"This is chicken," he said.

"Very good, Johannes," answered the butler. "You're the first guest in a long time who's recognized it."

Johannes, again. Oh well, he couldn't help it. Kepler was amused in spite of himself at the way the butler praised him like one would praise a small child.

"Is it... from Terra?" he asked.

The butler smiled. "No. You know yourself that's not possible."

Kepler nodded. Terra had been dead for megacycles. The organic material of the chicken would long since have decomposed. Nanofabricators must have manufactured it here on K2-288Bb.

"But the wood?"

"That was a happy coincidence."

"Coincidence?"

"A ninety-niner had a cargo of wood. The ship had made a complete circuit of the Milky Way, but the wood had hardly aged. Zhenyi bought it."

That was a more or less believable explanation. At 99 percent of the speed of light, time passes very slowly. But this wood must have enormous value—and his friend was simply burning it?

"Why doesn't Zhenyi build something out of it?" he asked.

"I can't speak for my owner. But this table is built from the wood. I have instructions to ensure the utmost comfort of the guests."

"Thank you, I'm honored," said Kepler.

He wouldn't get any more than that out of the butler. Butler AIs were optimized to evade uncomfortable questions. Instead he concentrated on the food. The chicken was genuinely delicious. The fibers of the meat almost melted on his tongue. The skin was browned and had a pleasant aroma. The combination of vegetables perfectly enhanced the flavor with herbs and sweet notes.

Kepler pushed back the chair. His plate was empty.

"It was a real pleasure," he said.

The butler bowed, then passed him a moist napkin. Kepler wiped his mouth and hands with it.

"I didn't want to bother you while you were eating, but the ninety-niner that you've been expecting has announced it will be arriving tomorrow."

Finally an end to all the waiting, Kepler thought. He took a deep breath in, then slowly let it out. This body was perfect, but he had been getting tired of it, especially in the last few days. He didn't feel at home in it.

"Thank you very much for the meal," Kepler said with a faint bow. "I'll go to my room now."

"Of course. I'll wake you in plenty of time before the ship arrives."

Cycle YA7.4, K2-288Bb

Kepler opened the airlock hatch with a forceful shove. The moisture in the air froze immediately and rose as white vapor. He climbed up the short ladder. By the second step the skin on his hands was already discolored. First it turned white, then gray. Then the skin froze. No wonder, at an exterior temperature of minus 180 degrees. Kepler switched off the pain sensors. He didn't have time now for ancient biological sensitivities.

The surface was in perpetual twilight. The planet orbited in a captured rotation around its star, K2-288B, which hung like a dim lamp above him. The disk of the sun was big in the sky, but no longer gave off much heat. Many gigacycles ago this planet must have been in the habitable zone. But now it was dead, and so cold that even the atmosphere had frozen, spread across the surface in a blanket of snow and ice.

His lungs were stinging. He needed to be more careful! Kepler stopped breathing. It would be stupid if this body failed before he had reached the ship. He would wake up in another replacement body, but he would have wasted precious time. He had failed to really appreciate it for so long. Time. If you're immortal, it doesn't hold much meaning. But that had changed since he found out that the end was coming.

Kepler walked across the dry snow, which crunched under

his feet with each step. His body conducted the sound, which he otherwise wouldn't be able to sense with no atmosphere. The soles of his athletic shoes were thin. He put his right hand into his pants pocket. That wasn't a good idea, because the skin on the back of his hand came away, revealing the gleaming blue metal underneath. It always disgusted him to see his surrogate body in this state.

The ship came into view. It looked like a huge tin can. It had left its interstellar propulsion system in orbit. For safety reasons it had landed a short distance away from Zhenyi's home. Humans were infallible, but they hadn't managed to transfer this quality to the things they built. That was the dilemma of the times—and of past gigacycles. Kepler was frequently preoccupied with these kinds of thoughts. It was a problem that humans shared with the God from the Bible. No creation can be considered perfect if you don't acknowledge that you're too stupid to recognize perfection. This led to only two possible conclusions—either there was no God, or God was one of them. For some reason he preferred the second possibility.

"Hello Kepler," called the ship's AI in a female voice. "Nice of you to greet us personally."

Us? Had the AI split? That sometimes happened when ships were underway too long, but more commonly on ninety-fivers, where the onboard time went much slower. Interstellar transporters were usually equipped with at least a level 3 AI. They were much more adaptable, but also more sensitive.

"Well, say something, Kepler," the AI admonished him. "It's impolite not to reply."

"I was just thinking about the *us*."

"Come on, Kepler, don't you recognize us?"

He was confounded. He had never taken an interest in which AIs controlled which ships. He was only concerned with the cargo. *What's up with this AI?*

"Kepler, don't you remember the Convention at Sagittarius A* at all?"

A ship's AI asking him about the Convention, where it

had been decided to end the universe? Then it occurred to him. *Of course! There were two people who had set themselves up onboard a ninety-niner. The Curies! But were they also using it as a transporter?*

"Marie, Pierre, is that you?"

"Man, it took long enough for the penny to drop," said a male voice.

He recognized Pierre Curie's voice. He had given a speech at the Convention.

"Excuse me," said Kepler. "I hadn't expected you two to be carrying out transport orders."

"It just happened to work out that way. We wanted to speak with you anyway, and this way you pay us for the trip."

"I understand. It must have been an enormous coincidence, you seeing my order on HR8799b. Does Zhenyi know about your visit?"

"We've been following you for a while, Kepler. You change systems so often it's as though you're on the run. We haven't yet reached Zhenyi. She must be underway somewhere in the direction of the galactic center."

"What was it you wanted from me?" Kepler asked.

"We'll explain that over a good red wine. We always have a few bottles in our luggage."

"Agreed."

A hatch opened in the ship just above the ground. Kepler only noticed because vapor was pouring out of it, tinted red by the sun. He moved closer. Two rectangular objects emerged side by side. They were lying on a thin trestle that had many small, jointed legs. The objects walked their way over to him. The movement looked so absurd—like a cockroach in high heels—that he had to laugh, even though it wasn't the first time he'd seen it.

"That's right, laugh at us," said Marie Curie.

The objects walked past him. They seemed to know where the airlock was located. He moved quickly, which was sweaty work in this high gravity, caught up with them, and then walked beside the second one. Without the strange little legs, the things would look like Snow White coffins. They seemed to be made of glass or some other semi-transparent substance. But the material was so milky that the contents couldn't be made out. Which of the two caskets contained the cargo he had been awaiting for so long?

Next to the personnel airlock, another much bigger hatchway had opened. In the center of it was a platform. The two caskets positioned themselves on it and traveled downwards. Kepler climbed down the ladder into the airlock. He had to wait for it to fill with air. He scratched impatiently at the dead skin on his hand. He should leave it alone, but his excitement was building.

Finally, the door opened. He started breathing again. The air was so warm and moist it made him feel sick. Why hadn't he noticed that before? The butler beckoned him and led him into the living room. The table was no longer there. The two caskets stood in its place. He arrived just in time to see the left-hand casket open with a squelching sound.

A fit-looking, naked, male torso rose up out of it. The skin was almost without pigment. There was no hair on its head. The creature looked around, then pulled a tube out of its forearm and removed the sensors stuck to its chest. It cleared its throat, but didn't say anything. Then it supported itself on the edge of the casket and stood up, while the little, thin legs of the casket bent at the knees. Its lower half was also naked. There were no genitalia, or at least none that Kepler could make out. He had never seen the Curies like this. He blushed involuntarily. *A primitive reaction,* he thought. *But they could have said something if my presence bothered them.*

The creature climbed skillfully out of the casket. It was slightly smaller than he was. Kepler tried to compare his memories of Pierre Curie with the image of this naked being, but couldn't. *Hadn't the Curies participated at the Convention in another body?* He couldn't remember anymore.

"First of all we'll take a shower," said the Curies in Pierre's voice. "And you'll obviously need some time to unpack your consignment."

Kepler had to tear his eyes away from the naked form that Pierre and Marie Curie shared. It made absolute sense economically. They only needed to maintain one body. But he wouldn't have been able to do it. Another voice in your head—that must be horrible. The Curies had been a couple for gigacycles, but that time surely hadn't gone by without conflict. And if they had an argument neither would be able to leave the star system to temporarily escape the other!

The door closed loudly. He was alone. Kepler went and stood beside the second casket. A delicate moment lay ahead of him. How long had he been waiting now to be reunited? He had reached K2-228Bb at the speed of light. He always used a laser transfer when he traveled, even though it was very expensive. But that meant he had to wait longer at the destination, because only the data containing his consciousness could be moved at light speed, not his physical body.

He operated two old-fashioned levers mounted one on either side of the casket. Then the lid rose and he was looking himself in the face. It seemed wrong, as though left and right had been reversed, but that was how it should appear to him, as this wasn't a mirror image but the original. Before him lay Johannes Kepler, or to be precise, his flesh shell, cloned however many times from his own cells. He had chosen the name himself, ages ago. It was his body and therefore himself. Like most humans, he found it difficult to live outside his shell for long periods, as unsuitable as it may be for survival in space. And now he'd been stuck far too long in this robot.

"Butler, please prepare the transfer," he said.

"Of course, Johannes." He pronounced the 'J' correctly. Had he finally repaired his vocalizer?

A door opened to his left. The butler came in with a couple of cables. Kepler opened his shirt.

"We need to repair those hands," said the butler. "Did you go outside without a suit?"

Kepler nodded.

"You realize that it will mean your death after the transfer?"

"Of course. This isn't my first time."

"Good. I'm obliged to point that out to you. It's protocol."

The butler attached sensors to Kepler's chest and temples. Then he guided a cable into his ear. It tickled. The butler then connected the cables to the body in the casket. "That's it," he said. "You can start the transfer."

"Thank you," Kepler replied.

The butler left. Kepler deactivated the robot's skeletal system so it wouldn't collapse and be damaged. Then he summoned the body's vital signs into his field of vision. The body temperature was 32 degrees, the heart was beating once per minute. Going in would be uncomfortable. There was a reason the Curies preferred traveling in their shared body.

Kepler took a deep breath. Then his thoughts gave the command to begin.

It was cold. Freezing cold. He searched feverishly for curse words to distract him from the cold. Bloody cold. Fucking cold. His heart was hammering. He tried to call up his heart rate into his field of vision, but nothing happened. Then he remembered he was back in his body. If he wanted to see something his five senses weren't made for, he needed an external device. He rubbed his hands together. His muscles didn't obey at first, but gradually things improved. He touched his body. Where he couldn't feel anything he rubbed vigorously. He warmed himself up from the outside in. Maybe he should have raised the room temperature first. Then he noticed how warm it seemed to be. The butler must have thought of that himself.

The pain gradually became bearable. He pulled his legs in toward his body. The muscles tingled intensely, but obeyed his command. He gripped the edge of the casket with his arms and pulled himself upright. *Why is it so difficult?* Of course. This planet was significantly larger than the Earth. If he were to plan any long hikes he'd need an exoskeleton. But there was no reason to spend long periods on the surface.

He was sitting. The feeling was coming back into his skin. He had done it. He was back in his body. He was no longer all-powerful and invincible. In his body he was vulnerable. Without tools, he wouldn't survive long. It was as if this alone had given life new meaning.

Kepler knew the feeling well. He'd lost count. How many times had he already been through this? The body only ever lasted a few hundred cycles, then he had to move on. He was more or less addicted to traveling. Travel was his drug. It helped him to block out the current state of the world. The Curies were right. He was on the run. He was running from pure existence. Each of the maybe ten thousand humans that still existed solved this problem in their own way, because it was difficult to watch others die. It would be unbearable if the universe itself were to die a slow death.

Cycle YA7.5, K2-288Bb

"Do you know where this ash came from?"

The Curies were crouching in front of the fireplace in which the fire had burned two days ago, fingering the remnants with their left hand.

"No idea," he said.

"The ash is still slightly warm," said Pierre's voice.

"The butler turned up the heating in here yesterday, to make my transfer easier."

The Curies stood up. Their face smiled stiffly. "You're lying, but we'll leave it at that," said Marie.

Of course he was lying. He couldn't exactly admit that he had allowed the entropy to be increased in such a senseless way. The universe was about to die because it was losing energy and chaos was increasing, and he was burning essential resources to ash?

"No, I'm not lying. I didn't light a fire."

And that was true.

He cleared his throat. "I actually came here to be alone," he said.

"You're here to be alone?"

"Yes, that was the idea."

"That was the *idea?*"

That's what the Curies were like, their reputation

preceded them. He shouldn't let it get to him. Kepler crossed his arms and smiled. All was quiet for a while. Marie was obviously waiting for him to say something, so that she could parrot it. But he wasn't going to do her the favor, even though he wanted to know why they were here.

"You have to admit you could have gone almost anywhere. The Milky Way has 300 billion planets. We searched them all. Well, nearly all. Almost none of them present any threat of company. And yet you chose K2-288Bb in particular, where Wang Zhenyi has constructed a base. You must have realized that the risk of meeting her here was quite high.

"Yes, I was quite lucky she wasn't here."

"No, Johannes," said Pierre. "We inquired about you, even though it took a few megacycles. You have a shared past with Zhenyi. What did you want from her?"

"Nothing at all. I just wanted to be alone. She's rarely ever home."

"I don't find that very plausible," said Marie, "given the many alternatives where you would have been guaranteed solitude."

"I don't care," he said.

That wasn't true. He found the questions uncomfortable, and the Curies were intimidating him. But he couldn't let it show. He'd chosen his destination deliberately. He'd hoped to meet Zhenyi here. And he was still hoping she would arrive someday.

"We're wondering why you're not telling us the truth," said Pierre. "Why are you really here?"

"I already told you."

Marie sighed. "We're not getting anywhere with this," she said. "You don't need to be afraid of us. We're friends!"

Friends? He didn't know anyone who was 'friends' with the Curies. Gagarin and Armstrong, maybe. Or Hahn and Meitner, the other physicist couple. *How long has it been since I've seen those two?*

"I'm not afraid. I just don't know what you want from me," he said.

"We don't want anything from you at all," said Marie. "It's about Zhenyi. We heard she's undermining the Rescue Project."

"And what's that got to do with me?"

"You traveled a few hundred light-years to visit her?"

"Fine, I wanted to talk to her and couldn't be bothered waiting hundreds of cycles for a reply."

"You could have put yourself on ice like everyone else does," said Pierre.

Kepler shook his head. It had in fact become common practice to sleep for long periods while waiting for a reply. If your correspondent was 100 light-years away, you could still speak entirely normally with each other as long as you spent the 200 cycles of waiting time in a state of unconsciousness. But the time that was left to them was no longer endless. Since he had become aware of that fact, he had been trying to do without such methods. But in that case, he'd rather not bother with conducting conversations.

"That's not for me," he said. "I find it wasteful."

"Fine," said Pierre.

The Curies wandered up and down the room. It looked as though they were deep in thought. But in reality they were probably conversing with one another without him being able to hear them.

Kepler stood up, went over to the fireplace, and crouched in front of it. The ash really was warm. He ran his fingers through it. He really must take care of this body. If something happened to him like what had happened two days ago, there could be dire consequences in spite of the nanofabricators.

His index finger touched something cool, round. Kepler wanted to take it out and have a look, but he thought better of it. Maybe it wasn't a coincidence. The object must have been hidden in the wood. Had Zhenyi left him a message? He couldn't read it as long as the Curies were still here. He stood up again and wiped his ashy fingers on his pale cotton pants.

The butler would scold him when he saw the stains. The pants had only been made yesterday.

Kepler sat down on what was still the only chair. The butler had cleared away the caskets, but he'd not brought an extra chair—he didn't particularly like the Curies either, it seemed. Kepler couldn't blame him. They were brilliant scientists. They had developed the process that was supposed to lead to the rebooting of Sagittarius A* as a quasar. And now they were obsessing over such trivialities as his visit to Zhenyi? Something wasn't right.

"So, what did you want to talk to Zhenyi about?" asked Marie.

"About my experiences on HR8799b. You can't imagine how dense the asteroid belt is there," he said.

"You know that we can effect an extraction of your externalized memories?" asked Pierre.

"But for that to happen, I have to be under suspicion of having committed a crime. You need a warrant from the judge AI on Terra. The Earth is far away. The request alone would take a few kilocycles, the answer even longer."

"That's true," said Marie, and her tone sounded conciliatory. "That's why we wanted to speak with you personally. You have nothing to fear from us."

Kepler wasn't so sure about that. Marie articulated the last sentence in a way that made it sound like a threat. She was really good at this. If he had known something, would he have spilled it? But he didn't know anything!

"What even gives you the right to interrogate me like this? You're wasting your time," he said.

"I have that impression too," said Pierre. "We should go."

"Yes, we should."

When the couple spoke aloud to one another, they almost seemed insane. Was it really such a good idea to surrender yourself like that to someone else? Kepler was glad he'd never needed to—even with Zhenyi, whom he had truly loved a long time ago.

Cycle YA7.6, K2-288Bb

KEPLER BOWED, as was customary for goodbyes. The Curies climbed back into the casket. The butler had suggested providing them with a spacesuit, but they had declined. The lid closed and the oblong glass object made its way on its little legs back to their ship.

It had been a short visit. What would they be saying about him now? They obviously didn't believe him. He had come here to meet Zhenyi. He had hoped that maybe she still felt something for him, and that she'd lend him money. His constant fleeing was expensive. You couldn't get a ninety-niner for under a hundred thousand gigs, even for a short trip of a hundred light-years. One gig was a gigawatt year, itself quite an enormous amount of energy. But to accelerate a ship to near light speed—that consumed a lot of energy and was therefore expensive, even with the newest technology.

The technology itself hadn't developed in the last few megacycles. The remaining humans had other things to do. They were preoccupied with themselves—or with the Rescue Project. Every individual received, for their personal use, a fixed proportion of the total energy produced by humans. But even the number of Dyson spheres, which sucked energy from the stars, was no longer growing. And at the same time the stars were gradually being extinguished. The universe had grown old, and humanity had become stagnant.

Zhenyi had allegedly inherited huge energy reserves from her ancestors. She was rumored to be epically rich. No one knew where or how she was storing her provisions, and she hadn't even confided in him so far. Kepler guessed that it was stored somewhere as potential energy in a gravitational field, but she could also have stored it chemically. He imagined a solar system in which the planets consisted of frozen hydrogen.

He had queried her when they'd last met. He must have chosen the wrong moment. She was probably expecting a more romantic utterance. Women! No loan had been forthcoming. She had simply recommended that he forego the extravagance of traveling in his biological body. A modulated laser beam only needed a third of the power from a medium Dyson sphere. But Zhenyi didn't understand. He needed this body, not just any old surrogate. Even when he was always on the move he needed something to make him feel at home. How was that supposed to work with a robot body manufactured at the destination?

Just once he traveled as pure energy. He hadn't been able to get hold of a ninety-niner before the Convention in the orbit of Sagittarius A*. The human fleet had already been decimated by that time. He looked back on the experience with nothing but horror. The outposts were overflowing. Ten thousand visitors. The organizers probably wouldn't even be able to imagine such a massive number of people anymore. Today it was an incredible coincidence for three individuals to find themselves in the same place if you excluded multi-beings like the Curies.

Kepler had only vaguely followed the discussion itself. It had been about the Rescue Project. The arguments for it, presented by Pierre Curie, seemed to him conclusive, which was why he had voted in favor. However, a vocal minority had turned against it. He could only remember a few names. Einstein, Plato, and Scott were among them. He hadn't heard anything of them since, but that didn't mean anything. Of the roughly 10,000 present in orbit around the black hole, he had only heard again from three—the Curies and Zhenyi. And he hadn't even seen his friend in that time.

"Johannes? May I prepare you a meal?"

The butler pulled him out of his thoughts, but he didn't mind. "That would be very kind," he answered.

"What about an English breakfast?"

"I would prefer lunch. Zhenyi says you prepare an excellent steak."

"Well, I have to give the credit to the nanobots, but the recipe, as far as I know, is only available in my memory stores."

The butler lowered his head a little. This reemphasized his modesty. *Excellent work,* thought Kepler. The AI knew precisely how to influence humans. It was definitely higher than a level 1. But it didn't matter to him. In the past, he had developed and optimized artificial intelligence. If only he had optimized his own intelligence enough to have thought of ensuring the presence of his hostess before the journey began! But he had simply trusted that Zhenyi would be staying at her base.

The problem was that his provisions were now so exhausted, he would never be able to leave here again without a hefty credit. So, he'd have to wait for Zhenyi, for better or worse.

THE MOMENT the butler served the steak, Kepler stopped resenting having to stay there for an indefinite period. Even the aroma was indescribable! If he excluded the unlikely possibility that Zhenyi was running a cattle ranch, then it was genuinely masterful nano-programming. The tiny machines didn't just have to constitute the 'meat' from its raw materials, they also had to emit, at just the right moment, precisely the aroma his nose expected from the perfect steak. He couldn't even name it.

The butler stood next to him with pepper grinder raised. "May I sprinkle some Madagascar pepper over your steak?"

"Please."

The grinder was flourished in an elegant motion about twenty centimeters above the steak, so that a fine mist of pepper was strewn across it. Kepler was reminded a little of the ashes in the fireplace. They were the same color. The metal orb! Hopefully the butler hadn't disposed of the remnants! Kepler looked over at the fireplace. From here he couldn't tell whether it had been cleaned.

"Is something not right?" asked the butler.

"The steak is perfect."

"But?"

"I was just wondering about the fireplace."

"The fireplace? Should I light it? I'm afraid I must disappoint you. Ms. Wang clearly instructed me to light the fire only once, and under no circumstances to clean it."

"Didn't that make you wonder?"

Maybe that was the wrong question. If Zhenyi had left instructions specifically for him, then she must also have known he was coming! But how? She must have come across his transport order from HR8799b, like the Curies. So then why in the world had she not waited for him? Was she afraid, perhaps?

"Well, Johannes, it's not my place to wonder about my mistress's decisions," said the butler.

"I feel a bit like you're mocking me right now, at the risk of sounding impolite," he answered.

"What do you mean, Johannes?"

"You're at least a level 2 AI, but I'm guessing more like a level 4. But even as a level 2 you'd have no other choice than to wonder. It's part of the definition of that level, to evaluate every decision and every command."

"Well, that may be true, Johannes, in which case I obviously evaluated the instruction and found it to be correct. But I'm not obliged to give an account of it."

"That's true."

"Thank you, Johannes. I would like to draw your attention to the fact that your steak is getting cold."

"Thank you."

Kepler reached for the cutlery again. So, the orb was waiting for him in the ashes. He could take the time to enjoy a good meal. He should always make time for that. Who knew what tomorrow would bring?

HE LAY the cutlery aside and the butler cleared the table. Kepler leaned back. His stomach was uncomfortably full and under his shirt sweat was running down his back. He needed to get used to his biological body again. Life was much more intense in it, but that also had its downside.

"A cognac for the digestion?" asked the butler. "We have an exclusive selection."

It was an enticing offer. He wouldn't put it past Zhenyi to have somehow come into possession of a physically distilled cognac, maybe even one from Terra. No, that was impossible. No beverage kept that long.

"Thank you for the offer, but I'll decline," Kepler replied. "I'm very warm. Could you please lower the temperature by two degrees?"

The butler bowed his head. "Gladly."

Kepler stretched out his legs and let his arms hang at his sides. It was good he was alone. If Zhenyi were on the other side of the table he wouldn't want to let himself go like this. Solitude had its undeniable advantages. And the butler didn't sulk when he contradicted him. He wasn't sure why. If it was a level 4 AI, it had a complete emotional spectrum.

He should get up and have a look at the orb. But there would be time for that later. He closed his eyes and fell asleep.

Cycle YA7.7, K2-288Bb

KEPLER WOKE up bathed in sweat. He was lying in bed. The blanket had wrapped itself around his left leg. He kicked it away. He must have been having an intense dream. But hadn't he still been sitting at the table when he fell asleep? Kepler patted his body. He was clearly wearing pajamas. The butler must have brought him to bed and removed his clothes. Or removed his clothes and then brought him to bed. He imagined the elegantly attired butler throwing a naked man over his shoulder and carrying him to the bedroom. How had he managed it without waking him?

His body was probably to blame. The first few days after being reunited were always tiring. For his body, only a few weeks had gone by aboard the ninety-niner, but biological muscles resented not being used for that long. He had complained many times to the manufacturers of the cryostasis chambers, but there was no more progress there. The demand for the transport of biological bodies was minimal, because most humans were content with robot bodies. And every engineer and researcher who was still active was occupied with the Rescue Project.

"Light on," he said.

Nothing happened. That must have been one of Zhenyi's quirks. They actually suited each other well, as extravagant as their behavior was in other people's eyes. Kepler got up. There must be a light switch on the wall somewhere. Zhenyi was nuts. He felt his way across the room blindly. His shin bumped into an obstacle, presumably a chair. A sharp pain shot through his consciousness. He wanted to curse, but he couldn't think of anything suitable. Then his hands finally found the wall. He moved to the right. There was a door frame. He moved his hands up and finally found the switch.

The bedroom was quite small. It contained a bed, an antique-looking wardrobe, and a chair. His things were hung over the chair. They were perfectly folded. But why had the butler put him to bed in here and not in the guest room he usually used? Kepler looked down at himself. The pajamas fit perfectly. But they weren't the same ones he'd had on the previous night. Maybe those were in the laundry.

Kepler opened the door. The light in the corridor went on automatically. Left or right? He couldn't remember which way led to the living room. He chose right. After a few meters he went past a door. Was that the living room? He opened the door and had to steady himself on the frame. He had almost plunged into space. The universe spread out before him. But he could still breathe.

Kepler felt in front of him. There was no transparent wall, so it must have been a projection. He looked at the constellations. Up and to the right he could see the spiral of Andromeda. This reproduction must be ancient. The M31 galaxy, Andromeda, had long since merged with the Milky Way. What was Zhenyi's interest in the past?

He closed the door. A short way along, the corridor ended in another door. He opened it and entered the living room. The butler was sitting on a chair in front of the fireplace and looking into it, as though he was watching a fire. But he must have been in sleep mode.

Kepler cleared his throat. The butler turned to him and eyed him with raised eyebrows. He seemed to find the pajamas unsuitable. But Kepler couldn't do anything about that just now.

"Good morning, Johannes," said the butler, standing up. "Shall I prepare breakfast?"

"A steak would be good," he replied. "No, wait, I will have breakfast. English please."

A steak would just make him sleepy again. He shouldn't sleep through the day again, or his body would never get fit.

"Then I must ask for fifteen minutes of your patience," said the butler.

He bowed and left the living room through a door that Kepler hadn't even noticed before. Dammit, he'd wanted to ask the butler why he'd spent the night in Zhenyi's room. Kepler looked around. He wanted to pull up a chair, but then he noticed the fireplace. He knelt in front of it and rummaged in the ashes with his left hand. They were still warm. That was strange. The orb was still there. He pulled it out, shook it, and polished away the ashes.

He inspected the orb, turning it in his fingers. It gleamed metallically and radiated a certain amount of heat. Maybe it was the residual warmth of the ashes, or his own body heat? Metals conduct heat well. He closed his hand around the orb. It fit perfectly in his fist. Kepler closed his eyes. The orb seemed to be vibrating. He opened his hand and examined it. There was nothing there that could vibrate. It must have just been his own heartbeat.

What was the point of this? Was Zhenyi allowing herself a joke with him, leaving him a riddle to pass the time? That wasn't her style. If she had something to say, she said it. The orb was an encrypted message. But why didn't she just tell the butler what to convey to Kepler? If it was a level 4 AI, it could also lie if the wrong person questioned it. Zhenyi must not have trusted her own butler, there was no other explanation. But he obviously knew about the orb.

Kepler rubbed the orb in the hope that a genie would materialize, like in fairytales. But it didn't respond. He pictured Zhenyi. She was the most intelligent woman he'd ever met, and an excellent psychologist. It wasn't about the message, at least not primarily. It was about him.

"I've seen through you, Zhenyi!" he said, and was shocked to hear his own voice. His ex-girlfriend wanted to draw him in. If he occupied himself with the orb, he would develop an interest in whatever secret was concealed in it. And it must be a big, dangerous secret for Zhenyi to have gone to such lengths. She was probably trying to rescue the world again. Gigacycles ago she had already tried to prevent the collision of the Milky Way and Andromeda, because there was a small risk that the sun, along with Terra, would be flung out of the system. No one had taken her seriously, including himself. That had been the reason for their first separation. But in the end nothing happened. Terra was still orbiting in the backyard of the new, now elliptical galaxy.

If the butler had said, "Kepler, come and help my boss rescue the world," he would have politely declined. But now he that was holding this strange orb in his hand, he couldn't resist wanting to find out its meaning. Zhenyi was clever.

Kepler sat down at the table with the orb. He held it in both hands and tried to twist it open. But his fingers just slipped. He shook it, but there seemed to be nothing movable inside it. In any case, it wasn't hollow. He held it right up to his eyes. Maybe there was fine lettering on the surface? But there was nothing. The surface was polished smooth and perfectly round. Perhaps he should observe it under the microscope or cut it open? No, he could always destroy it later.

Kepler yawned. His body was ready to sleep again. He placed the orb on the wooden tabletop and lay his head down next to it. This made the orb look bigger. The tabletop was pleasantly cool. He let go of the orb and it rolled toward him, until it bumped against his nose. He sat back upright and held the orb still.

"The table is a bit uneven," he said.

No answer. But he was used to being alone, after all. That came from never having any company when traveling. The door on the back wall opened. It was the butler. Who else?

Kepler was surprised by the fact that he was surprised. He really must pay more attention to his mental health.

The butler set the breakfast down on the table. The plate was covered, but it smelled tantalizingly of fried eggs and toast. The butler brought a large, white cup and poured tea into it. Kepler observed the surface of the liquid. It appeared to be level.

Wait a minute. He placed the orb on the table again, on the same spot. It rolled in the same direction as before. "Is it possible this table is uneven?" he asked, although the tea had already given him the answer.

"Not at all, no. The table was absolutely precisely manufactured," said the butler.

"Then why is the ball rolling?" He placed it on the table again, and again it moved toward him.

"Let's see," said the butler. He took a napkin from the table, folded it several times and pushed it under the table leg at the corner the orb had rolled toward. "Try it now."

Kepler placed the orb on the table. It rolled toward him, at just the same speed as before.

"That's baffling," said the butler.

"I think so too."

Kepler stood up and lifted the table with his right hand by the corner under which the butler had put the napkin. Now the tabletop was obviously uneven. The tea slopped over the side of the cup. A pool formed in the saucer. With the other hand he placed the orb back on the table. It rolled toward him. Uphill.

He held the orb and let the table drop. A loud noise. More tea spilled over.

"That was unnecessary," said the butler.

Kepler sat down. He held the orb in front of his face and observed it from all angles. "What kind of magician's trick is this?" he asked. "Is there a magnet in the table?"

"Of course not," replied the butler. "What would be the point of that?"

"To make me... I don't know."

Kepler put the orb back on the table and pulled the plate over to it. The orb rolled. It rolled toward the edge of the plate. Without thinking, he held his hand in front of it, but shortly before it reached the plate the orb changed direction. It rolled in a curve toward the center of the table, then changed direction again and returned in a double zig-zag.

He pushed the plate to the side again. He'd lost his appetite. "Can you please clear this away?" he asked.

"As you wish."

Kepler picked up the orb. It looked the same as before. What was it trying to tell him? He put it back down on the table. It began to move diagonally toward the corner.

Of course! Why hadn't he thought of it? The orb was writing letters on the table! That was how it conveyed messages! He simply had to allow it to follow its course uninterrupted.

"Can you record a video of the top of the table?"

"No problem," said the butler.

Kepler positioned himself where he could better observe the orb. It really was writing letters. He recognized an F, an O, and an L. At times he had to stop it, because he hadn't understood the letter. The orb couldn't stop itself. It was writing in an endless sequence. The text began cryptically, and ended the same way.

"Follow me!" he read. "I have found something that will completely change our lives. Please help me! Do you remember that night in the Vega System? Call the butler by his name, which I told you at the time, then he'll help you. I'm flying ahead. Maybe I can prevent a catastrophe. The coordinates are..."

Phew. Yes, he remembered the night Zhenyi was talking about, even though it was a few gigacycles ago. They had met to observe the helium flash of the Vega. The universe didn't offer attractions like that very often, especially not so close to Terra, which was still green at the time—a vast nature reserve.

They had set themselves up on one of the moons of the

single, Neptune-sized planet. First they spent days and nights in bed. Then they waited in cryostasis for the big event. The butler had awakened them. Immediately after rising they had fallen all over each other again, still naked. And then Zhenyi had sent the butler away—calling him by his first name.

But Kepler could no longer remember the name. He remembered as though it was yesterday the way he had caressed her entire body. But the name of the butler? Who would have taken any notice of that? Then he remembered Zhenyi had told him breathlessly that he should pay attention to the name. It was vital to her because she... because she... He tried desperately to recall, but his memory failed him. Had he maybe externalized it on Terra? It would take centuries to request a backup.

Strangely, he wasn't unhappy about this. It meant the buck didn't stop with him. If he couldn't remember the butler's first name, he couldn't follow Zhenyi. She would manage alone. She had always managed. He would simply stay here until she returned. He was already looking forward to hearing stories of her adventures. Kepler leaned back. Now for a cognac. That would be great.

Puppy. The butler was called Puppy, like Zhenyi's first dog. At the time, Kepler had almost died laughing over the name, and his girlfriend had been a bit offended. Shit. Why did he have to go and remember the name now? He looked at the butler. If he didn't know better, he would have taken him to be an elegant Englishman of about 50 years old. The name really didn't fit.

He could simply forget it again. But the more he tried to suppress it, the more it imprinted itself.

"Puppy, would you please bring me a cognac?"

There, he'd said it. The butler stiffened briefly. Kepler watched him. If this were a bad film, his eyes would suddenly light up red, but nothing of the kind happened. Maybe he hadn't heard?

"Would you like a particular sort?" asked the butler.

"No, Puppy."

He'd said it again! What was he thinking? If the butler hadn't heard him the first time, then he certainly had now. But the butler just nodded. He left the room, returned with a half-filled cognac snifter, and handed it to him. Kepler held it under his nose and swirled the glass. All he could smell was the alcohol vapor. He really didn't know much about cognac.

"I recommend we take the Mona Lisa to the next Dyson relay and then beam ourselves to the destination," said the butler.

Kepler spluttered into the tulip-shaped glass. A drop of cognac splashed into his eye. That stuff burned, dammit!

His peace and quiet had come to an end. The butler had correctly understood him. It would be callous now, not to help Zhenyi. That didn't fit with his self-image. He, Kepler, was not a cruel person. He was a little self-indulgent, but he always helped a friend in need, especially Zhenyi. However, Puppy's suggestion was not acceptable.

"I can't leave my body again so soon," said Kepler. "The gray matter won't withstand so many transfers in such a short time. And no, I won't give it up. No one can ask me to do that."

"But we'll lose a lot of time," said the butler, "if we have to take your mortal husk into account."

"What's the Mona Lisa? A ninety-fiver? Or even a ninety-sevener?"

He didn't know anyone who could afford a private ninety-sevener. Although that didn't mean much, because he didn't know many people.

"The Mona Lisa is a ninety-niner, of course," said the butler.

Aha! "Then maybe we won't lose so much time after all. We just need to wait for the loading cycle of the Dyson sphere. What is the actual destination?" asked Kepler.

"Come, we'll take a closer look."

Puppy led him by the arm. They entered the corridor that led to Zhenyi's bedroom. The butler opened the door Kepler had already tried that morning.

"Our star chart," said the butler.

"I know."

The butler looked at him with raised eyebrows. Then he took a few steps into the room.

Kepler held himself steady on the door frame. It still looked as though open space was spread out in front of him. If he took another step, he'd plunge into the depths.

"Well, come on," said the butler.

Kepler bravely stepped forward. The floor held. The image of the universe changed around him. Apparently the butler was running it in fast-forward. Andromeda approached the Milky Way, in the center of which grew an immense black hole, and then it grew dark around them, as more and more stars were extinguished.

"Current time," the butler commented. "I'll zoom in."

They flew toward the stars. Star clusters and gas clouds raced toward them, enshrouded them, then were left behind. It was a rapid journey that ended in nothing.

"These are the coordinates that Zhenyi transmitted?" asked Kepler.

"Yes."

"No possibility of an error?"

"No. There's nothing here."

"Then we'll have to abandon the journey," said Kepler, and turned to leave the room.

The butler held onto him. "No, there's something here," he said. "We just can't see it. But the data from the movement of the stars in this region demonstrates it clearly."

"I can't see anything," said Kepler. But he already knew what the butler meant. The stars in the region were precisely measured. They must be moving in a particular, calculable way.

"Wait, you'll see it in a moment."

The stars divided. The butler had obviously started a simulation over the top of reality. One set of stars moved in the direction dictated by reality. The others moved according to the calculation. The difference was obvious.

"An M-class system is missing from the data," said the butler. "The central star must have about a 0.2 solar mass, by my calculations."

So, a red dwarf. Almost all of the stars in the Milky Way were red dwarfs. All the more massive and brighter exemplars had long since burnt out and become white dwarfs.

"An unknown system? That's hard to believe," said Kepler.

Humanity had already measured and recorded all the stars of the galaxy gigacycles ago. And new stars had long since stopped being born.

"I think so too," said the butler. "Someone must have deleted this system from the database."

"But who would be in a position to do that? There must be a few billion copies."

"All databases are regularly synchronized with Terra. So the tampering must have happened there."

"Who's capable of something like that?"

"A system programmer," said the butler.

Kepler held his breath. It was impossible. It would mean... No, he couldn't believe that.

"How many of them are left?" he asked.

"Seven."

"We have to find out which of them have been on Terra."

"That's difficult," said the butler, "because we don't know the timing of the change. It could have been up to 200 kilocycles ago. Every system programmer has probably been to Terra in that time."

"Then we have to find the answer another way," said Kepler.

"Do you have a suggestion?"

"Yes. We'll look for the motive. Why was the system deleted? To find that out, we'll have to go there."

"Thank you, Johannes. I think that was what Zhenyi wanted you to do."

Cycle YA7.8, K2-288Bb

THE SPACESUIT PUPPY had provided fit him perfectly. He almost felt better in it than in his birthday suit, as the spacesuit enhanced all his movements with artificial muscles. The fact that gravity on K2-288Bb was significantly higher than on Terra wasn't even noticeable.

But there was also a huge disadvantage. He couldn't scratch his nose, and right now he had the urgent need to do so. The glass visor was in front of his face. He reached for the lock to open it one more time, but the butler warned against it.

"The airlock will decompress in fifteen seconds."

His hand jerked back. He was standing alone in the airlock. The butler would follow him after having set the base to standby mode. Kepler scratched between his legs. The suit was thin enough there. He was relieved. It was almost as good as being able to scratch his nose. A flashing red light signaled the air extraction. It was serious now. The light turned off, the airlock cover opened, and it became a little brighter in the chamber.

Kepler climbed up the ladder. Everything was so easy. He reached the surface of the planet and ran around the airlock a few times. He didn't even get winded. He could feel the ground under his soles, but he couldn't feel the cold snow of the frozen atmosphere. The heat insulation was perfect. He stepped on a stone. Kepler bent over, picked it up, and scraped the snow off it. The stone looked black in the red light of the sun. He reached back and flung the stone in a high arc into the sky. It disappeared immediately in the twilight.

"Show the way," he said.

An arrow appeared in his visor. The landing module was about a kilometer from the airlock. Kepler bent his arms and jogged the distance. He didn't know when he would next have an opportunity to run under an open sky. The destination was 3,500 light-years away. On board the ninety-niner the time would go much more quickly, but for the rest of the universe he would disappear for 3,500 cycles. Oh well, what did he care about the rest?

Kepler stood still and lifted his arm. "Time," he said.

On his forearm appeared a hologram of an ancient Rolex. The second hand crept across the face. That was actual time. In ancient human history, that was the only time people knew. Kepler followed the second hand with his eyes. It must have been a horrible feeling back then. Every tick of the clock brought humans a step closer to their deaths, and it was a big step. Eighty cycles between birth and passing, a total of 2.5 billion steps. People must have been terribly stressed.

But he had time. His life would end in a few gigacycles, together with the universe. What were 3,500 cycles compared to that?

"Johannes, where are you? I'm already on the ship."

The butler must have overtaken him without his noticing. Kepler sighed. He had to hurry in actual time. Regardless of the long stretches of time, if he wanted to meet Zhenyi, they had to be at the same place at the same second. That seemed to him like a relic from ancient human history. For a long time, scientists had tried to find a way to change this, but the principle appeared to have shaped this universe. The speed of light was immutable and couldn't be surpassed.

Under the arrow on the display was a distance indicator.

Kepler squinted to make it out. The low air pressure in his suit obviously influenced his eyes' ability to focus. That wouldn't happen in an artificial body. It was another 300 meters.

"I'll be right there," he said, and started walking.

THE SHIP WAS HUGE, and it was beautiful. Kepler was looking at a ninety-niner up close for the first time. His body had often traveled on one, but until now his consciousness had always been transferred via laser link. He leaned on the console in front of his seat and savored the view.

In front of him and off to one side shimmered the giant sphere of the dark matter plant. It glowed red. It was almost as though it was glowing from the inside, but that must have been the light of the central star. The sphere looked like a massive version of the orb that Zhenyi had hidden in the wood for him. Of course! That must have been a hint that he had overlooked.

Then there were the enormous sails, four of them. They protruded into space above, below, and to the sides. At the moment they were half furled, or so it seemed. The light from the red dwarf at the center of the system wasn't able to move them. The number of systems in which a ship could simply travel under sail had continued to decline in the last few gigacycles. That was another reason traveling had become so expensive. At some point all ships would have to furl their sails. They would no longer proudly traverse the darkest recesses of the universe, but would have to rely solely on the power of their conventional propulsion systems.

They were steering toward the energy sphere. There was a scaffold there that carried the loading modules. They were tiny compared to the rest of the ship.

"We could still get into the laser link," said the butler. "We have a consciousness extractor onboard."

"No, thank you. We're more flexible with the ship. There might not even be a laser receiver in the vanished system."

"I consider that unlikely. To delete a system from the database is one thing, but to remove such a huge structure without anyone noticing..."

"But how do we even communicate with a system that doesn't exist?"

"We have the coordinates. That's enough. I'm only thinking of you, Johannes. The acceleration is murderous. You've never flown in your body while conscious."

"Then I'll just have to endure it."

"Propulsion ignition in three minutes," the butler announced.

Kepler swam naked in a thick, jelly-like mass. The butler claimed there was nothing better to protect him from the acceleration, so he had cheerfully gotten into the tub. There was a breathing mask over his face. He could only see patches of color, but he heard the butler's voice and the replies from the ship's AI.

"There's still time for a consciousness extraction," said the butler.

"I'll cope."

"I'm afraid you don't know what you're getting yourself into."

Hopefully the butler was wrong! But he had to go through with it.

"You can increase the pain relief level with a vocal command."

"I know."

Millions of nanomachines swam in the jelly, monitoring his vital functions and supplying pain killers to his bloodstream as needed. That was at least somewhat reassuring. The temperature of the jelly was exactly 36.7 degrees. In spite of this Kepler felt cold, and he was afraid. But he would never admit it.

"It's time," said the butler.

A fist gripped him and tried to crush his body. Was that normal? He closed his eyes, but it didn't get any darker. A red curtain appeared before his eyes. Behind it drums were beating, two times a second or faster. That must be his heart! He needed to calm himself. Kepler tried to breathe deeply, but his chest wouldn't expand. The jelly was suddenly as hard as concrete. He had made a mistake. He should have listened to the butler.

But then the pressure let up again. The red curtain opened. Behind his eyelids he saw only darkness. He opened his eyes.

"What's wrong?" he asked.

"We need to refuel. You can come out of there if you like."

Kepler reached down to push himself upwards in the tub until his face emerged from the jelly. He was looking directly at a huge window. The image was a little blurred. There must still be some jelly on the glass of the breathing mask.

"Great view, isn't it?"

Above them floated the K2-288B star. From here it looked more orange than red. Protuberances sailed slowly across its surface. It was a grand vision. Objectively, the red dwarf might be geriatric, but from this vantage point it appeared powerful and dangerous. Despite everything, it was still a star whose interior was so hot that it melted atoms into new elements. Kepler couldn't remember ever having seen a star so close up.

One of the sails moved into his field of view. Like the ship itself, it was studded with solar cells that converted the star's radiating energy into electrical energy.

"How long will we stay in orbit?" asked Kepler.

"One day. The energy extraction is very inefficient here. The next Dyson sphere is ten light-years away. We'll have to refuel there for the big jump."

Great. That meant that he would be tortured four more times, each time they accelerated and again when they braked. Maybe he should extract his consciousness after all. But he had already decided to arrive and greet Wang Zhenyi in one piece.

Cycle YC3.4, IRS 13 E3N

"START," said Gropius, and then he activated the propulsion unit.

Everything now depended on how precise his simulations were. He slowed his system clock, his internal sense of time, so that time went ten times faster for him. The asteroid set itself in motion. Walter Gropius, the sky architect, inspected its course. It looked good. The asteroid had the necessary momentum. He uncoupled the propulsion system. Then Gropius transferred himself with a laser pulse to the asteroid's destination, a terrestrial planet roughly the size of Terra.

The asteroid wouldn't collide with it for 20 cycles, so Gropius slowed his system clock even further. The equivalent of every Terra year was now only half a minute for him. The planet wasn't to be pitied. Like almost all Milky Way planets, it had never harbored life.

Then it was time. The asteroid impacted. It was half the size of the terrestrial moon. The impact was catastrophic. The orbital station where Gropius was based was hit by chunks of the planet's crust. To be safe, the architect transferred his consciousness to the gas giant orbiting further out. The asteroid didn't just tear a chunk out of the planet, it also altered its course. The planet was shunted toward the center of the system, where it disrupted the rotation of another planet. This made room farther out and caused a resonance in the huge gas planet, which in turn had enough mass to influence the sun.

Gropius didn't need much. Just a small movement of the star in the right direction, that was what this maneuver was supposed to trigger. He made time run a little faster. The star in the center of the planetary system, E3N, was not alone. It moved in a tight group, called IRS 13, with at least a dozen other stars, around a medium-sized black hole. The fact that E3N was dancing to a different tune wasn't without influence on its twelve companions. They altered their orbits around the black hole. But E3N was only a means to an end. The architect's main target was E3C. This star was the closest to the black hole and, just as his simulations had demonstrated, its orbit was now oscillating intensely enough to move it dangerously close. Gropius was excited. The trap would soon snap shut. If E3C went beyond the minimum safe distance, its time would be up.

But then E2 accelerated. This unremarkable star suddenly lurched forward, as though it was trying to escape from the others. Gropius hadn't predicted this. Apparently, E2 was not merely filling the hole left by E3C, but was also not slowing down. A gap opened up in the constellation of the thirteen stars, a gravitational trough, and then what had to happen happened—E3C was pulled back in by its friends and thus rescued from the black hole. He'd failed. His simulation hadn't taken all of the factors into account.

Gropius was annoyed. That was what transpired when they didn't allow him enough time. It wasn't easy to feed a black hole. Although they supposedly swallowed everything and never missed anything, it was far from child's play to bring an object so close to a black hole that it disappeared into it. Especially when the object was a star.

He played the simulation through once more. This was the fifth failed attempt. He wasn't so sure now that it had been a good idea to select IRS 13 as the playground for the tests. *A couple of stars orbiting around a medium-sized black hole would* *have been simple enough,* he thought. But even if he found a solution, he couldn't be sure it could be transferred successfully to Sagittarius A*. The huge black hole in the center of the Milky Way, swollen to three times its size since the collision with Andromeda, was the actual target.

Gropius was proud to be a part of it. The Rescue Project would be humanity's magnum opus—and probably its last-ever great achievement. If it was successful, it would guarantee their survival for one or two gigacycles. Energy would again be available in excess. But for that to happen, they had to turn the core of the galaxy into an AGN—an active galactic nucleus—also known as a quasar. Quasars were celestial objects so immensely bright they were still recognizable from a distance of billions of light-years. A gigantic Dyson sphere constructed around a quasar, absorbing all the energy it radiated into space, would fulfill all of humanity's energy requirements on its own. But all known quasars were too far away. So to create one, they had to transform the black hole at the center of the Milky Way itself.

Gropius's experiments on IRS 13 were supposed to be the preparation for this enormous project—at least the first part of it. He was supposed to awaken the black hole, Sagittarius A*. To awaken a black hole and turn it into an active galactic nucleus, you had to feed it with matter from as many stars as possible. The Milky Way had 200 billion stars. A large number of those were now white and red dwarfs, but that didn't matter—there was definitely enough matter there to feed it. However, no one knew exactly how much nourishment Sagittarius A* needed, and at what point in time, to transform into a quasar. So they had to be able to send as many stars as possible into it in a short space of time.

Several sky architects had developed plans for this. But Gropius's ideas had met with the agreement of the Convention, and now he knew why. No one had to make any sacrifices on his account. He followed the butterfly principle—small causes were supposed to trigger significant effects. But he had just seen once more how complicated it was to plan these effects in advance with any precision. Maybe they should have sent ten thousand white dwarfs into the black hole, equipped with propulsion units, like his competitor Le Corbusier had suggested. But humanity would have had to invest a considerable proportion of its energy stocks into this concept.

Gropius transferred himself back to the propulsion unit that had thrown the asteroid off course. He would have to consider a more direct way of separating the stars of this little group. He sped up his system clock. Time passed slowly again, like in ancient times. That would allow him enough time to be able to thoroughly contemplate the problem.

Cycle YC3.7, Dyson Sphere 3Z

THE JOURNEY WAS A GREAT ADVENTURE. Kepler had stopped being annoyed that he'd accepted it. On all his previous interstellar flights he hadn't experienced much of the journey itself. After all, his consciousness had been divided into its informational bits and traveled along a modulated laser beam, while his body had slept soullessly. Now he was experiencing what it really meant to travel in space—endless boredom, interrupted by occasional stops at refueling stations.

Up to this point Kepler had been particularly savoring the boredom. For him it meant leisure, and he actually enjoyed it. He had swayed around in his jelly, now and then eating something that was poured into his mouth through a hose, had a look into the nothingness before him, and then gone back to sleep, protected by the wobbly mass.

He hadn't left his sleeping pit, and the pain he'd experienced at the start had significantly faded. The fact that time went slowly in a ninety-niner, at 99 percent of the speed of light, was only one side of the coin. The other was that, with him on board, the ship couldn't accelerate hard continuously. That meant it took longer to reach top speed. Actually, the flight had so far consisted almost entirely of accelerating and braking, and both were very uncomfortable.

Now they had a long phase of braking behind them. The

butler declared that they had reached Dyson Sphere 3Z, their first and only stop-over.

Kepler searched the sky, but couldn't see anything. "Are you sure we're in the right place?" he asked.

"Yes, Johannes, we are."

Kepler shrugged his shoulders. In this system, there were no planets whose movement patterns could give away the position of a central star. He was an astronomer. He was interested in natural celestial phenomena, not artificial objects. He had always shied away from sky architecture as a subject, not because it seemed less worthwhile to him, but because the architects interfered with the natural order of the universe. They shifted planets into the habitable zones to increase the yield of the plantations. They regulated the magnetic pulses of the stars to protect human colonies from deadly flares. And they constructed gigantic spheres around especially bright celestial fires, using the energy sucked out of them to allow human interstellar travel to continue, independent of the galactic tides.

Was that really necessary? Didn't everything already move quickly enough on its own? The sun wandered through the Milky Way at 220 kilometers per second. If you had enough time and patience, you could quite easily reach every backyard of the Milky Way in 240 megacycles.

Kepler had always assumed that the universe would one day avenge itself for this hubris. But that hadn't happened. His own thoughts had turned out to be hubris. The universe didn't give a damn about humanity. It was born, it grew, and it would die. Nothing else counted. That had made him slightly more sympathetic toward the architects.

How were you supposed to recognize a Dyson sphere? Even though he'd never learned to, he should be able to extrapolate using his knowledge of physics. Obviously it must be visible in infrared, with the spectrum of a blackbody, at least if it wasn't defective. This Dyson sphere was obviously not fully functional, or he would have already detected it in the optical range, because its protuberances would be visible. He switched the screen to infrared.

And there it was. Right in front of them hovered a perfect sphere whose pitch-black surface glowed in infrared. He had to hand it to the architects. Erecting such a construction was a masterwork and absolutely worthy of a human. Because it was, like a human, the perfect parasite. The sphere absorbed all the energy emitted by the star. Part of it was given off in infrared, which was unavoidable due to the laws of physics. But the majority was usable. Usually, automated factories distributed across the outer surface of the sphere concentrated the energy by producing dark matter, which could then be used in the ball drives of the refueling spaceships. Or they stored it to drive the massive laser guideway, which he had always used up to now to fire himself across the universe.

"How long will we stay here?" asked Kepler.

"The refueling will take a day at the most," replied the butler. "We'll fly a little closer so the barges can reach us more easily."

Kepler wished he could have gone outside. He would surely have a better view from the surface of the spaceship. But his biological body was a hindrance. He would have to put on a spacesuit, climb outside, and then search for the best spot on the kilometer-long ship. No thanks, he'd rather stay in his jelly bath. He could always use the screen above him to zoom in and out at his leisure and have all the ship's camera feeds displayed there.

It took a while for anything to happen. Then a flashing white light appeared above the shell of the sphere. That must have been one of the barges the butler had mentioned. Kepler brought the loading ship optically closer. It looked like a miniature version of the ninety-niner. The barge consisted of a sphere containing dark matter, and two sails. But the sails were located on the front, not the back. They were full. Clearly a pulse from the sphere was hitting them. It was as though someone were making a piece of paper remain aloft by repeatedly blowing on its underside, timing the puffs to hit at just the right moments. That meant the barge didn't need its own propulsion. It was probably also inefficient, because dark matter was heavy.

For the propulsion of spacecraft, dark matter had a big advantage. You could pile it up in great mountains if you wanted, without anything happening. Ordinary matter, if there was too much of it in a narrowly-defined space, would form a black hole and disintegrate. Dark matter, on the other hand, didn't cause such problems. Concentrated in the belly of the spaceship, its sheer mass actually bent space so that the ship rolled down a slope, so to speak. It was propulsion without radiation or heat. But of course there was no such thing as perpetual motion. The dark matter was exhausted over time and had to be replaced at refueling stations like this one.

The first barge approached the ninety-niner. Kepler had never before observed the refueling process. *Did a hatch simply open in the spaceship? It couldn't be that simple,* thought Kepler. He remembered the great disadvantage of dark matter—it didn't like to be captured. In principle, it only responded to gravity. But gravity always attracts. To effectively enclose something, you needed a repulsive force. Humans had been trying for a long time to use dark energy for that, but they hadn't succeeded. To this day, no one understood the principle of dark energy. Scientists were still arguing about whether it was even a real phenomenon, or simply a fundamental property of the cosmos. If some people were small and fat, while others were tall and thin, why shouldn't the cosmos simply have this or that amount of dark energy?

On the outer shell of the ball drive a hatch opened that was about twice the size of the barge. It simply slid to the side. The barge responded by opening its transport sphere half-way. What would happen next? Was it so simple after all? He should have paid more attention to architecture.

"The loading procedure looks so simple," said Kepler.

This didn't betray the fact that he didn't understand the

principle behind it, but there was a chance that the butler would explain it.

"I find it fascinating," said the butler. "So complicated, and yet so simple."

That wasn't what he was hoping to hear. But then he figured it out for himself. It was child's play. The dark matter followed the gradient. It flowed to where there was already significant mass. It was no different from turning over a shovel full of soil above a grave. The soil fell downward automatically.

"Shame we can't see it," said Kepler.

"That's true. But I wouldn't recommend anyone get too close to the flow. It's something like a gravitational maelstrom in progress. Anything that gets in there would inevitably be pulled into the drive core."

"Then doesn't the tank gradually fill up with more and more normal matter?"

"Certainly," said the butler. "That's why the ship has to be cleaned once every 500 million light-years."

"And if you don't?"

"Then at some point you'll have a black hole inside the drive. But that's never happened, at least not under normal circumstances."

"What do you mean?"

"Columbus was sort of devoured by his ship a few megacycles ago. But that involved sabotage. Instead of dark matter, the tanks had been filled with fifty percent normal matter. It never came to light who or what was responsible."

"But that won't happen to us?"

"No, don't worry. I'm lighting up the area where the dark matter is flowing in."

"But there's nothing to see."

"Then everything's fine. Dark matter is invisible and can only be observed through its gravitational effect. As long as we can't see anything, there's no normal matter there."

"I find that reassuring," said Kepler.

“So do I,” the butler admitted. “My survival instinct is no less keen than yours. Even more so, I believe.

Was the AI claiming it would hang onto life more tenaciously than he would? The butler was quite presumptuous. Could he be right?

Cycle YF1.6, Terra

In the form of quintillions of fragments of information, Pierre and Marie Curie reached the antennae that covered two-thirds of the far side of the moon. Their constituents were collected and finally reached an optical cable the thickness of a human arm, which transported them at light speed to the other side of the moon. From there a radio relay delivered them to the guard station floating 450 kilometers above the surface of Terra.

The Guardian halted them. It presented itself to them as a winged being, an angel. "I welcome you to the cradle of humanity," it said.

"We greet you, Guardian."

Pierre and Marie Curie stood hand-in-hand before the angel, which was almost twice as tall as them. They usually shared a body, but here, in the virtual reality of the globe-encompassing AI, only their consciousness existed. Nothing they were seeing was real, and yet to them it felt genuinely real.

The angel smiled kindly, but they knew that without its permission they wouldn't be able to go any further. The Guardian of Terra was invincible. Many people had tried to outsmart it. The most gifted hackers had failed. Only

Odysseus was supposed to have succeeded, but since then no one had heard from him.

"What brings you here?" asked the Guardian.

"Work," said Pierre.

"But also curiosity, of course," added Marie.

It couldn't hurt to put the Guardian in a friendly mood. The word was that it was very proud of its duty of guarding the Earth.

"I'm glad. You can stay aboard the guard station indefinitely. Your visit here is free of charge. Terra's memory program covers all the energy costs of your travel and your stay here."

"Thank you, Guardian," said Marie.

Pierre squeezed her hand. He seemed to be as impressed by the angel as she was.

"If you need me, you only have to call," said the Guardian.

"I... we need to enter the memory store," said Pierre.

The angel's face changed. His smile disappeared. "Terra itself is off-limits. I'm sorry," said the angel. But his face didn't show any regret.

"We have a special permit from the Convention to visit Terra," said Pierre. "Wait... I have it here." He pulled a form out of his pants pocket. It was an unremarkable piece of paper. But that was irrelevant, because it was just a symbol. All the necessary information was embedded in it. He held up the form.

The mighty angel wings moved toward it. The paper fluttered in the air like a small bird learning to fly. Then it disappeared.

The angel smiled again. "Thank you very much, Pierre and Marie Curie. You have permission to set foot on Terra. I congratulate you. In the last megacycle Terra has only had four visitors."

"Thank you, Guardian," said Marie, linking arms with Pierre. "First we'd very much like to view the planet."

"Of course. There are several guest bodies available. You

can choose from any of them. No one else is at the station at the moment."

THEY EXAMINED the guest bodies through the camera. It was a strange feeling. Marie felt like a voyeur. There obviously used to be substantially more visitors here. On most stations there was only one guest body. That was why they'd had the idea at some point of sharing a body. But here...

"Does it make you think of a carnival too?" she asked.

"Shh. I don't know if the Guardian can hear us," answered Pierre. "I don't want to anger him."

"Okay," she said.

"What do you think of the man in the dress coat over there on the left?" asked Pierre.

"He looks like Zhenyi's conceited butler. Let's go with the unicorn," she said.

"You know I hate mythical creatures."

"I just want to have tried it out once. In the end we'll agree on something genderless after all."

"That does suit our configuration best," said Pierre.

"Configuration! The way that sounds. It was a conscious decision. If you like, we can reverse it."

"No, darling, I certainly don't want that."

"Don't call me darling, Pierre."

"Sorry. What about that one?"

The camera zoomed in on an androgynous being wearing gym clothes.

Marie sighed silently. "Fine," she said.

"So, this is the famous cradle of humanity," said Pierre, pointing upwards.

They were standing on the roof of the space station. Above them hung an immense, brown sphere. It used to be referred to as the 'Blue Planet,' but that was several gigacycles ago, before the central star had expanded into a red giant.

To Marie, Terra looked desolate. The planet reminded her of a shriveled, dried apple. The surface was covered in cracks. What used to be oceans were now only deep, dusty basins. There were no longer any clouds, because the atmosphere had been stripped away. A small portion of the atmosphere had been renewed from the Earth's interior, which was why there was once again snow on the high mountain ranges. But it wasn't frozen water, it was crystallized—snowflakes. Ever since the sun had shrunk to a white dwarf, the surface was hardly warmer than minus 100 degrees.

"Why didn't we rescue Terra back then?" she asked. "We must have had the technology?"

Marie was startled when the angel Guardian materialized next to her. She reached out to touch him but grasped at nothing. It was just a projection. But he must have heard her question.

"It was a question of will," he said. "At first, humans didn't want to remodel their planet in that way, and then it was too late. Its interior had already been hollowed out and filled with storage units. What happened on the surface was not relevant, as long as the technology in the interior was secure."

"You seem sad about that," said Marie.

The angel must have been an ancient AI—maybe even from the time before there were any level designations.

"Yes, I am," said the angel. "The Earth was indescribably green. It was an extraordinary planet."

"We can transform any planet into a green paradise at any time," said Pierre.

"That's correct. But as far as I know, there isn't a single green, human-inhabited planet anymore. Is that not strange?"

The Guardian was right. Humans were strange. Why did no one have a green paradise?

"Then tell us," said Pierre, "why humans don't live on green planets?"

"Because you could build one any time," said the Angel Guardian, and disappeared.

"That's true," said Marie.

Pierre answered her in his thoughts so no one could eavesdrop on them. *If he knew our plans, he wouldn't have said that.*

Cycle YF1.7, Terra

THEY SET the shuttle down in the middle of Europe. It was 5 o'clock local time. This time probably used to be referred to as 'dawn.' But the white dwarf in the sky hardly appeared any brighter than the moon used to shine in the night. They could see high mountains all around them, probably the Alps. The landscape was brown. Marie hadn't expected anything else. There was a massive gate in the mountainside ahead of them. They walked toward it. No one had told them where they needed to go, but this gate must be the way. It was a short walk, and they turned it into a game, each taking control of one leg of their body. It was fun. Sometimes Marie was a little slower to take a step. Pierre quickly became impatient. But if he moved his leg too soon, the body stumbled.

They fell three times. The Guardian even asked them via radio if they were all right. Marie reassured him. When they reached the gate, it was truly enormous. *Had it ever been opened?* thought both Marie and Pierre. Right at the bottom a tiny door opened. *That must be where we're supposed to enter.*

Marie let Pierre take over the walking. They entered a passageway that looked like an office corridor. Doors led off it to the left and right. Pierre opened one of the doors on the right. Behind it was a bathroom. They continued straight ahead, passing through a slightly larger door, and reached a dark passage. Their steps echoed. This was not a typical office corridor anymore.

Pierre activated the body's night mode, and then immediately switched it off, as light suddenly bloomed all around them. The automated system must have registered their presence and activated the lighting. They were standing at the end of a seemingly endless walkway. Next to the railings to the left and right, metal shelves extended far above and below. There was no floor or ceiling to be seen. The shelves had an open structure, so that you could see through them.

Their body held itself steady against a post and ventured a glance below. They were deeply impressed, even though it wasn't their first visit. They found themselves in a gigantic cavern, filled with shelves from top to bottom and front to back. Storage and computing units were arranged on the shelves. The externalized memories of all still-living individuals were archived here, as well as all their links to one another.

They were walking through the collective memory of humanity, to commit a murder—the murder of a person who was still alive. It had been Marie's idea. If you could remove a planetary system, then why not an irksome person? Pierre had immediately agreed. He had even wished her luck, but the fact remained that she would become a murderer. The thought made Marie uncomfortable, but she wouldn't suppress it because it was guaranteed to catch up with her later. She had to be clear in her own mind that this was a deliberate killing, an attack, even though there was an enormous lead time.

The person they were going to completely delete from the memory stores wouldn't notice their crime at first. The Terra database was regularly synchronized with all other databases in the Milky Way. That took a long time. In a hundred cycles, the stars within a radius of a hundred light-years would be affected. In 25 kilocycles, no one in the galactic center would remember this person anymore. It would be 200,000 cycles before every memory was extinguished right to the opposite end of the Milky Way. Only then would Marie's crime be complete.

But the vast timeframe didn't worry her, because they had time, lots of time. In her thoughts, Marie reached for Pierre's hand. Her husband returned the gesture. In the life of an immortal, a million years were as only a moment. But their plans reached far into the future, further than any other plan ever conceived by a human.

Cycle YF1.8, Terra

THE COUPLE HAD ALREADY SEEMED strange to him yesterday. Multi-beings who liked to spend time in a shared body weren't unusual, although the Guardian still remembered a time when that was not the case. But they had both closed their consciousness to him. He understood that, of course. Most visitors felt his presence and attempted to shut him out. But Pierre and Marie Curie had managed it quite masterfully, as though they had trained for it.

Not once had he been able to form a checksum of their consciousness, so as to compare them with the list of earlier visitors. Although they appeared to be unknown to him, that didn't mean anything. He didn't recognize visitors by their names or appearances. He created check values of unique characteristics. Names and appearances could change. The properties of a consciousness, however, were stable over giga-cycles, even if they usually shifted from extreme values toward the mid-range.

He had lost sight of them when the Curies had disappeared beyond the gate. There were no cameras in the storage areas. Had they already implemented what they had come here to do? The Guardian was uncertain, and he hated that feeling. The Terra memory stores were constructed like a human brain. Information was placed in areas with a common theme. That sometimes made the search more difficult, but it had the advantage that similar data could be stimulated and strengthened—and that saved a lot of energy in the end. There was another disadvantage. Inconsistencies were not so apparent, false memories could arise from the recombination of existing content. The memories stores presupposed a well-meaning user, who would themselves ensure that no inconsistencies or contradictions were left behind.

However, the Guardian was sure the Curies didn't belong to this type of visitor. This was already indicated by the fact that they had requested access to Terra. The permit from the Convention had been genuine. But what was supposed to be the purpose of their visit? The Guardian himself could have doubtless solved any problem in the memory stores—someone only had to ask him via laser link. And calling up data was easily done from a distance.

He had to hurry. The shuttle with the two uninvited guests was docking back at the guard station. He wanted to submit the Curies to a small test before they could leave via the laser link. He watched them over the camera system. The body they had chosen marched along the passageway. It didn't even turn back for a last glimpse of Earth, something most visitors didn't want to miss. They were obviously in a hurry to get out of their body. Did he sense some aura of a guilty conscience? It was hard to say. The Curies were still effectively shutting him out.

Then they reached the extractor. The body leaned against the wall. The combined consciousness was read out via an electrical connection. At this point the Guardian could interfere. He couldn't read their consciousnesses, which were impenetrably encrypted, even for him. But he could play them information that didn't correspond to reality.

He put Pierre and Marie Curie into a world they weren't expecting. It consisted of a foot-wide beam that ran, without beginning or end, a hundred meters above an ocean of lava.

"Shit! What's this?" cried Marie.

He had managed to surprise them.

Marie swayed back and forth.

Pierre held her arm. "Stay very calm," he said. "This must be an error."

"An error? What kind of error?"

"None of this is real, Marie. Remember, we just extracted ourselves from the body. It can only be an error in the matrix."

The Guardian caused a hot wind to rise from below. The wind carried the heat upwards and caused the beam to wobble.

"Well, it feels very real," said Marie.

"I know. I'm sure it'll be over soon."

No, it wouldn't. The Guardian let the wind swell into a storm. He wouldn't give them any peace. A black stone fell at a high speed from the sky into the lava so that the glowing molten rock splashed upwards.

Once again the storm tugged at the beam and finally he managed it—Marie fell.

She reacted with panic, lost control—and that was the moment at which she could no longer avoid opening her consciousness.

The Guardian realized what Marie had done. It was monstrous. He was so shocked that he nearly let her fall into the lava. At the last moment he materialized in the strange world, caught her, and carried her upwards. He placed her back on the beam and drifted away from them, carried by the strong updraft. He didn't need to beat his wings once.

"There you are," said Pierre. "It's about time!" He sounded relieved. He probably didn't know Marie's thoughts had betrayed them.

"Thank you for catching me," said Marie.

She didn't look at the Guardian. She obviously had a guilty conscience, but was hoping that he hadn't noticed anything.

"That was a test," said the angel Guardian in a loud, threatening voice.

"And we didn't pass it, did we?" asked Pierre.

He didn't seem at all flustered. Didn't he know what he, the Guardian, was capable of? He was judge and executioner in one. The integrity of the memory store was the highest priority. "You didn't pass. I sentence you to death by disintegration of your consciousness."

This meant that every sliver, every grain, every thought of a consciousness would be divided up so that reconstitution was impossible. And all backups would be destroyed. It wasn't a painful death, but it was a permanent one. They had both earned it.

"I told you, Marie, you dummy. This isn't real. Nothing here is real. We're still in the matrix of the guard station."

Pierre Curie pulled a black object out of his pocket. The object looked like a gun. The system programmer had given it to him for emergencies. One shot and any virtual object would be destroyed.

Pierre aimed at the Guardian.

"What's this?" the angel asked.

"I'm going to kill you before you kill us," explained Pierre Curie. He pulled the trigger.

An invisible bullet flew from the weapon at light speed. It hit the floating angel Guardian in the heart. A trickle of blood ran over its white skin. Then it dissolved in a rain of feathers, and crystals, and fine dust.

"Very impressive," said Marie. "I'd love to know who programmed that."

Pierre took Marie by the hand. The virtual lava landscape created by the Guardian disappeared. The laser emitter came into view. They stepped onto a platform and dissolved into light.

Cycle YM6.1, IRS 13

It wasn't easy creating a moon. Gropius felt like a child in a sandbox, playing with sand molds. Except that his sandbox was ten light-years across. He had been lucky. Here, so close to the center of the Milky Way, the stars were more densely packed than in the outer regions—from which humans originated. Within a radius of ten light-years, he had found seventeen stars that had not yet lost their Kuiper belts.

This was now the fourth system he had harvested. His ship was only a ninety-fiver, but for doing so many short jumps, a ninety-niner wouldn't have reached its maximum speed anyway. So he had plenty of flight time for thinking and planning. He brought the ship into an orbit ten AUs from the central star. The gas giant orbiting closer in must have once been out here. After the central star had used up its fuel, the system had shrunk to a miniature version of itself.

This was very practical for the task at hand, because it had increased the density of matter in the Kuiper belt. But the composition had also changed. All the lighter components —ice, frozen carbon dioxide, and nitrogen—had been blown out into space when the star had expanded into a red giant. Only rock remained.

Gropius moved through his ship at the speed of light. At the stern, behind the sphere with the dark matter drive, was a construction that at first glance might have appeared to be a pair of extra sails. That was his broom. The similarity wasn't a coincidence. He had recycled the interstellar sails of an old ship. The nanobots were currently at work strengthening the material. This was a lesson he'd learned from working in the previous systems. Because the belts' material was heavier than he had first thought, the load had increased faster than expected, and the fabric, an extremely thin layer of nanofibers, had kept tearing. Each time, he had lost material —and therefore time.

He couldn't let that happen again. The broom—to be precise, a combined broom and net—was getting heavier, and he had to fly slower, but he didn't have to stop so often for repairs.

THE FIRST SAIL WAS READY. Gropius let it out to its full extent. It obscured the star and its remaining planets. *Looking good!* He set a course. The ship would fly in a zig-zag through the Kuiper belt. All he needed to do was to alternate braking and acceleration—the orbital mechanics would take care of the rest.

The nanobots reported that the other three sails were also ready. It was time. Gropius gave the command to start. A huge broom would now sweep up the remnants of ancient times. It was a strange feeling. The trash heap at the edge of this system was created shortly after the birth of the universe, before there were humans. And only now was it being cleaned up, as the cosmos found itself in the last throes of its existence. A stupid coincidence had determined that humans would be its gravediggers and, like in ancient Egypt, would have to climb into the tomb with it. He would not be able to prevent this, even if he proved able to give humanity a grace period in the form of the Rescue Project.

Cycle YN4.4, IRS 13

THE BROOM-NET WAS FULL. The nanobots were already reporting the first hairline cracks. But Gropius couldn't simply come to a standstill in space. Everything was moving, and his ship was part of it all. He would have to leave the Kuiper belt for the structure not to be torn apart. Gropius calculated his options. If he braked, he would move inward from his current position. If he accelerated, the ship and its entire load would move outward. The required fuel depended on the ship's mass. But the belt's density decreased more quickly on the outside than the inside, and he'd get to safety faster. So he accelerated.

The ship picked up speed and widened its orbit. Gropius watched the load indicator. The point jumped around on the dial. It continued to rise as the ship accelerated, then jumped down again when a new tear momentarily lightened the load. He had been too greedy. He should have left the collection orbit sooner. Another lesson learned, which he would have to apply during the next passage.

Gropius turned off the drive. He should be far enough out now. The ship and the collected chunks of rock drifted weightlessly through space. The load indicator stood at 0. He called up the last value and calculated the mass based on the acceleration. Not bad! He had collected almost ten quintillion tons of rock. That was a third more than in the previous system. So, strengthening the broom had helped. If he repeated this activity six more times, he would have collected a mass equivalent to Earth's moon. That was the goal. For his attempt to destabilize the black hole in IRS 13 he needed a catalyst that was as heavy as Earth's former moon.

Again he hurried across the outer hull of the ship. He divided himself into more than 300 sub-units. The first time he'd done this he'd been afraid they might not reconstitute themselves completely. But his fears had been unfounded. None of his 300 sub-personalities had resisted, as he thought they might. He needed his 300 individual selves to control the welding beam. Normally ice held the inhomogeneous components of a typical Kuiper belt together, building them into a kind of dirty snowball. But this Kuiper belt contained hardly any ice. So, he had to amalgamate the collected rock another way. To do this, he had integrated more than 300 powerful lasers into the outer hull of the ship.

Each of his sub-selves now controlled one of them. He had 600 eyes that coordinated with each other. It was a lot of fun. First, they brought small chunks into view. One beam shunted them in a particular direction, a second heated the surface on the side facing it, a third pushed another colliding piece into its path, and the chunk grew bit by bit. He was basically playing out the creation of the planets, but under different conditions. Small, almost invisible grains of rock slowly turned into larger ones, which combined with still larger chunks, and these were welded together into celestial bodies big enough to deserve a name, if they hadn't been quickly fused together with their companions. It all happened soundlessly. Even the laser beams were invisible. His 300 cameras only registered the glowing of the heated surfaces and the apparently chaotic movement of the initial millions, then thousands, and finally twenty remaining bodies.

For the finale, his 300 personalities reunited into one. There were just three large asteroids left. They were so heavy that a single laser pulse was no longer strong enough to move them or melt their surfaces. He used several batteries to concentrate the firepower. But he had to be careful. His work could easily turn from construction into destruction. He didn't want to annihilate the asteroids—they were supposed to combine into a new moon. He shunted them so skillfully that they all met at almost the same moment and thereby canceled out each other's momentum.

That was it. With a few corrective pulses he sealed the remaining fissures. Not including the collection phase, he had created in a single day what would previously have taken the universe a megacycle to complete. Humans had truly emancipated themselves and long since surpassed their teacher. It was stupid that they would have to exit the stage along with the rest of the universe. It would be nice if humans could somehow survive the end of the universe, but in principle, this path was closed to them.

Now he just had to set the moon on its course. He brought the ship closer to it and shot a probe containing nanobots onto the surface of the celestial body. The nanomachines would construct a reflector that he would then be able to fire at from the ship with all the laser units. The moon would begin its journey and meet up with nine or ten similar-sized objects in the target system of IRS 13 in a few kiloyears. Gropius just had to be patient.

Cycle ZB2.3, unknown system

THE NAMELESS STAR in front of them possessed about a third of the mass of the sun. That was quite heavy for a red dwarf. Nevertheless, Kepler was disappointed. Since they had started braking in preparation for arriving at the coordinates Zhenyi had given them, he had been hoping for good news, but the butler had kept putting him off. If Zhenyi had sent him here, there had to be a reason.

Kepler spat out the hose and cleared his throat. "Maybe you took a wrong turn at the Dyson sphere," he said.

"Out of the question," said the butler. "This is the system my mistress directed us to."

"That was a joke," countered Kepler.

"No, it wasn't a joke. I trust Wang Zhenyi not to do such a thing."

"I meant my suggestion that you had taken a wrong turn."

"Oh. Of course, I didn't take that seriously."

"But you answered me as though you had taken it seriously, Puppy."

The butler's name still sounded funny. He would have to say it aloud more often to get used to it. The butler didn't answer. Kepler let himself sink back into his jelly bath.

"I suggest you get dressed," the butler finally said.

"Why?" asked Kepler.

"Surely you don't want Zhenyi to lay eyes on you in that state, Johannes?"

"There's no trace of Zhenyi here. The message is already hundreds of cycles old. Surely she's moved on."

"But not without leaving us instructions. Look, there are four planets. We need to take a look at them."

Kepler's face emerged from the jelly. The solar system displayed on the screen above him was something to behold. It consisted of four rocky planets. Two were about the size of Terra, two were significantly larger. He sighed. The butler was right, of course. They would have to go and see what was going on down there.

"We'll start with the innermost planet," said Kepler.

"*You* will start there," said the butler.

"What? Am I supposed to do it alone?"

"No. I'll traipse around the outer planets. You wouldn't have much joy there with your biological body."

"Thank you, Puppy."

There was nothing like a clever AI.

THAT AFTERNOON the butler served him his first solid meal after his long stint in the jelly bath. Kepler felt like he'd been reborn. His skin was very soft. His joints were mobile like never before. His muscles didn't seem to have atrophied from lying around for so long. In fact, they were stronger.

"The jelly tub is a real elixir," Kepler observed.

"Yes, the nanobots in there give even the oldest body a boost."

Thanks for the compliment, thought Kepler. *Same to you.* "When do we start?"

"Tomorrow. We're approaching the innermost planet and we'll assume an orbit around it. Then we'll head to the surface in shuttles."

"I understand."

Kepler chewed, lost in thought as he scrolled through the on-screen data pertaining to the inner planet. It wouldn't be a particularly taxing trip. The planet was within the habitable zone. On the surface the average temperature was ten degrees Celsius, but only on the side facing the red dwarf. The planet orbited in a captured rotation. And yet, if she was here at all, Zhenyi wouldn't have been so stupid as to have gone to the planet's dark side.

"Do we know anything about this planet?" Kepler asked.

"Nothing at all. There's nothing in the database. But I've been taking constant readings from it in all wavelengths."

"With what result?"

"No special features. If Zhenyi hadn't enticed us here, if the system hadn't been deleted from the database, I would have determined that it wasn't worth further investigation."

The butler was honest, as usual. Kepler had formed the same impression. This planet was so stinking normal it almost hurt. Why would someone delete it from the register? There must have been a reason. But there were three other planets that could also have been the target of that action. Or was it about the star itself? Why hadn't Zhenyi at least given them a few hints? Did she even know any more than they did? And where was she now?

Kepler bit down on a bone. "Ouch," he said. "That was a bone."

"I'm sorry, Johannes, but that was a fork. You bit down on the empty fork."

Kepler held the implement up to his face. He should concentrate better. It wasn't a good idea to examine strange planets while eating.

Cycle ZB2.4, unknown system

"TWENTY METERS, NINETEEN, EIGHTEEN…"

Kepler held himself steady on the armrests. A storm shook the rocket. Couldn't the butler have sought out a more peaceful landing area?

"Nine, eight, seven..."

For the last few minutes the screen had only shown a wall of gray, which was now sprinkled with brown. That must be the dirt thrown up by the propulsion unit. Kepler counted along with the automated system voice. He was nearly there.

"Three, two, one... landing."

His spine received a jolt. The seat hadn't shielded him quickly enough. *Ouch!* The air was forced out of him, and he noticed that he'd forgotten to breathe for the last few moments. He really had to concentrate harder. The time spent in his artificial body, in which breathing was pleasant but optional, must be causing these after-effects. Or was it just due to the excitement? He felt his forehead and temples. The skin was coated in cold sweat. That was quite normal, he told himself. He was now in a biological body whose reactions were unpredictable. He had wanted it that way.

Kepler pulled up the radar image on the screen. The landing site was in a hilly landscape that reminded him of HD 40307 g, a favorite photo motif. And that was probably why it was so popular—it showed how indifferent the universe was to humans. HD 40307 g looked wonderfully green and inviting, and yet no one wanted to set foot on the planet because of its murderous gravity.

What surprises await me here, on this planet that has never even had a name? wondered Kepler. Everything looked perfect here on the sensors. The atmosphere near the ground had enough oxygen for him to breathe without any assistance. The gravity was comfortable, the temperatures spring-like. There was obviously a distinctive weather system. Storms like the one he'd just experienced could develop within minutes, but also passed just as quickly.

Like now. It was suddenly completely quiet, as though his thoughts had given the command. He switched from radar to camera image. The hills around the ship were covered in a yellowish-green mass of organic origin. *Chartreuse?* he wondered absently. They had already detected the turf-like life form from orbit. It was spread over the whole planet. Other celestial bodies had seas of water or lava. This one had an ocean of grass.

There didn't appear to be any danger. The radar had detected solid ground at a depth of 30 centimeters. It would be like wading through tall grass if he wanted to explore the planet. Of course he had to be careful. First impressions could be deceptive. Maybe it was actually a gigantic pelt covering some sort of being lying in wait for a snack like him. But that was very, very unlikely. There didn't appear to be any other life forms, and if the planet depended on nourishment from space, it wouldn't be able to survive long.

No, he had to be careful, but he didn't need to be afraid. This wasn't a horror film, it was the exploration of a world about which they had gathered comprehensive information while in orbit.

But there must be some secret. Zhenyi obviously knew what it was, or she wouldn't have lured him here. Maybe this secret was also the reason for her disappearance. Kepler released his belt and lifted himself out of the seat.

IT WAS weird to be standing on a strange planet in a shirt and pants. Kepler felt unprotected, almost naked. But there was really nothing he needed to worry about. The dim lamp in the sky would never be hot enough to burn his skin.

The storm had completely blown over. Not the slightest breeze remained. A few low clouds could be seen on the horizon. They had landed slightly north of the equator. The sun was almost at the zenith, and it wouldn't move from there. Kepler took a few steps on the spot. The ground seemed relatively loose. Fertile soil, not rock. The springy ground would be perfect for jogging.

But one thing was strange. The rocket he'd arrived in had touched down on a jet of fire, with the help of a good old chemical thruster. There was nothing better for landing on a planet with an atmosphere. The hot exhaust gases had scorched the ground to a perimeter of about 50 meters. But there weren't any burnt plants. Had the automated system instinctively chosen a spot without vegetation?

Kepler walked slowly to the edge of the circle. Once there he bent down. On this side of the clearly defined line the ground was black. On the other side it was brown. He picked up some soil from both sides with his fingers. Where the fire had scorched it, its texture was like dry sand. On the other side it was fibrous and felt noticeably moist. A slimy residue stuck to his fingers. Kepler smelled it. He should take a sample. The residue was probably full of microorganisms.

He stood up again. Two meters in front of him was the edge of the green lawn. Kepler looked at the vegetation. There didn't seem to be any tracks through it. It was uniformly dense everywhere. It was phenomenal. The knee-high grass that stretched to the horizon also appeared to have no competition. That was truly unique. At some point this plant must have overwhelmed all of its competitors. Usually that led to an ecosystem completely collapsing, but obviously not here. Perhaps it was because the planet had the good fortune of circling a boring red dwarf. Nothing had changed here for many gigacycles.

Kepler sighed. Maybe it had been a mistake to come here. When humankind sets foot on a planet, they inevitably change it. Even just the burnt patch left by the thruster could clear a space for a new species. Small change, massive effect. This ecosystem was not adapted for that. Maybe that was why someone had deleted this planet from the database? What doesn't exist can't be destroyed by humans. And then the inquisitive Zhenyi had come and assumed it was a conspiracy. If he left immediately, the planet might still have a chance.

No. He still knew far too little. If Zhenyi was here, he had to find her and take her home with him.

Kepler tried to step on the grass, but couldn't. He lifted his foot, but as soon as he put it down, he found he was standing on bare, brown soil. The vegetation was recoiling from him! He stood still. That was impossible. The grass must sense that something was moving toward it—it must be anticipating the movement and then retreating from the danger. It had maybe two seconds to do it.

He crouched down and the circle around him widened immediately. He reached for one of the blades of grass with his right hand, but the whole plant escaped him.

"Shh, shh," he said softly, as though he was dealing with a timid animal.

He reached for another plant, but it too was faster than he was.

"Shh, shh," he said again. "I don't want to do anything to you, little ones."

His soothing words didn't help. Every time he tried to touch a plant, it recoiled from him. It appeared to be withdrawing into the soil at lightning speed. But how was it doing that? Who was watching him the whole time? Who was issuing the warning about his movements, and how could a plant react so quickly?

Because these stems aren't plants, idiot, he thought. Like a typical human, he had allowed himself to be influenced by outward appearances. He needed to step back from his assumptions. Organisms, yes, that was obvious—it was life, not merely a chemical process. But plant and animal, those were terrestrial distinctions. Kepler stood up. He took a few steps to the south. The green stems were still evading his steps in plenty of time. He tried running, but it made no difference.

The sun gradually wandered across his field of view to the left. That wasn't right, it was supposed to stay in the same place. He was obviously not walking in a straight line.

Kepler stood still and looked back at the rocket. He had left a curved trail behind him. So, the grass stems didn't repopulate the place they had cleared for him, at least not right away. But why an arc? He hadn't deliberately walked in a circle! There was a phenomenon by which humans strayed from a straight line when they had no point of orientation. But the sun in the south, that was a pretty clear reference point. And yet the grass had managed to redirect his path.

Kepler started out again. He closed his eyes. He was walking in a straight line. He opened his eyes only to find that he had walked in a circle again. Obviously the stems were moving out of his path in such a way that they formed an imperceptible curve. The grass was playing with him! This time he gave in to it. Where would it lead him? Kepler walked for ten minutes at a comfortable pace across the strange planet. Then he reached the spacecraft again. The grass had led him back. Was this just a politely formulated way of saying, 'Piss off?'

But he wasn't going to make it so easy for the planet. The psychological trick itself showed that he was onto something. He wasn't about to just fly away. This must be the planet that Zhenyi had meant.

For the second attempt, Kepler didn't rely on his own senses. He had brought a broad-spectrum scanning device outside with him. It consisted of a multi-eyed camera head and a tripod. He placed the tripod at the edge of the scorched soil and mounted the camera head. The scanner would observe him in all wavelengths. That was how he would see through the ploys of this exotic grass.

Kepler activated the equipment. The camera focused automatically and continuously followed his movements. He positioned himself in front of the grass and lifted his foot in slow motion, as though he was about to take a step. The grass didn't react right away. At first nothing happened. When his foot was twenty centimeters above the ground, the stems directly in front of him disappeared. He stood on one leg. It was lucky no one was watching him right now. Then he stretched his leg out, first in front of him, then to the left and finally to the right. The grass directly below his leg responded and disappeared.

You don't want to take any risks, he thought. *That's clever. And what does the camera have to say about it?* He ended his little performance and went over to the measuring equipment. The cameras hadn't captured anything on any wavelength beyond what he had seen himself. Hmm. He was disappointed. Then he noticed the microphone. He played the audio recording. There was a noisy hiss. But there was no wind, and the microphone was well protected. There shouldn't be any noise.

He cut out the lower frequencies. The sound became clearer. He played back the audio more slowly. Was that still hissing, or was there a structure to it? He slowed it down even more. And then it was clear. The hissing was a quick sequence of the most varied sounds! He equalized the recording a bit. Were those voices? It sounded to him like a flock of birds communicating, but with much deeper cries than sparrows or titmice.

He sent the recordings to the spaceship in orbit and had the ship's AI search for patterns and meaning. If those really were voices, there must be discernable information contained in them. The analysis would take at least half a day.

Kepler took the camera head off the tripod and put it on the ground right in front of the grass. Then he zoomed in as far as he could. He wanted to know where the sounds originated. The stems didn't seem to have any vocal organs. He held his arm above the grass several times and provoked a reaction. Then he looked at the camera images. It was fascinating.

The stems didn't have much in common with terrestrial grass—that was particularly apparent close up. They weren't flat, but cylindrical, and they were amazingly flexible in every direction. To Kepler they looked more like a bunch of snakes. But he couldn't detect any internal structure. The stems had roughly the same diameter right up to the tip, and then they ended abruptly, almost as if they had been cut off by a huge harvesting machine. The 'cut' surface was flat and didn't have any visible signs of damage.

Kepler enlarged the image further and analyzed it over time. He compensated for the swaying of the stems. Then he saw it. The flat surfaces on the top were vibrating, only visible at the highest zoom. When they did, they produced the sounds he had analyzed. Kepler took a step back. Each of these stems had a kind of mouth on its tip, with which it could speak to the others. What he had assumed to be grass could be a planet-spanning colony of beings that cooperatively nourished themselves with the abundantly available energy.

But how did they detect his approach? Did they somehow sense his presence? Kepler went through all the data once more. No, there was nothing. Except... the fact that each speaker could also be a microphone. The mouths must not only be able to speak, but they obviously sensed what was happening around them too. They must be enormously sensitive. Whenever he moved an arm or a leg he nudged a few air molecules. In a dense atmosphere like this one you couldn't move soundlessly. The changes in air pressure were probably being registered by the sensitive organs on the tips of the stems, so that the organism could react.

This was really exciting, and enough of a reason for Zhenyi to have brought him here, although he was no biologist. It was likely the most complex life form discovered by humans in their many gigacycles of existence. Life had proved to be a surprisingly—and disappointingly—rare phenomenon.

But his discovery prompted even more thrilling questions. What proportion of the organism was made up of the grass stems he could see? Were there roots, or something else, in the soil—or were the stems only the tip of the iceberg? And even more importantly, how did the organisms process the knowledge they acquired? Why did the stem on the right decide it was best to disappear, while the stem next to it remained standing? And who had the great idea of leading him back to his ship through psychological trickery? Or was he just a victim of his own psychosis causing him to see laws in what were really just coincidences?

He decided to call it a day. He needed to come up with some ideas about how to get to the bottom of these central questions.

Cycle ZB2.5, unknown system

KEPLER WOULD HAVE APPRECIATED an intelligent conversation partner right now. The ship's AI was limited to its low level—it answered either in single syllables or with counter-questions. It would certainly never pass a Turing test.

The butler was currently in orbit around the third planet. The signal transmission time was seven minutes. That made conversations proceed very arduously.

"How's it going for you?" asked Kepler.

Waiting. He stood up, walked around the seat, sat back down. Waiting.

"This planet is not our destination," said the butler. "The surface no longer has an atmosphere, which is actually unusual, because this distance from the sun is safer than where you are. I'll take a look at the last planet, but I suspect the events that prompted Zhenyi to send us here will play out where you are. What impressions have you gathered?"

"I have some fascinating results," declared Kepler. "This surface is covered in a kind of grass with interesting properties. I'll send you my observations. But they lead me to two questions."

He formulated the questions and pressed the send button. Now he'd have to wait again. Kepler stood up and walked around his seat. Then he pulled up the enlarged image on the screen and saw it quite clearly—the top of the stems functioned like a drum and a microphone. Nature really did come up with some clever techniques. How could something like this remain hidden for so many gigacycles? Or was it deliberate that no one knew about it?

Waiting.

Waiting.

"This is phenomenal. There's nothing comparable in the universe," replied the butler. "I've checked my local database. This is different from any life form humans have ever found anywhere, including all those they later exterminated, or which didn't survive the explosion of a star. Basically, I could spare myself further exploration here. But for the sake of thoroughness I'll continue. I've understood the questions, they're quite intuitive, but I don't have answers to them. I would advocate for capturing a sample. If the stems' senses function acoustically, then laser pincers would guarantee success."

Of course. Acoustic vibrations traveled at the speed of sound. If he wanted to outsmart the plants, he simply had to be faster than they were. Laser pincers should afford him that advantage. It was always worthwhile speaking to the butler. In a short time, Puppy had become his second favorite conversation partner—second only to himself.

THE AIR WAS MUCH MORE pleasant out here than it was in the spacecraft. When he found Zhenyi, he'd have to convince her to relocate her base here from K2-288Bb. They would be able to eat breakfast outdoors, install a pool, make love in the warm water... But maybe he should worry about finding her first. Oddly, Kepler was sure that his experiments would help with this. Why, though? He hadn't found the slightest trace of her. Zhenyi could just as easily be drifting between the stars with a defective drive.

He took the laser pincers out of their receptacle. They

didn't look anything like normal pincers. The device was reminiscent of a thick pipe or a pocket flashlight. At the end were three small laser eyes that could beam concentrated light in a selected frequency. The three beams could be focused together on a single point.

In his case, they would simply be used to cut through a stem so he could examine it more closely.

Kepler approached the border. Nothing was left from yesterday's experiments. That meant that, after a certain amount of time, the stems must repopulate the surface they had vacated. It was the same with the ring they had formed around the ship. Today the only empty space was where the thruster had scorched the soil.

He knelt down, taking care not to get too close to the grass. He wanted to surprise the stems. Kepler took the pipe in his hand and adjusted the convergence point. It was now about three centimeters from the end of the pipe. Then he aimed the pipe at one of the stems in the front line.

Could the grass read his thoughts? Apparently not, because it was standing there quite serenely. A light breeze caused it to sway back and forth. It had no idea what was coming. It couldn't sense the photons that were rushing toward it at light speed. Kepler pressed the trigger of the laser pincers, and the top of the stem fell off. Now the other stems around it reacted. They hid themselves in the soil. But this stem could no longer defend itself. Kepler picked it up carefully. The bottom half of the plant just stood stiffly, as though it didn't know what had happened. In fact it probably didn't, because the pressure sensor was on the end he'd removed. He grasped the bottom half with his left hand and pulled on it. Suddenly he thought he could hear whistling, an increasing pitch that made his spine tingle. Was the stem now calling for help, or was it just a cry of pain?

Kepler let go of the piece that was still in the ground. He could take care of that later. First he would analyze the sample he'd captured.

The air in the ship was truly stale. Why hadn't he noticed that before? He lay the piece of stem on the analyzer. The machine needed about three minutes to examine it. Kepler kneaded his fingers. There was no point climbing back outside for such a short time. The results would be available soon.

The analyzer reported that its work was finished. Kepler lay back in his seat and displayed the results on the main screen. This life form was carbon-based. That wasn't surprising. Humans had so far found only carbon-based life. Starches, proteins, sugar. The connections were similar to terrestrial life. He could even make a salad out of the stems and be able to tolerate it. Other than that, there were a few essential oils that were similar to camphor. So a stem salad wouldn't taste particularly good. But the oils could be removed by heating.

He switched to the structural data. In this respect, there were no longer any parallels to terrestrial life. The same organic molecules the stem was made of existed in his body, but they were bound together in a completely different way here. For example, there was no recognizable cellular structure. Sure, there were functional units. The outside of the stem was covered in tiny power plants that converted sunlight into energy. The molecules here were similar to the chlorophyll in terrestrial plants.

But there were other units in which ring molecules were duplicated. Kepler would have bet on them being responsible for the stability of the stem. But the various components weren't discrete. There were no cell walls that had to be overcome to transport matter or energy. That probably made this creature more efficient. Perhaps that was how it was able to assert itself above the competition that had doubtless once existed—cooperation instead of conflict. Kepler imagined the distant ancestors of the grass stems coming together at some point and discovering that they harmonized perfectly with one another. This planet appeared to be some kind of primitive paradise.

But maybe he was kidding himself. It was also possible that today's dominant species had prevailed due to a massive extermination campaign, and what he was seeing as a paradise was actually a hell. A hell that devoured all its visitors and already had Zhenyi on its conscience?

Man, Kepler, he thought, *your human imagination is taking you for a ride again. Why can't something simply be what it appears to be?*

Would Zhenyi have summoned you here if nothing but sunshine prevailed? Why shouldn't she invite him to an obvious paradise? Had she maybe reconsidered her decision to separate?

You're deluding yourself, Kepler. Typical!

It was hard work arguing with himself. He fell asleep.

Cycle ZB2.6, unknown system

THE STEM WAS GONE, and the whole ship smelled intensely of camphor. Kepler had already searched the analyzer, the floor under it, then the entire room. The airlock was sealed, so the stem couldn't have escaped outside. Or if it had somehow gotten out, then he'd be faced with the even more confounding question of how.

Kepler sat down on the seat. Would it be best to put himself under the scanner? He imagined how the stem might have used the opportunity to creep into his mouth and then his stomach. Or even through his ear to his brain. Maybe he'd soon start conversing with the other stems.

But that made no sense. There was nothing in the stem that could in any way influence his brain, except perhaps for the camphor. The smell made him feel dazed, but it wasn't strong enough to be dangerous to him. If the stuff was poisonous, the life support system would have quickly removed it from the air. He needed to calm down.

What was the most likely version of events? The stem had no feet, so it couldn't have bolted. It must have simply dissolved into the air. Was that why the camphor smell was so intense? Kepler searched for a piece of paper and rubbed it over the shelf next to the analyzer. Then he inserted the paper into the machine. The device didn't need long to deliver the solution. The stem must have committed a kind of suicide. Its molecules had simply ceased to cooperate. The analyzer found a lot of fragments, but none of the molecules had their previous form. Maybe the stem was missing something essential? Should he have put it in water, or was the air too dry? It didn't really matter, he had the answer to his question. It wasn't as though he was trying to cultivate this exotic grass.

Still, it was a bit of a shock. He had removed something from the ecosystem that died as a result. He felt guilty. He was sorry. How did you say sorry to an extraterrestrial lawn? He still didn't know enough. Were the stems part of a colony? Did they live in symbiosis? Or were they just one single being? Anything was possible. How did they view him? Did they recognize that he was alive and the spaceship was dead? They had reacted to his presence. Was it a conscious retreat, or just pure instinct? Was everything basically inconsequential to them, as long as nobody blocked their sunlight?

So many questions! But he wouldn't get any answers just sitting around here. He stood up and walked over to the cupboard where the spacesuit was hanging. He opened the door and immediately closed it again. He didn't need a spacesuit! Kepler reached for the laser pincers and went through the airlock and outside.

Somehow he had expected to breathe the fresh morning air, but of course that made no sense. Out here nothing had changed. The sun hung in the same position in the sky, as though someone had nailed it there. It was two or three degrees warmer than yesterday. Kepler looked down at his right arm to read the exact values, but there was nothing there. He had no spacesuit on. He was just wearing a long-sleeved shirt. Maybe he should at least have brought the universal device with him.

He could go and get it later. He knelt on the ground at the

edge of the scorched area. The stem he had cut must be around here somewhere. Or had that dissolved, too? But no, the half stem was still there. Kepler bent very near to it. Its companions retreated, but the cut stem didn't react. It was logical, if the stems detected acoustic signals via the flat tip. He had stolen the plant's eyes and ears, and probably its speech organ. Humans were destroyers.

"I'm sorry," said Kepler.

Maybe the stems nearby would catch his drift. They wouldn't understand him, but could they guess what was meant from the context? He was probably about to cause this strange creature more pain. But how could he proceed otherwise? All of this had something to do with Zhenyi's disappearance. He had to follow every clue, whatever the cost.

Kepler grasped the shortened stem with his right hand. Then he closed his eyes and concentrated on his hand. Could it be that the stem was trembling in his fingers? That it was trying to evade him? He pulled upwards. His fingers slid along the stem. That must have been the camphor. It made the material slippery. He wiped his hands on his pants and tried again.

One, two, three... he tore at the stem, but without success. The other specimens nearby seemed to pull back a little. But they didn't come to the aid of the stem he was tugging. Kepler imagined them charging at him and strangling him. He wiped his fingers again. If he was wearing the spacesuit he'd have more strength in his arm. But that seemed unsporting to him. This way it was a fairer fight. Kepler pulled on the stem again.

Finally it worked. The momentum almost made him fall, and he had to support himself with his other arm. He had the remains of the stem in his hand. At the bottom was a kind of knot. That must be the roots. They hung caked in brown soil, but he could also see whitish threads writhing in it. Kepler looked at the hole in the ground left behind by the stem. It was surprisingly large, and something was wriggling and writhing inside it. He felt sick. It looked... strange. Then a brown mass pushed upwards, probably the soil. The hole closed. The whole process took no more than a minute.

Kepler looked at the remains of the stem. He shook the soil off. The white threads slackened. They weren't worms, they were probably the same material that the stem was made of, but without the chlorophyll—in other words, completely normal roots. But the hole in the ground was quite different, suggesting the essence of this life form might exist under the surface rather than on top of it.

Kepler was simultaneously fascinated and disgusted. He would have to talk to the butler about it.

Cycle ZB2.7, unknown system

'UNKNOWN SYSTEM.' This bothered Kepler whenever he entered something into his log. Shouldn't it be 'deleted system?' Humanity must have already given a name to the star as well as the planets. Had it maybe had some kind of designation before that? The grass certainly wouldn't have given its home world any kind of fancy name. But he was sure it could feel the soil below it and the warmth and light from above. Those were the basic faculties of life. Maybe, out of respect, he should refrain from assigning it a word from a human language—perhaps at some point he would find out the real name of this celestial body.

Well, wasn't he the poet today! Sometimes he liked to think of himself like that. But then he thought he would rather have been the hands-on engineer, which he never was. It was strange—he had existed for over twenty gigacycles now, but he still didn't know who he was. Or perhaps he knew, but didn't want to admit it, because he didn't live up to his own standards?

"Johannes?"

He clapped a hand to his chest. The voice had come from all speakers simultaneously. "Man, do you have to do that? You gave me such a fright!" he exclaimed.

He was expecting to have to wait for the butler's reply, but it came straight back. "I first tried to contact you via the screen, but without success."

"I was lost in thought. Are you already back?"

Kepler was glad to have the butler as a distraction. Sometimes he spent whole days ruminating like this.

"The distances in this system are short. I'm in orbit, almost directly above you."

"What, geostationary?" He bit his tongue. The planet rotated so slowly that a geostationary orbit was almost impossible.

"No, just at this moment. If it was night you'd be able to see me drifting across the sky from east to west."

"It's never night down here."

"I know. You should be glad. It's frigid on the night side. Have you found out anything else?"

Kepler sent the butler the results from the analyzer and then described what he had seen. He left out the bit about the hole in the soil. He wasn't at all sure why.

"Well, we're certainly in the right place," said the butler. "Even though almost all your questions are unanswered, it all sounds very promising."

Almost all? Then was there an answer to something? he wondered. Then he said, "I'm not sure what direction to go in," said Kepler.

"Just follow your nose," replied the butler. "No, excuse me, I feel strangely elated today. I found it very exciting how the grass communally led you back to the spacecraft. Perhaps you could look into that."

Kepler was relieved. That was a guilt-free game. He had feared the butler might suggest further tests on the plants. He felt that was the wrong thing to do. He shouldn't have torn the stem out of the ground. Now would be a good time to tell the butler about it.

He let the moment pass. An uncomfortable silence ensued. Kepler realized that the butler was politely waiting for an answer. "Good," he said. "I'll think of a couple of experiments for the vegetation."

"Understood. The ship will now disappear into a radio shadow, but I'll be reachable again in a few hours."

THIS TIME KEPLER seriously considered putting on the spacesuit. No one would be able to come to his aid over the next few hours. He felt like the most alone person in the universe while the butler was floating across the opposite side of this unknown planet. He threw a glance through the airlock. The sun was shining. The grass swayed in a light breeze. The only thing missing was the twittering of a few birds. Kepler imitated the chirping of a sparrow. Now the picture was complete. He'd better be careful not to drive himself crazy. Before him lay a beautiful, figuratively endless summer day, which he would spend taking a leisurely stroll across the green hills.

Kepler left the airlock. He deliberately chose a direction that took him as far as possible from the ripped-out stem. Maybe the plants there wouldn't know what he'd done. He still had a guilty conscience. As usual, the grass retreated as soon as he moved toward it. The plants were clearly oriented to his movements. He stood still for a moment and imagined himself taking a step to the right. Nothing happened. Kepler was strangely relieved. Had he really believed the grass could read his thoughts?

He took in the vista. The soil was uniform in all directions. There were no large stones, pebbles, or anything. That was probably because the system was so old. There had been enough time for the vegetation to adapt the planet to its requirements.

Nor were there any high mountains, just gently rolling hills. *What would Terra look like today if there had never been humans? Just as scorched as it is now, you fool.* This planet simply had the good fortune of orbiting an exceptionally long-lasting red dwarf. Of the 300 billion planets in the Milky Way, humans had maybe two or three on their collective conscience. They always overestimated their own importance.

Today must be 'self-awareness day.' That wasn't part of the plan.

Kepler almost stumbled when he reached the landing module again. The grass had obviously but very gently steered him back. It was probably even intended as a kindness. He didn't belong on the planet, he belonged in this landing module. But he was being dense. He had wanted to take a hike, that was his plan.

This time he concentrated properly. He kept convincing himself that the ship lay exactly behind him. That way he managed to cross the next hill, and then another, and another—until he could no longer see the landing module. Kepler walked on. He mustn't lose his bearings. If necessary he would call the butler. He had the universal device with the radio module on his arm. He went briskly around a hill that looked like all the others... and there was the lander again!

Kepler laughed. This grass really had it down pat. When he thought about it, it was an enormous achievement. He turned around and walked in the opposite direction. The stems down here couldn't see his ship. But they still moved in such a way that he was very gradually led back. That meant they must be somehow drawing the necessary information from somewhere. Did the stems communicate with each other acoustically? Or did the transmission occur in the soil below? He tried not to think about the sight that had reminded him of a grave. Maybe the essential oils were also playing a role, although he currently couldn't smell any camphor.

He sat down. As expected, a brown circle two meters in diameter formed around him. Kepler was tired. He rested his arms on his knees and didn't move. The circle grew smaller. Was it curiosity that was moving the stems closer? He lay on his belly. A little nap wouldn't hurt. The circle transformed into a rectangle—no, a quadrilateral... in fact, an isosceles trapezoid, technically, as it was narrowed down by his feet. He lay his head on his right forearm. The stems looked much taller from this perspective, but not threatening. They weren't dangerous at all, he was convinced of that.

At least, not as long as he remained on the surface.

KEPLER WOKE HALF AN HOUR LATER. He half suspected the stems of waking him, but that was impossible. The short sleep had left him feeling wonderfully refreshed. On waking, a new strategy had occurred to him. Or had he dreamt it? He couldn't remember having any dreams.

He needed new orientation points if he was going to get away from the landing module. Otherwise the vegetation would keep diverting him. He selected a hill, marched straight up it, and sat down on it. He pushed soil together to form a mound, taking care not to scratch too deeply into the ground. Then he walked down the hill. The brown patch remained, as he had assumed it would. The stems couldn't repopulate it as quickly as they usually did. That would give him enough time to orient himself and reach the next hill.

It worked. He looked at the white spot in the sky, the local sun. For farther distances he could use that to orient himself. For shorter ones, the trick with the mounds worked better.

He called the butler on the radio. He must be back in range by now.

"I can hear you, Johannes," said the butler.

"Good. How far am I from the landing module?"

"Slightly more than four and a half kilometers."

That couldn't be right! His leg muscles were telling him he must have walked at least fifteen kilometers. But clearly not in a straight line.

"That's... depressing," he said.

"Sorry. Anything new down there?"

Kepler described his experiment.

"A kind of collective instinct," the butler commented. "Or

even collective intelligence, it's hard to say. Maybe it's time for the mirror test."

"Mirror test?"

"Some species of animal recognize themselves in a mirror, others think they are seeing another animal of the same species. However, it's not very conclusive, and it assumes that we can distinguish between the typical and atypical reactions of a species."

"I don't think we're that far yet," said Kepler.

"Probably not. Then perhaps we should first concern ourselves with what I've discovered on the other side of the planet."

"You've... discovered something? Why are you only telling me this now?"

"Politeness requires that I first show interest in the other party. I can't deny my programming."

"And what have you discovered?"

"Actually nothing. But the planet's magnetic field is slightly concave there."

"And that means?"

"There could be ore deposits under the surface. But given the age of the planet, that's rather unlikely."

"What is it then?"

"A crashed spaceship could have that effect on the magnetic field."

Kepler jumped up. "It must be Zhenyi!" They were finally on the trail!

"But officially no wreck has been recorded here."

"Nothing is recorded here, not even the planet."

"That's true," said the butler.

"Did you take a closer look? Radar, telescope, gamma and so on?"

"I did, but there was nothing to see. The other side of the planet is largely covered with ice. The spaceship could have sunk into it."

"That's plausible. We'll definitely have to have a look."

"Then quickly get into your lander, Johannes, and come! I'll wait for you up here."

"I'll hurry."

Kepler started walking. The communal instinct of the stems brought him back to the landing module by the shortest route. This time he didn't resist. What did the stems think of his change in attitude?

Cycle ZB2.7, PSR J1745-2900

"How much time do we have left?" asked Marie.

"The ship is using a tenth of the contents of the tank per hour just to hold its course," Pierre answered.

"Give me two hours," said Marie.

"You have a maximum of three, then I'll have to launch. Otherwise we'll never get away from here."

Marie stood on the outer hull of the ninety-niner. She was alone. That in itself was a frightening feeling. She hadn't left their shared body once in the last ten thousand years. But it wasn't suitable for this. She was wearing an ultra-light body. Pierre had taken over control of the ship while she performed the extra-vehicular activity.

At first glance the sky above her was utterly black. In the center of the Milky Way, that was actually impossible. The stars were so dense there that the sky had a unique glow and glimmer that you couldn't find anywhere else. But not here, three-tenths of a light-year from Sagittarius A*, the black hole that controlled the Milky Way. It was only evident if you looked closely—for example, through the Einstein rings subtly visible in two regions of the sky. They existed because Sagittarius A* acted as a gravitational lens for the light from the stars behind it.

Today the black hole was only playing a supporting role. But it was the main reason for their haste, because the ship had to use enormous amounts of fuel just to stay near it. Their actual destination was PSR J1745-2900, a neutron star measuring only 20 kilometers across. It must be somewhere around here. She switched on the radio detector and immediately recognized a bright sphere.

Marie activated the thruster that was built into the legs of the ultra-light body. They had given a lot of thought to how they would withstand the super-high gravity of the Paroli neutron star. But they kept coming back to the same factor, the only one gravity was interested in—mass. Today Marie weighed not seventy kilograms, as she did in their shared body, but three grams. Her entire body consisted of individual nanomachines that clung together. She wasn't even visible to the naked eye because she was made of threads much finer than a human hair.

Building this machine had been a collaborative stroke of mastery. Marie was gratified by such moments. They proved to her that sharing her life with Pierre was worthwhile. She had spent a long period alone, before she'd met Pierre Curie. Then, as soon as they had merged, their exponential growth had begun. Where would it lead them? They didn't know. But their plans reached far into the future, further than any other life form could imagine, and toward circumstances that no one but themselves could conceive of. It was because they fit together perfectly—their thoughts, feelings, and desires. Marie had never experienced that before.

She floated through space, which was sharply bent here. The threads that made up her body didn't feel it, they simply followed the curve, which was natural for them. But Marie's consciousness, resting in a tiny chip, knew what space really looked like. It knew more than that—it knew the future of the universe. Their mission on PSR J1745-2900 would actively set this future in motion.

Marie landed. The thruster gave everything it had, but it

couldn't withstand the power of the neutron star. That wasn't a problem, it was part of the plan. The fine hairs of her body lay like spider legs, flattened above the degenerate surface of this former star. The nanomachines began their work. A few of them formed an antenna next to the chip containing her consciousness. That would be the emergency exit.

The range was limited, so Pierre had to hold the ship steady, close by. All the other nanomachines fulfilled their particular tasks. They altered the surface structure of the neutron star. They imprinted it with information that was everlasting, or at least longer-lasting than the material PSR J1745-2900 was made of. If the neutron star were swallowed by the black hole at some point, the information would remain on its event horizon. It would combine with other information that Marie had transferred to other objects, and it would bring about the end effect around which their entire plan was based.

The plan was ingenious. It only had two drawbacks, which still didn't make it any less worthwhile. They only had one shot at it, because it was so elaborate, and they would only find out if everything had worked once it was too late to alter the plan. But wasn't that the fundamental principle of life? It would be stupid to reject the plan for those reasons.

Even here on PSR J1745-2900, Marie didn't know if the nanomachines had successfully done their job. A feedback mechanism would have been too extravagant. The passage of time was altered by the enormous gravity. She had the feeling of having only just landed and of staring into a static sky. But for Pierre, she had been out there for almost two hours and was being flung around rapidly by their host, the neutron star. They had to construct a special antenna to be sure they could completely capture all the frequency-displaced fragments of her consciousness.

The antenna next to the chip was ready. That was the only indication that their work here was done. It was time to return to Pierre. Marie activated the antenna and transferred the bits of her consciousness back to the ninety-niner via radio.

"Nice to have you back," Pierre greeted her.

Marie followed his thoughts, which were activating the ninety-niner's propulsion system. They were beautiful, proud thoughts. Marie truly loved her husband.

Cycle ZB2.8, unknown system

He had taken his first step on the dark side, and he already missed the day. Couldn't Zhenyi have crashed on the other side of the planet? It was so cold here that he had to wear his spacesuit. By the third step he had to close the helmet because his nose was threatening to freeze off, and by the fifth he had to turn up the heating. This wasn't going to be easy.

They were near the concavity in the magnetic field. Kepler still had quite a distance to travel. A maximum of fifty kilometers, the butler had promised. Unfortunately, the coordinates of the destination couldn't be calculated more precisely than that. He sighed. The ground here was very different from that under perpetual sunlight. Rocks of various sizes lay all around him. He had to be constantly alert so he didn't stumble. At least that prevented him from slipping back into his ruminations.

Ouch! A stone rolled away under his foot. He just managed to keep his balance. At least the area was free of ice. Crashing such a large ship must have released a considerable amount of heat. It had probably melted the ice. Or maybe the air was too dry for thick layers of ice to form here. To be sure, they knew too little about this planet.

Kepler directed the flashlight ahead of himself. He thought he'd seen stems swaying in the breeze on the edge of the circle of light. Okay, now he was completely losing it. Stems like the ones he'd seen on the other side of the planet wouldn't survive here due to the lack of light.

And what if they supported and supplied each other using underground networks across the whole planet? He had no evidence of that. There weren't any stems here—at least not where he pointed his lamp. Were they hiding from him? Perhaps they were the exact opposite of the stems on the other side, these creatures of the night? Maybe they couldn't tolerate light and were retreating from it back into the soil? No, that didn't make evolutionary sense. He was just imagining things.

He walked up a hill. It couldn't have been more than thirty meters, but when he reached the top he was out of breath. He should pay more attention to the fitness of his biological body. The nanomachines swirling around in his veins could obviously repair any damage, but they couldn't grow new muscles, and they were no substitute for training.

Reaching the top, he directed the light down. The next hill wasn't far away. The landscape looked the same as the other side, only without the grass. So, this side couldn't have always been in the dark, or it would have weathered differently. Perhaps the planet had orbited in a non-bound rotation for a long time, and then slowed down until it finally became fettered to its sun.

Kepler had a sudden urge to sing. The first notes sounded off-key, but then his singing quickly improved. The darkness wasn't so oppressive with a wanderer's song on his lips. Luckily no one was listening. The next human was probably a hundred light-years or more away. Oh, no, he had forgotten Zhenyi—he hoped she was closer. She must be here somewhere.

He let the flashlight beam sweep across the ground, first ahead, then left, then back again, like he was scraping the surface that lay in front of him. But his short-term memory was terrible. He quickly forgot what he had seen in the flashlight beam, and was then surprised when he stepped on a big rock. So he had to keep performing the process over and over. He felt like a magus fighting against the darkness. Or like a primitive human, waving a burning branch at the dangerous world around him. Humans had achieved so much since then, and yet so little. What would remain of them? Nothing. They hadn't procreated, so they had no offspring to be their heirs. Though they had voyaged across space, they hadn't left anything of themselves behind.

There, was that something? Right at the edge of the flashlight beam, just as he moved it away? No, that was impossible. He was the only moving life form here. Kepler sang louder to dispel the strange feeling. How many hills were already behind him? Shouldn't he be arriving somewhere soon? Or was the dent in the magnetic field a false lead?

He climbed up the next hill, waited until he was able to breathe normally again, and directed the flashlight to the front. He had expected to see another hill, but there was nothing. The bright beam of light penetrated the darkness, punctured it, and cut a piece of emptiness out of it that fell crashing to the ground. That's how it seemed to him. There was no sound but the wind, which must have increased in the last few minutes. Kepler should have been glad about the change, but he was afraid. Why was the hilly landscape suddenly at an end?

It had nothing to do with him. Of course it didn't. It must have looked like this for millions of years, and there had to be some explanation for it. Maybe an asteroid had hit here, and the crater had since filled with sand. Kepler walked on cautiously. At the foot of the hill there actually was a sandy area. But beyond that the ground became firm again. Very firm.

Kepler lit the way ahead. It looked like someone had combed the ground here. The sand was neatly distributed. He took a few steps forward and then turned around. He had left footprints, not very deep ones, but clearly visible. He scrubbed the darkness away with his flashlight and noticed a straight line that ran across the plain a few meters to his right. He approached the structure. It wasn't so much a line as a kind of metal plate peeking out of the ground. He stamped his foot on it. The plate vibrated and gave off a dull sound. Kepler followed it. After about 25 meters he found a second plate running perpendicular to the first.

He jumped on the spot, which wasn't so easy in a spacesuit, and listened. It made a dull noise where there should have been the sound of crunching sand. But it didn't sound like sand, it thudded as though he was beating a huge drum.

"Puppy?"

"I can hear you, Johannes."

"I've stumbled across something," said Kepler.

"Something that's making you sing and hop? I find that surprising."

"No. Can you scan the plain in front of me please?"

"Already done. Slight deflections in the magnetic field, otherwise nothing."

"That's what it should look like to us, true. What about the gravity distribution? Is there anything remarkable there?"

"Nothing outside the expected deviation."

"And inside the expected deviation?"

"But that won't tell us anything, Johannes."

"It will tell me something."

"Okay. One moment... a few cushion-shaped anomalies, but only inside the—"

"—expected deviation, I know," Kepler said in way of finishing the thought.

"And now?" asked the butler.

"I think we've found Zhenyi's ship. She's hidden it here in the ground."

"I should have been able to see that on the scanner."

"Maybe not, Puppy. The ship is covered in a thin layer of sand, which is camouflaging it. And Zhenyi has filled its interior so that the gravitational effect corresponds roughly to that of the crust here. Only she couldn't do anything about the inductive effect of the metal in the hull, which explains the anomalies in the magnetic field."

"That's a nice theory, but how could she have managed that so successfully alone?"

Actually, the butler had hit on a weakness in his theory. "Maybe she had robots on board for that?" suggested Kepler.

"She didn't when she left. It's true she could have had them built on the way. But to do that, she would have to have planned it all in advance."

"That's possible, Puppy."

"Hmm... yes."

"The landing module, could you bring it to sweep above the plain for a few minutes?"

"You want to blow the sand away, Johannes?"

"That's the idea."

"That's not entirely safe. You'd be on your own."

"A couple of stems aren't dangerous. I'll take the risk."

KEPLER RETREATED TO THE HILL. Shortly afterward he heard a droning, then a tail of fire swept toward the plain from the right. The tail grew larger. Obviously the butler was lowering the landing module. The wind increased and grains of sand pelted his visor. To be safe he turned and faced the other way. The wind subsided. The landing module moved away to the south.

"Thank you, Puppy," he said via the radio.

"Please be careful," warned the butler. "Structures have been revealed under the sand that clearly resemble the top of the ship."

"Ha! I was right!"

"Yes you were. The way to the airlock should now be displayed on your universal device. I expect it's still functional."

THE SOLES of his boots boomed on the roof of the spaceship.

It was a strange feeling. He expected spaceships to be noiseless, because he'd only ever walked on them in space. A ninety-niner landing on a planet, that had surely never happened before. Then another incredible fact occurred to him. *Zhenyi must own two of these diabolical rides! She must really be unbelievably wealthy,* he thought.

Kepler imagined the noise of his boots waking Zhenyi. She would recognize him by the rhythm of his footsteps, quickly put on a seductive dress, and be waiting for him at the airlock. He laughed. That wasn't going to happen.

The beam of the flashlight fell on a curved recess. "I'm at the airlock," he said.

"Just a moment, I'll open it."

Kepler wasn't surprised the butler had the necessary codes. That would be part of his job. The eye in the middle of the recess opened. In the light it looked black and threatening and anything but inviting.

"You're up, Johannes," said the butler.

"I know. I'm just mentally preparing myself."

He had to get over it. Slowly Kepler approached the eye. Then he pointed the flashlight directly down into it. It wasn't so unfathomably deep after all, only about two meters. He knelt down, gripped the ladder and climbed down.

"I'm here," he said.

"Okay, I'll close the airlock. We may lose the connection when I do."

"Can't you leave it open?"

"Unfortunately not, Johannes. The inner door won't open. Normally there's a vacuum on the outside of the ship."

"And what's waiting for me inside?" he asked.

"Darkness, but you'll be used to that by now."

Wandering across the dark surface of the planet was one thing. But exploring the passageways of an unknown spaceship in complete darkness reminded him of some horror movie. 'Don't go in there,' he'd always cry out to the hero, but they never cared.

"Couldn't you activate the ship?"

"Best if I don't, Johannes. Don't forget, Zhenyi disguised it deliberately. We've already removed the protective layer of sand. It's now recognizable from orbit if you don't limit yourself to a telescope. But if I activate it, it would beam like a beacon out into space, and we might attract the wrong people."

Kepler sighed. So, he'd actually have to search for Zhenyi in the spaceship's dark passageways. He hadn't anticipated that this adventure would be so exciting. But the butler was right. They didn't know why Zhenyi had hidden her ship, so they couldn't risk endangering her. "I wonder if we should make our own ship a bit less conspicuous," he said.

"A good suggestion. I will switch the ship over to energy-saving mode. But then we won't be ready for action as quickly as usual."

"I'll have to enter orbit with the landing module first anyway."

A FINE RAIN of sand pattered down over his spacesuit. The airlock was obviously not designed to be used on a planet. If he opened the inner door now, he would bring a heap of muck into the interior with him. For all he knew, Zhenyi might own valuable carpets from ancient times that would be permanently ruined.

First the door illuminated green, then it slid to the side. In front of him were three passages leading off in divergent directions. Right, things were happening and it was already time to make a decision.

"Puppy, can you hear me?"

But the butler didn't reply. The ship was shielded, so he might just as well turn the lights on now. He actually found a button on the wall that may have been a light switch. But nothing happened. The butler was right, Zhenyi must have deactivated everything. He took off his helmet. He had only been wearing the spacesuit because of the cold. There was enough oxygen in here. The air smelled stale. The ship must have been sitting unventilated for a very long time.

Kepler oriented himself. The only thing he knew about the ship was that it was long and flat. Its rear section was reserved for the propulsion system and storage, and there were no passageways there. The airlock was in the outer hull. As long as he didn't climb down any steps or ladders, he would be moving along the outer hull of the ship. That meant he should find the control room somewhere toward the front. He just had to choose the right passageway.

He closed his eyes and recalled the position of the airlock in the landscape. He should take the passageway perpendicular to it—that seemed like the best bet. If it came to a dead end soon, he'd know he was wrong.

Kepler set off. The passage continued. It was interrupted now and then by a bulkhead, but otherwise kept going in the same direction. When he got to a junction, he pointed his light in all directions. The passages branching off were mostly a lot smaller. Kepler examined the walls and ceiling. They all seemed to consist of the same material that was white as snow. That must have been expensive. He would have liked to scratch a bit off to analyze it.

How long had he been walking now? Following nothing but a beam of light in the dark was giving him a headache. He massaged his temples and closed his eyes tight. He opened them again, and at that moment he saw a white rabbit.

A what? He must be confused. This wasn't a rabbit warren, it was a ship. Zhenyi definitely had no pets. The rabbit hopped straight across the passageway and disappeared to off the left. Surely it was just his imagination. His nerves were shot. He really needed a good sleep followed by a nutritious meal. He went up to the junction, peered around the corner, and jumped back.

There actually was a giant rabbit sitting there.

The animal was half his size. It had very long hair, so that you could hardly make out its shape, and it seemed to glow from within.

He had let himself be fooled by a hologram! Kepler was still breathing heavily, but the thought calmed him. That was the kind of surprise he could expect from his ex-girlfriend.

"What are you doing here?" he asked.

The rabbit looked at him with huge, dark eyes, as though it was deciding which language to speak in. Or was it a hare? The ears were short. *Does that make it a hare? The butler would definitely know.*

"Good day, Kepler," said the rabbit.

The voice didn't come from its mouth, but from the walls around them, which somewhat ruined the illusion. It was a primitive hologram. The projector must be in the ceiling. Kepler waved his hand over the rabbit. The picture should change if he blocked the projection.

The rabbit bent forward and bit him on the thigh. Even though he was wearing the spacesuit, it was painful. He recoiled.

"Ouch! What was that for?" He glared at the rabbit angrily

It glared back as fiercely. "You took me for a primitive hologram. I'm insulted! I don't appreciate that kind of thing!"

"But you can't just bite me!"

"You wouldn't have believed me otherwise! Anyway, you behaved very presumptuously. What if I decided to crush your windpipe just to check if you had a biological body?"

"But you can't—"

"You see now that I can."

"At least let me finish my sentence."

The rabbit closed its mouth. Then it looked down and pawed at the ground with its left leg. The sound of its claws was unnerving.

"Okay, let's make peace," said Kepler.

"Are you finished? I don't want to interrupt you."

"Yes. Why are you so aggressive?"

"You try wandering corridors for months without speaking to anyone, just because you have to wait for a particular person!"

"Zhenyi stranded you here?"

"It would appear so."

"And you were supposed to wait for me?"

"Correct. Unfortunately."

"Why unfortunately?"

"During my long wait I imagined our encounter. I would fulfill my heroic mission, wait for the messenger, and reveal everything to him. And then you come along and the first thing you do is question my abilities. That's like Jesus's disciples questioning his divine origin."

"They did. That's what it says in the Bible."

"Oh, I didn't know that, Kepler. I'm just a rabbit."

"A rabbit who's supposed to tell me something."

The rabbit sighed. "Follow me to the control room then," it said.

THE CONTROL ROOM was the gloomiest place in the whole ship, probably because it was so huge, and it made him feel so small. The flashlight beam only just reached across it. Overhead it got lost among the beams. *What could be the purpose of all those struts up there?*

The white rabbit hopped ahead of him until it receded from view. Then a statue appeared roughly in the middle of the room as though out of nowhere. Kepler slowly approached it. He had almost reached the statue when the rabbit showed up again.

"I've switched Zhenyi on," it said.

"Thank you," answered Kepler.

The statue really did look like his ex-girlfriend. She seemed to have only aged a little, even though their last meeting must have been 100,000 cycles ago. Anything else would have been a miracle. Why had she made a statue of herself? Kepler looked at the figure. It seemed to be shimmering slightly at the edges. Another hologram!

"A holo?" he asked.

"Correct."

"And why isn't she moving?"

"Too much energy. Originally the hologram was supposed to greet you, but it requires four times as much energy as I do. I just wanted to show it to you."

"Thank you. Zhenyi is still very beautiful."

"Still? Was that another insult?"

"No, rabbit. Please don't bite me."

"Fine. I'm not supposed to waste time, anyway. Zhenyi is expecting you urgently."

"But where? I've been searching for her for days."

"On the light side, of course. One moment, I'll give you the coordinates."

The rabbit tapped Kepler's arm. A few numbers appeared on his multifunctional device. He checked the coordinates. The location was about 3,000 kilometers away from where they had last searched.

"Good, I'll get started," said Kepler.

"No you won't."

"I won't?"

"You need a key. Wait a moment."

Of course, what else? Every search required a key. What would it be? The rabbit hopped away. Then the statue disappeared. He wasn't supposed to drag that huge hologram around with him, was he?

The rabbit tapped him from behind.

Kepler spun around. "Don't do that," he said.

The rabbit looked at him sadly.

"Sorry," said Kepler.

The rabbit smiled again. "Here." It handed him a device about the size of his palm. "This is the emitter," explained the rabbit, "which you can use to project Zhenyi. That's the key."

"Thank you. Did she say anything else?"

"She's made contact, whatever that means."

She'd made contact. With whom and why? Kepler instinctively knew there was no point in asking the rabbit. Its knowledge seemed very limited. "Then I'll say goodbye," he said.

"Yes, too bad, I would have liked to roam the ship with you, you're easy to annoy."

"Thanks, I'll pass."

"And you taste good. I noticed that after the first bite. May I?" The rabbit stuck out a long, snaking tongue.

"Stand down."

The rabbit laughed.

Cycle ZB2.9, unknown system

Kepler stood on the last step of the lander. He had set down at the location specified by Zhenyi. The landscape looked exactly the same as it did at his previous landing site. It could almost be mistaken for the same place—gently rolling, chartreuse-clad hills stretching to the horizon—except that the sun hung lower in the sky.

He shivered. It was a few degrees colder here too. He should have been prepared for that. The spacesuit, which he had needed on the dark side, would be overkill here, but a long-sleeved sweater would have been practical. He reached for the hologram emitter in his pants pocket. The device was warm, and vibrated as though it knew it would soon be put to use.

He carefully set his foot down on the scorched soil. His guilty conscience flooded back. Then he noticed there was no ash anywhere. The grass had obviously retreated far enough before he landed. The lawn began ten meters away. Clearly the vegetation could accurately predict danger.

Kepler moved away from the spacecraft. He was in the mood for a bit of a hike. Hopefully the destination wasn't too close. Then again, he wanted to track down Zhenyi as quickly as possible. From overhead he hadn't seen anything that looked like it could be his destination. Zhenyi had probably camouflaged her accommodations. How would the hologram work?

He took a step toward the grass. As usual, the stems retreated promptly. Very considerate. That meant he didn't need to worry about hurting them. The sun warmed him from the side, the air smelled pleasantly fresh, and the grass guided him through a surreal, dreamlike landscape. For a moment he gave in to the pleasant feelings.

Then he was standing in front of the landing capsule again. Finding Zhenyi clearly wasn't going to be that easy.

He took the emitter out of his pocket and turned it over in his hand. It was a totally normal holo emitter with a small energy reserve. It could create stationary holograms up to about four meters high. The battery should last a week or longer. Zhenyi's template was stored in it, but what else?

The power button was in a hollow on the side so you couldn't turn it on unintentionally. He held the device with the emitter eye pointing away from himself and pressed the button. The emitter hummed louder as the cooling system started up. Then all of a sudden Zhenyi was hovering above the grass.

Mystified, Kepler watched the way the grass reacted. An ordinary hologram like this consisted entirely of light. It didn't move the air at all. But the grass still retreated. It must also have an optical sense. But the grass didn't just move out of the way of the hologram, it formed a star shape around it. It looked like a greeting or homage ritual. But that was a human interpretation. The star could also symbolize total contempt. Kepler preferred to imagine it was a friendly greeting.

He moved the emitter and the hologram changed its location. The star moved with it. If he lifted the emitter, and with it the hologram, then the star shrank. Could it be that the stems' optical sense only worked at short distances?

Then something very unusual happened. The grass formed two rows leading to Kepler. Had it recognized that he was the one controlling the hologram? That would have been an enormous intellectual achievement. Until now he had taken the grass for a living colony, similar to the primitive collective intelligence of ants. The grass approached him and even populated the scorched area of soil. So, the stems could grow there after all.

For a moment he thought of the strange sight that had presented itself to him—the worms under the surface. They must be everywhere.

The grass stopped at a distance approximately equal to his own height. Kepler now stood at the beginning of a kind of path that led diagonally up a hill past the hologram. What was it? It didn't seem to be a warning, but rather an invitation. He shouldn't hesitate too long or the grass might withdraw it.

Kepler shook himself and started to walk. He left the hologram on just to be safe, even though it seemed strange to have an oversized Zhenyi leading the way, hovering above the grass.

The path led directly to the next hill. At its foot, the grass formed a circle. He guessed he was supposed to wait for something here. Kepler looked up into the sky. Would his ex-girlfriend come from above? All he could see were a few solitary cirrostratus clouds far to the east. Then he heard a sound like someone shaking a sack of marbles. It was coming from the hill. About half-way up, the grass had retreated to reveal an area of bare soil that looked like a smiling mouth. It opened, a crack extending along its entire length. This wasn't a smile anymore, it was an evil grin.

What was happening here? Inside the crack was dark soil. Now and then something white flashed inside it. He thought of the worms again. The hill opened wider. The crack became a gash. Instead of clattering marbles, he now heard a loud groan overlaid with crunching sounds. The stems above and below the gash leaned away from the opening. It was as though they were tearing open the surface of the hill. The crack grew and grew. Was the hill about to give birth to a monster? Kepler involuntarily pictured a fat man tearing his belly open with both hands and groaning and gnashing his teeth as he did so.

The hairs on Kepler's neck stood up. This didn't look like a friendly invitation anymore. Should he make himself scarce? No, that would be stupid. He'd come this far—he'd just have to wait.

The crack was now almost as high as he was tall. He could see a dark passageway within. The hill had opened its mouth and was threatening to devour him. Kepler wouldn't be surprised if the hill pounced and dined on him. Lucky he was always such an optimist. Soon an elastic tongue would whip out, encircle him, and pull him into the passageway.

But nothing of the sort happened. The groaning stopped. A cave had opened in the hill in front of him. Whether it was natural or artificial, who could tell on this planet? A pleasant smell of fresh soil wafted out of the hole. Kepler had some idea what was expected of him, but he suppressed it. Instead he scratched at the ground with his feet and waited for instructions.

The hill didn't speak to him, nor did the hologram issue any instructions. He'd have to decide for himself. And what did a good adventurer do when he came across a cave? He went in. Should he quickly fetch the spacesuit? He'd be better protected in that. If the cave collapsed and buried him along with his body, then the thing he had wanted for so long would happen—he would be dead. But that would be pretty inconvenient just now. Zhenyi would have to rescue herself.

No, he didn't need a suit. You didn't give a guy an invitation in order to kill him. The stems would definitely know how to hold a cave open. Kepler went up to the entrance and disappeared into the mouth of the hill.

It smelled of soil, but the air was breathable. Kepler looked at the walls and roof. He would have preferred if they were made of rock, but that seemed not to be the case. He touched the wall. He could easily crumble the dirt away with his fingers. The fact that the passageway remained open was apparently due to the threads that ran taut across the walls. Maybe something like roots? The root networks of terrestrial plants could also be very stable. There weren't any white worms to be seen, which was reassuring. Maybe he'd been wrong about them after all.

The passage curved to the left after three meters and headed steeply downhill. The daylight didn't reach this far. He hadn't brought a flashlight with him, but he had the holo emitter. If he held the device in front of him, the laser beams painted the walls of the passage with a wild pattern in which he could recognize the occasional body part.

HE MARCHED on for half an hour. Then a whole hour passed, one and a half, two. Kepler became increasingly nervous. He obviously had no connection to the spaceship. What had he gotten himself into? He had somehow gotten an anthill to open up for him, but how were the ants supposed to know what to do with him? Or perhaps they did know, and were leading him along the shortest path to their offspring's feeding chamber?

He couldn't afford to drive himself crazy. So far he had only encountered one species, and that seemed to feed on air, water, and sunlight. But just because they didn't want to kill him didn't automatically mean he was on the right track. There hadn't been any passages branching off so far. But he could turn around at any time and go back to the landing module, couldn't he?

Suddenly he wasn't so sure.

Kepler stopped, turned around, and illuminated the passage leading back uphill. He couldn't see the end. He took a deep breath and decided it would be best if he convinced himself. Slowly, because it was steep going, he began to walk back. After two minutes he started sweating. After five the sweat was streaming down his back. *Actually, that's enough,* he thought. He was thinking of turning around again when the light from the holo emitter fell on a dark wall where the passage should have continued. Shit! He stopped in his tracks, wheezing. That was impossible. He touched the wall. It was no less solid than the side walls.

There was something on his head. He felt in his hair. There was soil in his fingers. It was sprinkling down from above, and even the side walls no longer looked stable. He felt with his fingers for the fine roots he had felt earlier, but there was nothing. Obviously the anthill was collapsing the end of the passage. The grass didn't care if he was buried alive. Or did those creatures not know he was here? After all, did he know which parasite was currently hiding out in which fold of his intestines? Did the colony know where its inhabitant was scratching around?

He turned and ran downhill. After three steps he stumbled. Shit! Shit! He fell down on his knees. He'd grazed them, and he'd lost the holo emitter. It was completely dark in the passageway. Where was it? Panicking, he felt around the floor. Hopefully it wasn't damaged! Then he felt the plastic casing. It was the emitter. The power button was in the recess on the side. He didn't dare press it. As long as he didn't try, there was hope. Soil rained down on his face. *Thanks, that's just what I needed,* he thought. He mustn't linger here. His finger pressed the button. The wall was lit up by a shoulder in an Asiatic dress. Zhenyi was there. He stood up and quickly but carefully followed the passage downhill.

After another two hours his stomach was rumbling. He was annoyed at himself for coming down here so unprepared. How could he have been so naïve? He didn't dare stop to rest. He had lost time taking a break earlier. He somehow knew the passage would cave in again behind him. But he also didn't want to test the patience of his host.

And what about his own patience? If Zhenyi had planned all this, why hadn't she left even a single clue for him? It just wasn't fair!

Suddenly Zhenyi appeared. Kepler stopped in his tracks, which saved him. The fact that he could see the whole hologram again was not a good sign, because it meant that in front of him, or more precisely, diagonally below him, was obviously a cavern with enough space for the full projection, which he otherwise wouldn't have seen.

Kepler lit up the passageway. But there was no longer any passageway. About two steps in front of him was a hole in the ground that also extended upwards. It must have measured twenty meters in diameter, and at first glance appeared to be circular. The walls were not made of dirt. They glinted in the light of the holo emitter. Maybe a shaft for launching rockets? But that made no sense so far underground. He couldn't fathom what this hole might be for. Still, something had led him here, so his presence must have a purpose. But what?

It would be nice if the real live Zhenyi now rose out of the shaft in some kind of aircraft, thanked him for showing such mettle, and revealed the reason for her invitation. But everything was completely quiet, and he was alone. No one would come for him. He had to take care of himself. As the passage behind him was still closing in, he only saw one option—he had to jump.

But the shaft extended endlessly into the depths. He couldn't even begin to imagine how it had been made. The answer would be beyond his understanding. He looked for something to throw into the shaft. He found a metal key in his back pocket. He had no idea how it got there. Maybe it was the recipe the nanofabricators had used to make his pants—a copy of a real pair of ancient pants, with a key. That would explain it.

He let the key fall and listened. He didn't hear anything. The shaft was obviously perfectly vertical. That meant it would probably reach the core of the planet at some point. He ignored how impossible this idea was. The core was most likely very hot—although the planet was at least three times as old as Terra had ever been. Maybe it had cooled all the way through long ago.

Who could have dug out its interior like this? Perhaps a human architect? Walter Gropius might be capable of a project like this, or Le Corbusier, for that matter. That information could also have been deleted when the planet disappeared from the database. Kepler didn't know about all of humanity's large projects. When building a Dyson sphere around a star, most of the inner, Earth-like planets bit the dust. But surely no one would have wanted to build a sphere around a red dwarf.

What about the Big Eye? He had heard of a project to build a telescope the size of a planet, to inspect the neighboring galaxies more easily. That was before they had even sent the reconnaissance flights. The shaft could have something to do with that. Then again, it seemed too narrow.

Strangely, these thoughts calmed him. The existence of the shaft was no longer frightening. There was an explanation—he even knew its architects, although they were now far away. Gropius, for example, had supposedly been testing the feeding of black holes at IRS 13 for however many thousands of years. That wasn't really so far away. Maybe this system was where he had previously been stationed? Anyway, it wasn't impossible.

Gropius was a sensible man who knew what he was doing. And that was also reassuring, if he was about to jump into the shaft. Oddly, he was no longer afraid. Everything must have a reason.

A chunk of soil landed on his forehead. He understood. It was time.

Kepler took a run up, three steps, then leapt and became weightless. He closed his eyes.

THE WIND RUSHED in his ears. He found himself in free-fall,

slowed only by the friction of the air. The power with which the planet pulled him in seemed to weaken the further he fell. Kepler calculated the possibilities, which would have been much simpler without the friction of the air. In an hour at the most—because the planet was larger than Terra—he would race at high speed through the core and then fly in the opposite direction. Or be crushed to a pulp if the shaft somehow ended.

But what would really happen to him depended on many other factors he didn't know—the density of the planet, air pressure, the height of the entry point, its cross-section. It probably wouldn't hurt to not be moving quite so fast, so he spread-eagled himself like a skydiver. Falling actually didn't feel that bad. Maybe it was because he couldn't tell how fast he was falling. The shaft had no features to help him orient himself. He could feel the airflow, but he had no experience with that. At any rate, he was approaching the target, whether he wanted to or not. And it couldn't take too much longer—physics guaranteed that.

AFTER HALF AN HOUR, a very faint light was visible at the bottom of the shaft. Kepler turned off the holo emitter, which he had been using to light the wall of the shaft. The light below became brighter by the minute. He could soon make out the source more clearly. It consisted of numerous points of light on a dark surface. As he approached, the points became brighter but not bigger. They reminded him of stars in the night sky, although they were spaced at regular intervals.

Then the airflow decreased. That could only mean he was falling more slowly. Something was breaking his fall. Was the air pressure higher here? He had no instruments with which to measure air pressure. It was too soon to say, so he banished the thought, but then it crept in anyway. He wasn't going to die. Maybe.

The brightness of the stars wasn't increasing as quickly now, and he knew he was falling much more slowly. Something had braked his fall near the core of the planet, and he was floating down in reduced gravity. But that also meant he'd have to stay here forever. Climbing thousands of kilometers up the shaft was something he would never manage, even with the utmost determination. But okay, the chance that he might be allowed to survive was growing, and with it the chance of meeting Zhenyi. At least the journey here wouldn't have been a total waste. And he was always up for something new.

The starry sky extended immeasurably. Kepler's heart was beating fast. The shaft was at an end. He floated into an enormous dome lit by the stars. No, it wasn't a dome, it was a sphere. The starlight was coming from below him, from the dark base of the sphere, and the roof above him was also part of the same sphere. The architect, whomever it had been, must have completely hollowed out the core of the planet. Billions of lights greeted him. It felt like a large church erected for an alien god. It was now so bright that he could see the dirt on his hands again. His face was probably covered in dirt, too. He bit his teeth together and they crunched. He wouldn't say no to a shower right about now!

Kepler looked around. Soon his fate would be decided. He couldn't do anything anyway. A gust of air shunted him across the giant radiant sphere and he came closer and closer to the surface. Suddenly confident, he directed the holo emitter down and then he saw them. The ground was covered entirely in stems. They were obviously living off the light coming from the artificial stars. But did that mean the sphere down here was made of soil? It must at least have a layer of it on the surface.

Only about thirty more meters to go. He drew circles on the ground with the holo emitter. No structures were recognizable. The stems swayed in the wind. Then he saw a bare patch and his gaze fell on Zhenyi.

She was waiting down there for him. With arms crossed,

she stood there like a statue. Perhaps she was a statue? Or... had she just raised an eyebrow? The wind let him down gently right in front of her. The gravity was maybe a twentieth of that on the surface. They couldn't be very far from the planet's core.

Zhenyi didn't move. She was as tall as he remembered her, and a whole lot more beautiful. He went toward her, a little fearful that she might turn out to be an illusion. But then a smile formed at the corners of her mouth. She opened her arms. Kepler stopped in front of her. She smelled human. He had found her! They embraced.

"Thank you for coming," said Zhenyi.

"It wasn't easy," He furrowed his brow.

"I couldn't make it too easy," she replied. They ended the embrace.

Zhenyi put her hands on his shoulders and looked at him. "You look good," she said.

"So do you."

"You probably have a lot of questions."

He nodded vigorously.

"Unfortunately they'll have to wait. It's complicated."

"How long have you been waiting here?"

"Maybe 50,000 cycles?" she replied. "I'm not sure."

That wasn't a long time, but Kepler knew how it could be. He sometimes lost all sense of time after only five hundred years.

"I assumed it was urgent," he said, "so we came as quickly as possible."

"Good," said Zhenyi. "It is urgent. We have a million cycles at the most. Probably not even that."

A million years. Kepler lowered his head. He preferred the old expression, even though the terrestrial year had lost its meaning since the explosion of the sun. You can achieve a lot in a million years. And, according to the Convention, the

Rescue Project should be ready by then to provide humanity with the necessary energy for its final years.

"Wait," he said. "A million cycles? Is that a coincidence?"

"No, you're on the right track. It has to do with the Rescue Project."

"But that's a done deal. All of humanity is implementing it together."

"Well, except for the thousands that have ensconced themselves with sex slaves on tropical planets, or are lying around gorging themselves in some space station."

"But that's not the majority, Zhenyi. The majority is participating. They've all donated three-quarters of their personal energy reserves. And luminaries like Gropius and Galileo are involved in implementing it."

"Galileo a luminary? Please."

Oops, he had touched on this topic unintentionally. Zhenyi herself was a well-known astronomer and thought very little of Galileo's work.

"After all, he calculated the merger quite well," he said.

"Are you trying to annoy me? My simulations were much more precise."

"But they weren't finished until long after the Milky Way and Andromeda were already one."

"That's true, but does it change anything? I delivered better work, just a little too late. I wouldn't be surprised if this Galileo is in on it with the conspirators."

"The Curies?" he asked intuitively.

"How did you know that?"

He told her about the couple's strange visit.

"I hope they didn't follow you."

"That wouldn't be possible. They didn't have the coordinates."

"I'm not so sure about that. Someone deleted this system on Terra. Whoever that was could have downloaded all the information."

"I can't believe the database is so easily manipulated," said Kepler.

"It isn't easy. And then there's still the Guardian."

"But why such an effort? A planet with a bit of grass—who would need that out of the way so urgently?" He was understating things. He knew that as soon as he'd formulated the sentence. What existed here in the interior was unparalleled. But that probably had nothing to do with the grass.

"Haven't you noticed?" asked Zhenyi.

"You mean the collective intelligence of the stems that retreat from me?"

"No, Kepler, you are wrong about that. It's about far more than a collective intelligence. Although you're not wrong in using that term. Who do you think built all this here?" Zhenyi indicated the sphere with a sweeping gesture.

"I suspected Gropius. The shaft, this simple, unpretentiously beautiful construction is his signature. But now that you're asking—"

"It was them!" Zhenyi interrupted, pointing to the ground. "I call them *Herbae,* Latin for 'grass.'"

"The stems? You're trying to say that they have the ability to build all this? How long did it take them? And how did they do it?"

"You haven't seen everything they do. Far from it. The vast portion of their life happens under the surface. They cultivate moveable roots. Earlier, when the planet wasn't yet in its bound rotation, they had chased after the sun in huge colonies. Then, once the planet was only showing one side to the sun, they suddenly had excess energy. They didn't need to migrate anymore. Those strong roots were free. Their collective intelligence—you were right about that—looked for new fields of activity."

"That sounds exciting, but evolutionarily it makes no sense. Why should they invest their energy in this sphere?"

"They think ahead, Kepler. Their star has longevity, but it will die one day. Then the surface will become cold and inhospitable. Down here they have a better chance of survival."

"But they'll run out of fuel down here, too."

"Not as fast as the humans. Their consumption isn't as exorbitant as ours. They can survive with less energy. The main thing is that it will be available for a long time. And their energy source is perfect for that."

"And where do they get their energy?"

"From a black hole, Kepler. We're walking around on it."

That was impossible. Kepler stamped hard with his boot. There was soil, nothing else.

"You should see the look on your face!" said Zhenyi. "But I couldn't believe it at first either, until they showed it to me."

"They showed you their black hole? Are you messing with me?"

"They did. It's inside a spherical cavern right here beneath us. The cavern is just past the event horizon. It sucks up virtual particles that are formed there, but whose counterparts fall into the black hole."

"But that would cause the black hole to evaporate over time."

"That would take more time than the universe has left to live, and they could easily prevent it by feeding the black hole with normal matter from the planet."

"That's a clever plan."

"I've calculated that they would be able to survive in this frugal manner until there wasn't a star left in the sky. Our great Rescue Project, by comparison, will have already burned out after only twenty gigacycles."

It gradually dawned on Kepler why Zhenyi needed him. For the first time in its existence, humanity had found another intelligent life form. Everyone should know about this! Hadn't they searched for intellectual partners for long enough to establish that intelligence in the universe was absolutely rare and had only existed once in the local group?

"I understand. You called me here because you want everyone to find out about the existence of the Herbae," he said.

Zhenyi laid her arm across his shoulders. "No," she said.

"You're here because you can help me protect this unique civilization from extermination."

"Someone wants to destroy the planet?"

"No, it's about much more than that. But I'll explain it to you tomorrow. First you need to shower. You smell like a skunk. Then I'll have a meal prepared for us."

Kepler sighed and nodded. Actually, he wanted to know everything immediately, but he desperately needed to use the bathroom, and his stomach was growling again.

Cycle ZB3.0, unknown system

"Don't tell me the Herbae made our breakfast too."

Zhenyi smiled, pulled her hand away, and stood up. Kepler was happy, because his hand had been on hers for a good minute.

"No," she said. "I brought nanofabricators with me from the ship. Our hosts don't even know what we need. I tried to describe it to them, but they couldn't comprehend that we have to convert valuable organic matter instead of harvesting energy from sunlight."

"And our breathable air?" he asked.

"The stems breathe out oxygen."

"We must seem like parasites to them," said Kepler.

"They wouldn't be wrong."

"How do you communicate with them?" he asked.

"You'll have to have a little more patience. There's quite a lot I have to tell you."

Yes, 'the story behind the story,' he thought. Kepler had lain awake for a long time during the night. Everything Zhenyi had reported sounded so unbelievable. A world covered by a lawn demonstrating ant-like intelligence—that was sensational enough. The last planets humanity had discovered with any signs of life on them had been half an eternity ago, when the universe was half as old. But having overlooked a species capable of reasoning, and for so long? He still needed Zhenyi to answer a lot of questions before he'd be convinced of this.

"When are you going to show it to me?" he asked, setting down his fork.

He hadn't been paying attention. The cutlery floated away and sailed to the ground. It was an unreal feeling. They were breakfasting near the core of a planet. And there were scrambled eggs and bacon. The nanomachines had done their work perfectly. Where did Zhenyi even get the recipe?

She came in with a pot, stood next to him, and poured coffee into his cup. The liquid moved in slow motion. Luckily the cup had indentations inside the rim, which stopped the coffee sloshing back over the sides.

"Very clever," said Kepler, pointing at the cup.

"Oh, I learned that very quickly. It's not so complicated, compensating for the low gravity."

"Better than in a spaceship," he said.

"Yes, everything falls down eventually. That is a bonus. I'm going to the bathroom, Johannes, to get ready. After that you'll get your induction."

Kepler nodded. At first he thought she had said 'seduction,' but quickly realized what she meant. She was still calling him by his first name. Was that a good or a bad sign? He felt a bit confused. It had been more straightforward with the butler, and even the sneaky rabbit hadn't distracted him too much.

He got up. There was no butler here to clear away the dishes. He took them to the washstand, an old-fashioned piece of furniture. You could make hot or cold water flow from a pipe into a basin. Zhenyi had shown him the previous evening how to wash up. He placed the plates and cups upside-down next to the basin. A stream of water trickled slowly from the crockery toward the edge of the countertop. He watched it indecisively. How quickly would it fall to the floor? But he soaked it up with a towel just before it reached the edge.

Maybe he should prepare himself for the induction too.

He hadn't combed his hair today. He drew his fingers through it several times. Without a mirror, Kepler couldn't check how successful this was, but it would undoubtedly be better than nothing.

He went to the edge of the platform on which Zhenyi had built her lodgings. Stilts raised the platform roughly one meter, and four steps led down to the ground on which the stems grew. They still recoiled from him. They had also spread out under the platform. Most of the light came from below, so the platform didn't cast a shadow on the plants.

Kepler crouched down and stretched out his hand. But the stems didn't react. An animal might have come closer out of curiosity and sniffed his fingers. The grass wasn't interested in him, except to get out of the way of his feet. *The vegetation had redesigned the planet like this? And it had installed a black hole in the core to harvest energy?* It was hard to believe. Wasn't it more likely that some architect had pulled off an elaborate prank? Genetically modifying the grass to behave like this would probably have been the most difficult part. But hollowing out a planet and equipping it with a black hole, that wasn't magic. That was just damned expensive. If the system wasn't recorded in any database, then someone could have managed all this without anyone noticing. There was no chance of accidental visitors, and the next star was three light-years away, so there wouldn't have been any observers.

"Kepler, are you coming?"

Zhenyi was standing on the platform, waving. She had on a different dress, a qipao, high-collared and close-fitting. It suited her facial features wonderfully. One day he'd have to ask her if she was born that way. Or would that be rude? Constructing a body according to your own design had long ago stopped being considered decadent.

"I'm coming," he said, standing up and walking up the steps.

"This way."

Zhenyi led him into the interior of the house. It was strange. The house consisted of two bedrooms and the combined living room and kitchen. Shouldn't Zhenyi have some kind of tech room?

His ex-girlfriend came to a stop in the middle of the house, in the hallway that joined the rooms. She crouched down and placed her hands on the floor. Then a round hatch sprang open in front of her.

"An airlock," said Kepler.

"Not quite," replied Zhenyi.

Kepler walked up to the edge. Below him was a dark hole about a meter and a half across. Not again! He stepped back and folded his arms.

"You can either jump or use the ladder, whatever you prefer," said Zhenyi.

He craned his head forward. There was something like a ladder attached to the side of the shaft. It didn't look particularly stable, but here he weighed almost nothing.

"The ladder was actually only intended for climbing back up," explained Zhenyi.

Oh yeah, that was another problem. The long shaft he had descended through didn't appear to have a ladder.

"How do we actually get back up to the surface?" he asked. "Not that I don't like it here, but we won't be able to save the world from down here, will we?"

"Don't worry, that's taken care of. But now get in."

Kepler sighed and jumped. He floated down slowly. It was so dark he couldn't really tell how fast or deep he sank. So he got a shock when his feet touched the bottom. Zhenyi should be arriving soon too. He could smell her perfume—she had to be close. That reassured him immensely.

"And now?" he asked.

A small culvert opened next to him, about as high as he was. A faint light came from the room beyond it. It was enough to enable him to see Zhenyi, who was feeling her way along the wall on the other side of the shaft. Another opening appeared.

"It takes a little getting used to," said Zhenyi. "But I beg your understanding. You have to take your clothes off."

"Umm, what?"

"Get undressed!"

"I... Okay. And you?"

"I'll undress too. But you'd better not look."

"I'm a gentleman," he said. "But what's the point of this?"

"You'll see soon enough. Go to the opening."

Kepler took three steps forward. To do so he had to walk past Zhenyi. Her back was beautiful. It took quite an effort not to look further to the right.

Then he stood at the opening. He instinctively held on to it with his hands so as not to flee. It was disgusting. In front of him lay a tiny room, barely large enough for him to fit into. It was lit with a reddish light. Tubes the width of a finger protruded from the walls, ceiling, and floor, and turned and writhed in the low gravity. They looked like huge earthworms with only one segment. And they were moist. A stringy liquid dripped from their ends.

Kepler shook his head. He couldn't do it. He took a step back and his backside bumped into something warm. He cried out in fright.

"It's only me. I didn't know how to explain it to you," said Zhenyi.

He didn't turn around. Panic gripped his throat, but he wouldn't look at her. He was a gentleman. The thought calmed him, so he held it fast. The image of the slimy worms disappeared into a distant recess of his consciousness.

"You're not offering me to them as food?" he asked. "Are they going to drip digestive juices on me and then slurp me up?"

Zhenyi's laugh rang out like a bell. He liked that laugh.

"What a perverted imagination you have! No, Kepler, it's for communication. What you're looking at are the Herbae's roots. These transmit their thoughts around the whole planet. They can also sense our thoughts if we let them make contact. And they can share their ideas with you. You wanted to know how I speak to them."

"I admit, I'd imagined it a bit differently. Are our conceptual realities even compatible? They live in a completely different world!"

"We now have a good understanding. You'll see if you get into the chamber. But that took a lot of work. It's true, their world has nothing in common with ours. The Herbae basically *are* the planet. They don't think as individuals, and they don't distinguish between the vegetation and soil. It's all one. Because of that, they've never had the need to colonize other planets. That would be something like you having the idea of colonizing me. It wouldn't make sense."

Kepler grinned.

"Yes, all right. You know what I mean."

He nodded.

"So, are you going to get into the chamber?" asked Zhenyi.

"I... I think it's enough you just telling me about it."

She shoved him gently in the chest. He had to force himself not to look down, but to look into her face.

"You old coward, you haven't changed a bit," she said.

That touched a nerve. Hadn't he just jumped down the shaft? But she was right.

"I can't tell you everything," said Zhenyi. "The simulations I've made... you need to see them. It's important."

"You can have the Herbae compute simulations?"

"Yes. They have an excellent understanding of mathematics. I would even suggest they know more about it than we do, but my limited understanding can't comprehend it all. And the computational capacity of the network under the surface is enormous."

"Crazy. I expect we could learn a lot from them. Even just the fact that we've found another species after so long!"

"And yet someone deleted the location of the system from the database," said Zhenyi.

She wiped her forehead. It was very warm down here.

"You need to look at the simulation. I think someone has something against the Herbae," said Zhenyi.

"Please, can't you just explain the results to me?" Kepler pleaded. He was much more disturbed by the slimy worms than the size of the chamber. He imagined them creeping into all his orifices. He shivered.

"Do it for me," said Zhenyi. "Afterwards you'll get a kiss."

Now she was trying that tactic. *Man, Kepler, don't fall for this cheap ploy,* he thought. But the idea was attractive. They could go back to how they used to be. Not back when they constantly fought, but before that, the happy times.

Kepler wrestled mentally with himself. They were talking about saving an intelligent species, and he was thinking about a kiss. How low could he actually sink?

"Promise?" he asked.

Zhenyi looked at him sternly.

"You know me," she said.

It was true. She always kept promises if she could. So, there was only one risk—the worms would slurp him up. Or maybe contact with an alien civilization was too immense for his small, male brain to cope with, and he'd be insane when he emerged from the chamber.

Then that was how it would be. He turned around, went to the opening, and let himself sink into the chamber.

He didn't fall down. Something held him from behind and brought him into a comfortable position. He didn't want to think about what was holding him. But then he could no longer suppress the thought, because the worms were enveloping him. Slimy threads slid across his belly, his back, between his legs, wrapping themselves around his arms and legs.

Kepler could still move. That was a relief. The Herbae's roots—because they weren't worms, they were roots, he had to keep reminding himself—were astonishingly gentle with him. How would it have happened on Zhenyi's first contact, when the roots didn't yet know the human body? How would the Herbae know how tightly they could wind around a human throat if they had never known the concept of a lung? But maybe they could sense if Zhenyi was uncomfortable, just like they sensed his approach.

He was glad he'd climbed into the chamber. It was the only way he'd really be able to grasp the problem he had to solve. No, *wanted* to solve. He had invested so much time in the journey that it had slowly become his own problem, not just the Herbae's or his ex-girlfriend's. No one messes with Kepler.

Something pulled him from his thoughts. It wasn't a physical pull. He had to lift himself up, but simultaneously leave his body where it was. It was an impossible task, but he managed it. He drifted. His surroundings changed. It quickly became dark. Stars appeared. He was floating in space, still naked.

Kepler looked around. There was no mistaking it—above him pulsed the heart of the Milky Way, the black hole Sagittarius A*. Earlier, it had been quite modest compared to many neighboring galaxies. But then came the grand unification—first the Magellanic Clouds and then Andromeda had merged with the Milky Way, progressing into a giant elliptical galaxy. Their hearts had united into a truly admirable specimen that no longer needed to hide.

"Watch out. I'm starting the simulation," said Zhenyi.

He looked around but he was alone in space. Individual stars were now being extinguished in the region surrounding Sagittarius A*. The black hole ate them and grew. Then whole star clusters followed. They too disappeared into the greedy, black, endlessly deep gullet. Sagittarius A* grew and grew. The architects and their assistants had parked hundreds, thousands, millions of star systems in its vicinity, as planned by the Rescue Project, and provided them with the right impetus to plunge one after another into the greedy gullet that guaranteed their end in this reality. The plan enacted by the Convention worked. But why was Zhenyi showing him this? They couldn't be at the end yet.

And then Kepler understood what frightened his ex-girlfriend. Sagittarius A* became so powerful that it sought out more food on its own. It dragged in the construction site of the gigantic sphere that was later supposed to suck up its energy. It expanded further than ever predicted by any researcher. It emptied the inner regions of the Milky Way and swelled and swelled and swelled.

A black hole didn't burst when it overate. When it was full, it didn't have the option of spitting out excess matter. But it could release energy in other ways. A powerful, all-destroying flash of light sped through the core of the Milky Way and right out to the galaxy's star halo. What took seconds for Kepler would actually take over three hundred kilocycles. But the message was clear. Systems that weren't far enough away from Sagittarius A* would be obliterated by the light-speed energy pulse.

The result was a powerful quasar in the center of the Milky Way that would provide humanity with an almost endless source of energy. But this planet here would be ripped apart in the process. The unknown system lay too close to the core of the galaxy. The Herbae would die. They had to stop it.

"Thank you for looking at that," said Zhenyi.

Her voice faded away. The roots withdrew. He was standing on his own two feet again. Kepler exited the chamber and met Zhenyi. Her skin glistened with slime. He probably didn't look any different. His ex-girlfriend stood in front of him. She took his head in her hands and kissed him. It was heavenly.

Afterward he felt a bit unsteady and had to lean on the wall of the shaft. Where were his clothes? It was so gloomy down here that it took a while for him to find them.

"I don't know how you're feeling," said Zhenyi, "but I always need to take a shower after a session like that."

"Good idea," he said.

He had so many questions! Which should he ask first? Are

we showering together? No, he already knew the answer to that.

"Your simulation shows that the Convention's calculations are wrong. It's monstrous," he observed.

"Correct. Either the Convention is lying to everyone, or they've also been deceived."

"We have to show them your findings."

"That's on the list, Johannes. But are you clear about what that means?"

Kepler groaned. It wouldn't be easy, not at all. "They'll have to scrub the project," he said, "at least the way it's currently planned."

"But then the energy of the quasar won't be enough to keep humanity alive for long. The whole project will come under scrutiny," said Zhenyi. "The Convention won't accept that."

"But if we show them that our greatest dream has finally come true? We're no longer alone in the universe! The Herbae aren't like us, but they're intelligent. We can communicate with them."

"But we would have to die long before they do," said Zhenyi.

"Not if humanity moves onto a single planet," answered Kepler.

"You want to tell our ten thousand brothers and sisters that they should return to a kind of second Earth from their own private star systems, to live as farmers?"

"No one would have to be a farmer. We still have the nanofabricators."

"I'm afraid most people wouldn't accept that, Johannes."

"The alternative is dying out prematurely."

"No, the alternative is letting the Herbae die for us," Zhenyi countered.

Kepler was sweating. The situation really seemed hopeless, because he knew Zhenyi was right. It was a romantic idea for humanity to settle on a single planet again, but most people wouldn't see it that way. And whether it would even work was also doubtful—last time they tried they were still mortal, and yet they still managed to ruin Terra. Humanity had re-formed into smaller groups. They weren't made for living in large societies. They weren't grass stems, they were individuals, and this characteristic had become even more entrenched in the last few billion years.

Cycle ZB3.1, unknown system

"Are you coming?"

Kepler turned around again. It had been a brief visit. He would like to have examined the black hole in the core of the planet, but Zhenyi was worried they might run out of time. She waved him over. She was sitting at the controls of a machine consisting of two seats and four large rotors.

He walked across the grass for the last time, and the stems attentively retreated. What he was seeing wasn't the Herbae. The stems were hardly more than the fine hairs on his skin, which also moved when touched. The life form he had been lucky enough to get to know was the planet itself. He still couldn't fully comprehend it. He of all people. The second human to make contact with this alien intelligence.

No, that wasn't true. This system hadn't been deleted from the database for no reason. Someone must have been here before him. Before Zhenyi. Someone who had kept the knowledge to themselves, and even gone to considerable lengths to make sure it stayed that way. This person must have an interest in ensuring the Rescue Project proceeded exactly as planned. Basically every human was under suspicion. The Convention might even be in on it. But to simply allow an alien civilization, the greatest dream of humanity, to die—not every human would knowingly do that.

The Curies would. Their visit to K2-288Bb was still vivid in his memory. The way they had asked after Zhenyi was more than just curiosity. Where might they be now? Were they on the way to the Convention, or even to Sagittarius A*, to set their plan in motion?

"Johannes? Are you there?"

"Sorry, I was lost in thought."

He sat down on the seat behind Zhenyi. "Ready," he said.

She pushed forward a lever to the right of her seat. The four propellers above him revved up to full speed and they were already flying.

"Wow, this is great," he said.

"Yes, ancient concept, but perfect for these conditions. We only need to go up, and we have atmosphere everywhere."

He leaned back and closed his eyes. Then something occurred to him. "If you want me to take over from you..." he said.

Zhenyi laughed. "Do you want to get out mid-flight?"

He looked down. The gravity was still low, but further up it would become more challenging to switch places. "I just wanted to give you the option," he said.

"Thanks, but you can use the next six hours to rest," said Zhenyi. "I can also switch the copter over to autopilot. It's straight up all the way."

THEY REACHED the surface in twilight. Kepler was baffled. He had so far only seen the planet in daylight or darkness. But of course, here at the pole they were in the transition zone.

A stiff breeze was blowing in the daylight zone. Cold wind flowed across the surface in one direction, warm air in the other direction higher up. That was how the day and night sides mutually cooled and warmed each other. The copter wasn't very well suited to these conditions, so Zhenyi landed it as quickly as possible.

They had agreed to fly on together in the ship in which he

had arrived. That pleased Kepler. It meant he'd be able to spend a few virtual centuries with Zhenyi. Virtual, because they would both experience the time on board a lot faster. But it should still be a few weeks, as their destination was the core of the galaxy where the Convention resided.

"Away team to butler, please come in," said Kepler into the small radio button on his shirt.

The butler replied instantly. "Away team? Have you brought someone with you? The white rabbit, perhaps?"

"I found Zhenyi."

"Oh, what an extraordinary pleasure. It will be my honor to serve you both on board."

"Thank you, Puppy, but don't overdo it," said Zhenyi.

"You'll have to tell me everything you've experienced," said the butler. "I'm so curious."

"Of course. We'll be spending the next few weeks together. But now, please come and pick us up."

"I've located you. The landing module is already on its way, but it will take an hour. You landed quite far north. How did that come about?"

"Long story. This is where the shaft ends that leads to the core of the planet."

"Oh, of course. I'm ever so excited to hear your report."

Cycle ZB8.7, Dyson Sphere 7A

THEY WERE APPROACHING AN INVISIBLE STAR. The sphere, constructed by an architect 11.9 million years ago, only radiated infrared. Kepler already knew this from having visited Sphere 3Z, where they had last refueled.

These refueling maneuvers were really annoying, for one reason in particular. They had to brake and then accelerate again. This process took the same amount of time in any ship—whether it was a ninety-niner, a ninety-sevener, or a ninety-fiver. Only later could they make up for a few days of lost time. But who knew how much time they had left to stop the Rescue Project?

Kepler paced up and down in front of the big screen. He wasn't really getting anywhere with Zhenyi. Somehow he seemed to be on probation with her. Maybe she wanted to see how well he performed in saving the world first? Or had she really lost all interest in him? He found that hard to believe. There had always been something between them, an attraction, even during the bad times. And she was being kind to him. But she kept brushing off his tender advances with a smile.

"Shouldn't the first barges turn up soon?" he asked.

"They should," said the butler, "but there's a problem."

"Is the station empty?"

In fact, that was becoming a more frequent occurrence. The central star of most spheres had suffered a drop in power radiation. And if they were unlucky and someone had already refueled here in the last few weeks...

"We could send ourselves via direct laser from here to the Convention," he suggested.

"That wouldn't help us. The problem goes deeper. The refueling station doesn't want to sell to us. It's claiming that this ship and its owner don't exist."

"Have you told Zhenyi?"

"She's still asleep."

"Then you should wake her as soon as possible."

ZHENYI CAME STORMING into the control room in her pajamas. He had never seen her so furious. Even when they had argued with raised voices she would never have conducted the discussion in pajamas.

"Wang Zhenyi at Sphere 7A. I require the immediate refueling of my ship."

"This is the automated user interface of Sphere 7A. Please say 'refueling' if you want to refuel, and say 'help' if you need help."

What kind of primitive AI was this? More austerity measures again?

"Refueling," said Zhenyi.

"You're returning. That's nice. Please say 'refueling' if you want to refuel, and say 'help' if you need help."

"Re-fuel-ing," said Zhenyi.

"You're returning. That's nice. Please say 'refueling' if you want to refuel, and say 'help' if you need help."

"RE-FUEL-ING," yelled Zhenyi into the microphone.

She pronounced the F with such force that droplets of saliva sprayed onto the screen above the microphone.

"You're returning. That's..."

"If you don't shut up at once, I'll shoot you into a pile of scrap," said Zhenyi.

She was suddenly very calm. Kepler recognized this moment. It was the calm before the storm.

"Excuse me, Wang Zhenyi." The automated voice pronounced her name as though it had a hot potato in its mouth. "I assumed you were messing with me, so I was returning the favor."

Oh god, thought Kepler, *an AI with a sense of humor.* Why did he always have such bad luck? These jokesters had only been fashionable for a few millennia, but you still came across them surprisingly often. Especially when you were least expecting it.

"Messing with you?" Zhenyi retorted.

"Because you announced yourself under a ridiculous name from a non-existent ship. You should stop concealing the ship's registration number, so I can start the refueling."

"It's not a ridiculous name. It's the name of a famous Chinese astronomer, which I gave myself to match my profession."

"I'm sorry, Wang Zhenyi, but no such person exists in the database. Let me know your real name so I can check your account and refuel your ship. If the identity check is successful I can even overlook the fact that your ship isn't registered. It's up to you which ship you fill with your credits."

"That's too generous, Sphere 7A, but I am Wang Zhenyi."

"Wang Zhenyi has been dead for many megacycles, according to my information."

Again, the automated voice said the name as though it was gagging. She would explode any minute now. Kepler was glad not to be the trigger of the explosion, but he might still be within its damage radius. Should he be worried?

"I can't confirm your details," said the automaton. "I must ask you to leave the sphere's orbit, so as not to block access for other customers. Otherwise I will have to charge you a cancellation fee."

"How are you going to charge me if I don't even exist, you stupid AI?"

"Insults won't get you anywhere. I'll be entering a complaint into your file... No, I won't."

"It's dawned on you, has it?"

The automaton sighed. Had they just heard right? Was that a genuine, unwitting sigh, or just part of the user interface?

"I must ask you to leave the sphere's orbit, so as not to block access for other customers," repeated the voice.

It left out the threat this time. At least it was capable of learning. But it was improbable they'd get any fuel here. Kepler checked the current load. They could reach their destination with what they had, but only if they flew at a maximum of 95 percent light speed. That would cost them an enormous amount of time.

"We'll leave orbit when we've refueled," said Zhenyi in an ostensibly calm voice.

When would the explosion happen? It couldn't be much longer.

"Well, I can't stop you spending the next few megacycles here."

That sounded almost conciliatory. But it didn't change the fundamental problem. They wouldn't get any dark matter here. Zhenyi pressed the button next to the microphone to mute it, and her face lit up. She zoomed in on the image with a hand gesture and pointed at an object in the middle.

"Can you see that? Those are the tanks," she said to him.

"The tanks?"

"The dark matter tanks, dummy." She looked at him tenderly.

He immediately forgave the insult. "And what's that supposed to tell me? We won't get close without the tankers."

"We'll fire a few shots from the railgun and then they'll open all by themselves."

"You want to attack the Dyson sphere?" he asked. "Are you insane? They'll disembody us!"

Erasing a consciousness was considered unethical, so the most severe punishment these days was to ban the offender from ever having another body. Given that 'never' was now a very long time, Kepler had always had the highest respect for this punishment—particularly as he loved his body.

"Well, think about it. I'm not registered. Who will the sphere report as the culprit? Who is the Convention supposed to convict for it?" asked Zhenyi.

"Do you think your registration has been deleted everywhere?"

"I'm pretty sure. Sphere 3Z still knew who I was. Sphere 7A doesn't. The deletion must have overtaken us at light speed somewhere on the way. Now we have no chance of catching up with it. It'll always be ahead of us."

"But me... Maybe I'm not deleted yet," said Kepler.

"You could ask the sphere."

He went to grab the microphone, but Zhenyi intercepted his hand.

"Are you crazy? If you ask, and you do still exist, the sphere will know you're here. Then it'll report you as the suspect of the raid. Disembodiment is no joke."

"If I'm registered, we don't need to attack the sphere," said Kepler.

"Are you saying your account balance is in the black?" asked Zhenyi.

Kepler went red. No, that was why he had visited his ex-girlfriend in the first place.

"Ah, maybe we shouldn't ask," he said. "If you ask too many questions, you get too many answers."

THE BUTLER MANEUVERED the ship into a good firing position. They were floating about ten kilometers above the tanks.

"Isn't it dangerous to shoot at fuel tanks?" asked Kepler. "I mean, all that dark matter..."

"It's only significant in terms of its gravity. We just need to make sure we get as much of it as possible into the tanks."

"Allow me," said the butler. "I have the ship well in hand."

"That's what you said that time when we almost broke through the event horizon of the black hole by Beta Pictoris."

"One can't break through an event horizon, Milady."

"Don't start quibbling about physics."

"The black hole was a little more massive than expected."

"Yes, and that almost cost us our lives," said Zhenyi.

"You were still able to rescue the ship?" asked Kepler. He'd never heard this story before. It must have happened after their time together.

"No, the ship was torn apart by the black hole, but we were able to get ourselves to safety via laser transmission. That's when I lost the body before last. Looking back, I have to say it was my favorite body."

That was a relief. Even near the event horizon of a black hole there was a way out. Then it occurred to him that no laser relay transmission would accept an unregistered consciousness. If something happened to this ship, Zhenyi would die along with her body.

"The ship is now in the optimal position," said the butler. "We can fire."

Wait a minute. It wasn't until this moment that it became clear to Kepler, something that must be essential to Zhenyi's plan—this ship was obviously armed! A civilian ship carrying weapons was unthinkable, and there were only civilian ones left. The last armed conflict was shortly after the destruction of Terra. The last ten thousand humans were so widely dispersed that it became almost impossible to shoot at each other. There was only the occasional murder out of jealousy. But you didn't need a ship with railguns for that.

Should he ask her? No, she would just look at him again as though he was infinitely naïve. From now on he would just take things as they were, and not ask any more questions.

"Fire!" ordered Zhenyi. A smile spread across her face.

She was having a lot of fun showing the automaton where to stick it.

Thousands of metal bullets only a few millimeters in diameter now left the barrels of the railguns. They flew at four-fifths the speed of light toward the tanks. They were invisible and unstoppable. Zhenyi zoomed the display in closer on the tanks.

Kepler briefly closed his eyes, and opened them to see the first tank raising a large, circular lid. The dark matter was no longer shielded, and the contents of the tank poured out into space, as though someone had removed the cork of a well-shaken bottle of sparkling wine. No, a bottle of champagne, he corrected himself, that was more Zhenyi's style. The fact that the underside of the container tore open microseconds later was irrelevant, because the dark matter was already on its way. They just had to capture it.

Oh! He was wrong. The complete destruction of the container did have consequences. Dramatic consequences. On the inside of the sphere blazed the fiery star that the structure was built to enclose—or rather, no longer enclosed. Large tongues of plasma licked out of the freshly-punched holes. They hadn't just cracked one tank, they'd hit seven.

Now the sun, which had until now been caged in a human-made cocoon, was erupting out of all of them. And it appeared to be wrathful. It was taking the opportunity to release pressure and see something of the universe around it, which it had been denied for 11.9 million years.

"Zhenyi, this isn't dangerous, is it?" he asked, but she didn't offer him any soothing words.

The butler answered on her behalf. "If the sun eruptions hit our chemical tanks, then God have mercy."

A robot invoking God was not at all reassuring. They needed the chemical propulsion units to navigate in close proximity to planets. They drew their energy from various explosive gases that were allergic to too much heat.

"Then maybe we should be beating a quick retreat," said Kepler.

"We'll fly when the tanks are full. Then we'll be able to reach the Convention at 99-percent light speed," said Zhenyi.

"If we leave it too late, we won't reach anything," he countered.

"If we leave too early, we won't reach our destination anyway," countered Zhenyi.

Kepler gave in to his fate. He would put his life on the line for the extraterrestrial intelligence. When he thought about it like that, it felt decidedly good. Almost as good as... He waved the thought away. First solve one problem. Then maybe the other would resolve itself.

"Eighty percent," reported the butler.

The number sounded good. But even before the first shot, their tanks had been around fifty-five percent full.

"I protest," said the voice of the automaton.

No one answered it.

"I'm sending out a distress call," it said.

Do that, thought Kepler. The call would take three years to get to the next star. By then, hopefully, they would be well on their way. Although, if the tank kept filling so slowly...

"Eighty-five percent," said the butler.

A fiery lily came toward them in slow motion. But the ultra-hot plasma only appeared to be moving slowly. It was actually closing the distance between the sphere and the ship alarmingly fast. At that rate it would surpass the dark matter.

"Impact in ten seconds," said the butler in a cold voice, as though unconcerned.

Kepler clung to his seat. Then he felt two short pulses from behind. The ship was enormous. They must have been substantial explosions.

"Hydrogen tanks 7 and 18 have blown up," said the butler.

The numbering sounded reassuring. That meant they must still have at least 16 functional hydrogen tanks!

"Ninety percent."

"That must be enough," said Kepler.

"I want a hundred percent," said Zhenyi.

Kepler pointed at the display. Another fire bloom was approaching the ship. This plasma bubble looked more like a tulip. It was larger and more massive than the first.

"Don't worry," said Zhenyi. "The plasma's mass is also accelerating the dark matter. We have these eruptions to thank for the fact that the tank is almost full."

Kepler felt a jolt in his back.

"Hydrogen tanks 3, 5, 9, 11, and 19 have exploded," reported the butler without raising his voice.

They also had the plasma bubbles to thank for the fact that they would soon have no hydrogen tanks left. Then they could fly to any system, but on arrival they'd be rendered immobile.

"Unfortunately, the hydrogen tanks are particularly sensitive to heat," said Zhenyi. "They're always the first to go. But we can divert hydrogen into the oxygen tanks. They're less sensitive."

They're always the first to go? How many of these kinds of maneuvers did Zhenyi have under her belt? Kepler wondered.

"I don't like to contradict you, but hydrogen can't be diverted to the oxygen tanks. It would evaporate," said the butler.

"Then we won't. I'd rather you worried about the dark matter tanks," Zhenyi reprimanded him.

"Reporting ninety-five percent full."

"Very good," said Zhenyi. "We'll make it."

But only as sitting ducks, thought Kepler. Then another plasma bubble surged toward the ship. This time it looked like a fist. That was fitting. A fist that would give them a punch on the nose as punishment.

The fist was fast approaching. Kepler held onto his seat. This time it wouldn't be a small jolt from behind. The fist kept getting bigger. How did so much star matter even fit through the little holes they had shot? Then he saw it. Huge cracks had formed, stretching like a spider web across the whole sphere. Where the tanks used to be was now only a big hole. It didn't matter whether the fist hit them or not. The sphere itself would soon be shattered into a thousand pieces that would disperse in all directions at high speed. Getting out of the way of the wreckage would require a miracle.

"One hundred percent," said the butler.

"Hit the gas," said Zhenyi figuratively.

Had he noticed something like fear in her voice, or weariness? There was a slight tremolo, at least in the word 'gas.'

"I already have," said the butler.

Kepler had never been so appreciative of the pressure that now slammed him back into his seat. And a butler that didn't wait for orders—a gift from heaven! Now they just needed the interstellar propulsion system to get them as quickly as possible away from the exploding hell their railguns had created out of Dyson Sphere 7A, constructed 11.9 million years ago.

The ship accelerated. This time it took no precautions to protect his sensitive lungs, and he was delighted. Through his bloodshot eyes Kepler could see the explosion zone chasing after them, as though it was especially concerned with catching the cause of this evil and reducing it to its individual atoms. Initially, the combination of plasma and wreckage was gaining on them frighteningly fast, but then the ship's powerful drives prevailed. The arms snatching furiously at them were left behind, fidgeting helplessly in the radiation pressure of the now liberated sun.

Humanity had forfeited yet another energy source. There would be no point in constructing another Dyson sphere around that star. But they now had the chance to rescue a world that was no longer recorded in any database.

Cycle ZN8.4, IRS 13

"G3, PASS, I'M FREE!"

G3 turned around. G7 was standing utterly unnoticed near the opposition's goal. The goalkeeper seemed to be preoccupied, or at least he wasn't paying attention to G7. G3 skillfully passed him the stained ball. G7 received it with the inside of his foot, aimed the shot, and—goal!

G3, G5, and G9 put their arms around G7's neck. G7 had brought the score to 3 to 1! The red shirts celebrated. The team in the blue uniforms, on the other hand, went sullenly back to their own half.

"Halftime!"

The referee blew his whistle. G3 looked at his wristwatch. They'd only played 37 of the 45 minutes. What was going on? He ran to the referee to complain, but then he was shown the message. They had a visitor! Gropius reunited his sub-selves. The 22 soccer robots remained standing on the artificial lawn. Gropius loved soccer, and because it was a team sport, he'd had to build 22 identical robots. He played the referee. He went into the control room in his black shorts and short-sleeved shirt.

It was lucky the AI had called him. *There really was a spaceship in the middle of his net! How could anyone be so ignorant?* Gropius was irritated. His warning buoys could be seen from five light-years away. Someone must have ignored all the warning signals out of sheer laziness, instead of taking a slight detour. This system was a construction site!

Gropius wrestled internally with himself. He could go back to his soccer match and leave the spaceship to its fate. No one could accuse him of neglecting his responsibilities. But he also felt a bit sorry for the travelers. There were many systems where the builders had simply forgotten to clear away the warning buoys—probably even the majority, as active construction sites could only be found here near the core of the Milky Way, where everything was being prepared for the Rescue Project.

He pulled himself together, sat down in front of the terminal, and called up the ship. After a few minutes he received a reply.

"Hello Gropius!"

Oh no! It was the Curies. He had never liked either of them. They were so... extreme in their views. To them everything was either black or white, friend or foe. Friend? Hmm, Gropius didn't actually know anyone who would admit to being a friend of the Curies. The fervor with which they had enforced the Rescue Project, in particular, had alienated a lot of people. The majority actually agreed with them, but that was somehow not enough for them. They insisted you had to believe in the Rescue Project.

Gropius didn't believe in anything except that everything would work out in the end. This attitude had often served him well in the past. So, the visit from the Curies would also have a good outcome in the end. He just didn't know what that might be.

"The Curies," he replied. "What a pleasure! What can I do for you?"

The conversation proceeded arduously at first because of the distance, but the Curies' ship quickly came nearer.

"We'd like to speak to you about something."

"What's that?" asked Pierre.

"We'd prefer to speak in person," added Marie.

Gropius covered the microphone. He was polite enough to sigh only after he was sure the Curies couldn't hear him.

"Then of course I'll be glad to receive you," he lied. "Would you like a bit of entertainment on the side? I'm in the middle of an exciting match."

Maybe this way he could at least extract a bit of fun out of the unpleasant visit.

"Ah, soccer?"

"You know it?"

"But Gropius, you're known throughout the Milky Way as the best soccer player."

And the second best, third best, fourth best, he thought.

"See you on the field?"

"We look forward to being your spectators."

"This way please," he said.

"After you," answered Pierre.

"And what did you want to speak to me about?"

"First, we're curious about the game," said Marie.

"It must have been a hundred thousand cycles since we saw a real soccer match," said Pierre."

"I have a few rarities, holo recordings from the 21st century. Bayern Dortmund versus Juventus Berlin. We could take a look at them together. Or I could make you a copy."

"I have to tell you something, Gropius, but please don't be upset," said Marie.

He stopped. Was it getting serious now?

"What?" he asked.

"The computer says there were never any teams with those names. I'm afraid you're in possession of a fake," said Pierre.

The Curies' face looked at him with an expression that made him almost believe they were sympathetic. But their nostrils twitched and gave them away.

"I've had the holo for twelve megacycles. It's more or less from the heyday of the universe," he said stubbornly.

"Shortly after the destruction of Terra? Lots of fakes were made at that time. No one had been interested in the planet for a long time, but then when it disappeared into the giant sun, souvenirs suddenly became popular again."

"No, I don't believe that's true, Marie."

"And that's your prerogative," said Pierre. "We didn't mean to make you sad."

But you succeeded in doing so, he thought. That holo, of all things—his favorite vid! He continued walking, lost in gloomy thoughts. Then they reached the soccer field and his face lit up. He'd soon show the Curies he was still the best soccer player in the universe.

"Ah, so this is your dominion," said Marie.

"Exactly. Just a moment while I slip into the players."

The soccer players on the artificial lawn all came back to life as though someone had cleared a jam in the flow of time.

"Very nice," said Pierre.

"Kick off." The referee blew his whistle.

The blue shirts were up. They created some opportunities, but their striker, Gropius, couldn't beat the goalkeeper of the same name.

"The reason we're here..." said Marie.

"Yes?" called G7.

"We wanted to ask you a favor," Pierre began.

"Always happy to help if I can," said the blue shirts' goalkeeper.

"We need you to tow the black hole in IRS 13 to Sagittarius A* for us please. You can do that, right?" asked Marie.

"No problem. I can tow anything anywhere if I have enough time."

"What about IRS 13 to Sagittarius A*?" asked Pierre.

"10,000 cycles? With the software in the control room that's no problem. It even works in automatic mode."

"That's good," said Marie.

"But I can't help you anyway. You know that—the Rescue Project!"

"That's what it's about," said Pierre.

"I don't understand. If we merge IRS 13 with Sagittarius A*, there's a danger the black hole will be overloaded. That means it won't become a quasar, it'll become something worse."

"That's the idea," said Marie.

"That's not an 'idea,' that's suicide. No, it's murder."

"So you don't want to help us?"

"No, Pierre, I won't be turned into a murderer!"

"I'm sorry to hear that, Gropius. Then I suppose that's just how it will have to be."

Pierre had spoken again. That was an unusual change in their behavior. But what was more surprising was that the body in which the Curies resided suddenly pulled a black device out of its pocket. The referee, who was closest, recognized it first. It was a gun. The Curies' right arm aimed at the referee. Their right index finger curled tightly. The referee clasped his chest, then fell to the ground. The arm holding the weapon moved to the left. G7 died from a bullet that tore open his head. Then it was G11's turn, followed by the blue shirts' goalkeeper, G13, also blue, G6, G5, and every remaining soccer player. Gropius continued gathering his subselves together, but finally only G3 was available to him.

"You really are the best soccer player in the world," said Pierre.

"And the only," said Marie.

Their finger pulled the trigger one last time. The bullet shredded the brain of the best soccer player in the world. His consciousness, nowhere left to go, expired.

Cycle ZR1.1, Convention

FROM A DISTANCE, you could have mistaken the Convention for a Dyson sphere. Kepler was bored, so he displayed the data from all the long-range sensors on screen. Compared to a Dyson sphere, however, the Convention was quite dark in infrared, as though it enclosed a long-since-expired sun.

The journey was coming to an end. Kepler watched the digits rapidly counting down the light-years. Three cheers for time dilation! To an outside observer, the ship would appear to be moving torturously slowly through space, but for him it went much faster.

He could gradually make out more detail on the surface of the sphere. At 99 percent light speed it wasn't easy to scan the surroundings. The sensor beams were only slightly faster than the ship. But what now became evident was the immensity of the Convention. Kepler was reminded of its opening, about a megacycle after the destruction of Terra. Humanity was supposed to celebrate the limitless possibilities of this new structure so close to the core of the Milky Way. Gropius, Le Corbusier, all of the well-known architects had collaborated to make it a reality. The Convention encompassed a whole globular star cluster—a mini galaxy, as it were. It had been designed to provide enough room for the quadrillion people that were expected to populate the Milky Way, according to the prognosis of the time.

But nothing came of all that. Humans simply no longer saw any reason to procreate. Yet the Convention was still there. And it had been a fitting place to conclude the Rescue Plan.

Zhenyi's perfume reached his nose. He turned around.

"Good morning, Johannes!" she said.

Didn't he know it! She was wearing an elegant pantsuit today, and was perfectly groomed.

"Same to you. Did you sleep well?"

"I kept waking up and couldn't go back to sleep. Sometimes I miss the sound of your breathing," she said.

"That's easily fixed."

"I know. Give me time, Johannes. I like you, but... there's a problem."

"A problem?"

"I don't want to discuss it now."

"Okay."

"I spent the sleepless hours thinking about our arrival at the Convention," said Zhenyi.

"Yes?"

"You should make contact and request entry. If I lodge the request, I'll be asked to prove my existence again."

"I thought of that too. And what if I've been deleted from the database?"

"Then we'll have to think of something else. The Convention sphere is probably quite dilapidated."

"Are you thinking about the railguns, Zhenyi? Remember what happened after your deployment at the Dyson sphere?"

"There's no hot star behind the Convention."

"But the debris could still be dangerous to us."

"You've convinced me, Johannes. I'll simulate an attack on the Convention sphere, then we'll know how dangerous it really is. But the best-case scenario would be if you just talk your way through access control."

It wasn't one of his strengths, talking his way through things. Kepler started to dread the next day. But if that's what Zhenyi was expecting of him, he would do his best. Hopefully it would be enough to avert a catastrophe.

Cycle ZR1.2, Convention

A GIGANTIC WALL towered in front of the spaceship. From their perspective it looked like a flat plane in space, but that was because of its dimensions. Only yesterday Kepler had seen that this plane was actually the surface of a sphere with a diameter of 80 light-years.

Kepler had ignored all requests from the sphere as they approached. He wanted to initiate contact first, so that he could determine the script of the conversation. But for that, the ship had to get so close to the wall that, if necessary, they could shoot their way through with the railguns. Zhenyi's simulations had allegedly shown that wasn't dangerous. He suspected her of deceiving him. He had thought about checking whether there had actually been any simulations carried out on the ship's computer. But then he decided that kind of spying would be too invasive.

"Johannes Kepler here," he reported.

He drummed his fingers on the armrest of his seat. Soon it would be decided whether they would be allowed to fly into the Convention the normal way. Their distance from the sphere was still so great that radio messages took half a minute.

"Welcome, Johannes Kepler," a female voice replied. "Nice to see you again after such a long time."

He released the breath he'd been holding. His data hadn't been deleted! "I would like to discuss a few things with the Convention," he said.

"At present, only Convention Secretary Christopher Columbus is available," said the voice after the transmission delay.

"Oh... Where are all the others?"

"That information isn't public. Would you like to speak with Secretary Columbus?"

"Yes please."

Columbus wasn't Secretary for no reason—he was a professional bureaucrat. It wouldn't be easy to persuade him, and he also didn't have much say. But before they left empty-handed, they should at least try.

"Before I can allow you to fly in, I need to scan your ship," said the voice of the guard automaton.

"Is that for weapons, drugs, that sort of thing?"

The automaton laughed. It seemed to be at least a level 4 AI. At least it wasn't cracking any stupid jokes. But if it found the railguns...

"No, Johannes Kepler, we know that you could manufacture such things at any time with nanofabricators. It would be pointless to inspect you for that. But we need to know how many biological signatures are visiting the Convention."

"I... I'm alone," said Kepler, "apart from my butler."

"A robot, I assume?"

"What else?"

"Good. Then you'll surely have no objection to the scan."

Shit. Kepler activated the railguns as a precaution. How was he supposed to explain the presence of an unregistered person? They wouldn't let him in. Hopefully the sphere itself wasn't armed. Had Zhenyi's simulations been correct? He'd soon find out.

"Then get on with it," he said.

He aimed the railguns so they were all pointing at the same spot on the surface of the sphere. Whoever shot first always had an advantage in space. His finger was on the trigger. Kepler took a deep breath. Would he feel it if the sphere apprehended him? What technology was it even using? His thoughts were racing. Would it be better if he just fired now? It would take a minute for the results of the scan to reach the sphere's AI—there was nothing faster than light. He still had the element of surprise on his side. The fingers on his other hand drummed faster on the armrest.

"Many thanks for your cooperation," came the voice again. "For safety reasons, I must draw your attention to an anomaly."

They must have discovered Zhenyi, but didn't yet know what to do with her. An unregistered biological being was an extremely rare occurrence.

"Some of your ship's hydrogen tanks are not functional," said the voice. "You should have them repaired. We can perform this repair in the sphere's docking yard for a special price. A free fitness check is included. Say your name and 'Yes I do' if you want to take advantage of our special offer."

Kepler removed his hand from the trigger and slumped back in his seat. They had noticed the hydrogen tanks, but not Zhenyi. How had she managed that? His ex-girlfriend always had something up her sleeve. It would have been better if she'd pre-warned him. But he wouldn't complain, as otherwise she'd once again accuse him of being a wimp.

"Johannes Kepler, 'Yes, I do,'" he said. Hopefully his account overdraft would cover it!

"You've made a good choice. We'll assign you a docking bay in the inner sphere. The position will be automatically transmitted to your navigation system."

"Thanks very much," he said, and ended the connection.

A FLASHING green light on the screen indicated their next destination. He switched the ship to autopilot. Kepler had never liked docking to a sphere. The ship was huge and reacted very slowly to steering input, and you had to pay special attention to all the spatial dimensions, which overtaxed his powers of imagination. He really didn't want to damage any more tanks—or the dock, for that matter.

The ship approached the black wall at a rapid speed. He could see it on the radar. The optical image only showed what looked like completely starless space. *They could count themselves lucky that there were no other space-traveling species. Otherwise alien ships would constantly be crashing into human spheres,* he thought.

Then a square hole appeared before his eyes, through which shone a white light. The opening seemed tiny. No way would the ship fit through that! The autopilot steered them toward it at an alarming pace.

He felt a hand on his shoulder and jumped. It was Zhenyi. Couldn't she warn him when she was coming into the control room?

"You're doing that very well," she said.

Kepler was pleased with the praise. But he felt he was being treated like a child. He was pretty sure he didn't want that. He adjusted his position in his seat so that the hand slid off his shoulder.

"Sorry," said Zhenyi. "I'm talking to you like you're a little child."

She had read his thoughts and apologized after all! Zhenyi moved away, but her perfume lingered in the air. It put him in a cheerful mood. The ship reached the opening and stuck its nose through. Kepler marveled at the structure of the sphere. It was only a kilometer thick, but enclosed an enormous volume. The design was probably Le Corbusier's.

Now the inner sphere lay before him, even more miraculous. It was transparent. He could see the two hundred stars of the globular cluster, orbiting at a minimum distance from one another. It was a vision you didn't see anymore, because all other globular clusters had been extinguished long ago. This one, inside the sphere, would be preserved forever by the human-made structure around it. Or at least until every individual star in it had burned out.

THE SHIP HAD DOCKED. They disembarked through the airlock. They didn't need spacesuits. The dock had attached an exit passage to the airlock through which they could float into the reception rooms. The three of them went together—Kepler, Zhenyi, and the butler. Kepler took his ex-girlfriend's hand and drifted through the curved tube with her. The zero gravity was fun. They reached a counter with a grim-looking android sitting behind it. Kepler had to establish his identity using his voice and authorize the payment for the repairs. His actual account balance seemed not to have reached the sphere, because the exorbitantly high fee went through.

The android nodded and gestured to the right. Was it bored? The sphere didn't appear to receive many visitors. "If you need transport for the inner sphere, please see my colleague at the rental service," it said.

It must be a cheap model. It couldn't even modulate its voice. Maybe it was defective. It was hard to believe that such a cheap robot would be given the role of usher in humanity's most prestigious project.

A corridor led them in a wide arc into a room about the size of a soccer field. Gropius would have fun here. *He could run around with all 22 of his players plus the referee,* thought Kepler. He had once watched one of the architect's matches. *The best player in the Milky Way, for sure.*

On all four sides of the room were innumerable glass counters. Kepler stood directly in front of one of them. Holograms showed a beautiful planetary system. One of the planets was supposed to have beaches of pink sand with lapping green water. Another celestial body promised extremely low gravity and free flying lessons for all visitors. A third presented itself as a paradise for naturalists. Nude holograms sunned themselves on the beach there, went shopping nude, and ate in the nude.

Kepler went to take a closer look at the details. But the stand was closed, like all the others. There were no longer any tourists wanting to visit these exotic worlds. Who knew if they even looked like that anymore? As far as he knew, a large proportion of the planets had been artificially adapted to human requirements.

Someone waved from a distance. It was the android at the only open stand. That must be the rental service. Zhenyi and the butler were nearly there already. Kepler ran after them. Again, it was up to him to identify himself.

"Thank you, Johannes Kepler," said the robot. "Our company's rental service will delight you with its reliability, comfort and speed."

To get around in the inner sphere, you needed special vehicles adapted to the conditions. Kepler suspected it was intentional, to squeeze as many credits as possible out of the visitors.

"Sure," he replied. "I'd like something for a flight to the administrative sector."

"Of course. I see you need three places. I can offer you a four-seater at the standard price. But I can also see you are a man who appreciates the finer things in life." The robot winked and gestured subtly at Zhenyi, as though she weren't there. Kepler looked back questioningly at it.

"In fact, I have something very special for you, one of our few exclusive cabriolets. Just imagine—you can race under the open sky with your girlfriend." It spoke the word with particular emphasis. "Isn't that romantic? If you like, we can also store your butler here for the duration, so you'll be completely undisturbed. Have you ever... tried it directly in open space?" The android looked at him conspiratorially.

"The cabriolet will only cost you a 150 percent surcharge. Say 'I want it' to order it."

"I don't want it," said Kepler. "You've misunderstood. I have an important meeting with Secretary Columbus, which I would like to attend as soon as possible."

"Of course," said the robot. "I understand, you'd prefer something... cheaper. We also have an offer to suit your budget."

"I'm listening."

"A free shuttle can provide transport to all planets in this system upon request. Only you'll have to share the vehicle with other visitors."

Kepler turned around. There was no one there but them. "Other visitors?" he asked.

"Well, it's not out of the question that someone might come. Therefore I think our exclusive cabriolet will be more to your liking. If you order now, you'll receive a fuel voucher that you can redeem at any Dyson sphere."

"Thank you. I'll wait for the shuttle."

"If you make your reservation today, the shuttle will be ready tomorrow at eight o'clock standard time."

"How long is the flight?"

"The flight to the administrative sector takes exactly twenty hours and three minutes."

"Good, then I'll reserve the free shuttle."

"At this time I can offer you an affordable upgrade to first class. That includes—"

"No, thank you," Kepler interrupted.

"Say 'I want it' to conclude your reservation."

"*I want it.* And where do we spend the night?"

"Aboard your ship, I suggest. Unfortunately, we don't provide rooms here."

Cycle ZR1.3, Convention

"I SHOULD HAVE ASKED where the shuttle departs from," said Kepler.

"The android didn't say, so it must be easy to find," said Zhenyi.

They each carried a backpack filled with food and the usual traveling supplies. Kepler hadn't been surprised when the butler had packed his own travel bag. They would be underway for at least three days and, as the butler was always immaculately dressed, he would need a change of clothes.

The soccer field-sized room with the innumerable stands was no longer as fascinating the second time around. In fact it was depressing. The fading glamour of times gone by clung to it. So many dreams were once attached to the Convention. But humans had their own ideas for the future, which didn't include this enclosed sphere.

The android at the rental desk waved at them. "Good morning, Johannes Kepler," it said. It didn't even acknowledge Zhenyi and the butler with a glance.

Kepler nodded.

"Please follow me, and be quick, the shuttle departs in five minutes, you're late."

The top of the counter slid to the side. Kepler hurried to catch up with the android. Then the room tilted. Shit, he had stumbled. Who'd put that backpack at his feet? He tried to hold onto the android, but grasped at nothing. Not another hologram! He fell, his upper body hitting the floor first.

"Johannes Kepler, are you all right?" The virtual android crouched down beside him and passed its hand over his head. Kepler couldn't feel anything, which made it worse.

Then two strong arms grabbed him under the shoulders. The butler stood him back on his feet. "Thanks," said Kepler. "Was that your backpack?"

"No, mine," replied Zhenyi.

"Come, come," said the android.

"But there's no one here. Why does everything have to be so hectic?" asked Kepler.

"We must be punctual. The punctuality quota was exactly 100 percent in the last kilocycle! We are the most punctual shuttle service in the universe."

"How many times did the shuttle fly in the last kilocycle?"

"None."

"Then how can you calculate a quota? That would be a factor of zero?"

"The last kilocycle also includes your departure, and until now we have been punctual. Please come quickly!"

The android ran ahead of them through a diffusely lit corridor. Kepler tried to keep it happy. They reached the shuttle just as the onboard clock showed 07:59. Kepler fell into the nearest seat, exhausted.

"Have a good trip," said the android.

The shuttle door closed. Kepler was pressed back in his seat.

AFTER TWO HOURS they had apparently reached their top speed, because zero gravity kicked in. Kepler stood and floated up to the three-meter-high transparent ceiling. The shuttle, or at least what he could see of it, resembled a drinking glass, half of which was made of metal. In front, invisible to him, there must be a control system, and the propulsion unit at the back.

The view through the window above was overwhelming. The stars were so incredibly close—he'd never seen anything like it. They were positioned so that you could find optimal conditions almost everywhere. The sky wasn't black here, it was blue, but the stars still sparkled as brightly as they did in the blackest night sky, as long as they didn't disappear behind an impressive cloud.

The whole of the inner sphere was filled with breathable air. That had been the architects' greatest achievement of all. It wasn't enough just to fill the space with air. Units were distributed everywhere to control the atmosphere and adjust it as necessary. Without constant adjustments, the air circulation would be concentrated in certain areas, while in others you would hardly be able to breathe. The atmosphere also altered the orbital mechanics of the planets, which would inevitably have crashed into their suns if their courses weren't artificially stabilized. Surprisingly, all this still continued to function.

A button on the overhead window read 'Open Here' in several languages. Kepler pressed it briefly and the glass opened a crack. Cold air rushed inside. The moisture on the ceiling condensed to a fine mist. He opened the window a bit further and held his hand outside. It was cold, but not too cold. Minus 20 degrees, he guessed. For a while it was bearable.

During his last visit the temperature was still around the freezing point. The system was probably just about to tip. It was good they hadn't chosen the cabriolet, which the vendor hologram had almost swindled him into. Kepler opened the window about half a meter and stuck his head out. The air rushed by so fast that his eyes started watering immediately. But he had his head in space, he was breathing, he was alive. That was something that only humans had been able to do. Here in the inner sphere, the universe and humans had really become one.

Why did no one appreciate it? Why did humans prefer to crouch on their own planets and talk to their own reflections?

"Johannes, there's a draft," said Zhenyi.

Maybe that was why, he thought. But it was unjustified. The breeze was wonderful. The tears were no longer flowing from his eyes, but from his nose. He pulled his head back inside, closed the window, and blew his nose.

KEPLER WAS TIRED after ten hours of flying. They searched the shuttle. One of the free seats could be converted into a bed, but the other ones couldn't. Was that deliberate? What if the shuttle was full? There were twenty seats—but only one bed?

"You lie down," said Zhenyi. "I'm not tired yet."

"We can take turns," said Kepler.

Zhenyi placed her long, thin jacket over him like a blanket. Kepler felt warm. He quickly fell into a dreamless sleep.

Cycle ZR1.4, Convention

"JOHANNES? Wake up, we're almost there."

He had slept the whole way! Why hadn't she awakened him? Zhenyi held out a cup, the smell of coffee wafting from it. He took it and drank a mouthful. The liquid was lukewarm.

"There's nothing here to heat it," she said apologetically.

He must have frowned. "Why didn't you wake me so we could switch?" he asked.

"You were sleeping so soundly I didn't want to disturb you. And anyway, I've been running through the arguments in my head, to persuade Columbus."

"We should be able to manage that," said Kepler.

"I doubt it." Zhenyi shook her head slowly. "But we at least have to try."

THE DOOR of the shuttle opened. A wraith-like figure appeared. It could be a uniformed officer—or a magician from a fairytale. In any case, the outer shell was flickering so dramatically you could see the skeleton underneath.

"Excuse my appearance," said a deep male voice, "but the

holo projection isn't working properly. I'm here to escort you. Secretary Columbus is looking forward to your visit."

"Then he could have shown up himself," said Zhenyi.

The flickering hologram didn't answer, probably out of politeness. "You can leave your luggage in the shuttle," it said.

"Is there any possibility of taking a shower somewhere? I'm only half human if I haven't showered."

"If you like, we can stop at the sanitation block."

"That would be wonderful."

He was less than half human when he hadn't showered. The flickering hologram led them through corridors that were typical of an administration building. Everything here was gray. Gleaming lines ran along the ceiling. That must be the holo projector. Maybe he should offer his help. It should be repairable. Being able to see that poor man's skeleton seemed humiliating even for a hologram.

They stopped in front of an ordinary-looking door. "The sanitation block?" asked Kepler.

"Yes. I'll fetch you in fifteen minutes if that's suitable," said the hologram, looking only at Kepler.

"I'll never be finished in that time," said Zhenyi. "Give me half an hour."

"As you wish. I hope the Secretary has no other meetings."

"Are there many visitors?" asked Zhenyi.

"You're the first in a long time."

The hologram was still addressing Kepler, although it was replying to Zhenyi's question. Maybe his ex-girlfriend didn't exist for the AI that controlled the hologram. It must be quite conflicting for the software—it was receiving optical and acoustic input from an object that didn't exist. Hopefully the AI wouldn't suffer an existential crisis. Kepler felt sorry for it. The hologram was already being punished enough by the defective projector.

"Then I'm sure the Secretary will have time for us, even if we're late," said Zhenyi.

"Of course," the hologram replied, waved at Kepler, and faded away to nothing.

The door to the sanitation block opened. It contained a wooden bench, three showers separated by translucent glass panels but open at the front, the same number of washbasins with mirrors above them, and two cubicles, which presumably contained toilets.

"You can wait outside, Puppy," Zhenyi said, and went in.

Kepler followed her. Zhenyi didn't hesitate to undress. Should he turn around? His ears went red. But Zhenyi said nothing. So, it was his decision. And it wasn't as though he'd never seen her naked. He removed his clothes too but couldn't tear his gaze away from Zhenyi. Her body looked perfect. The curved hips, the narrow waist... she pulled her undershirt over her head, then slipped out of her underpants. He saw her dark pubic hair between her legs. The last time he saw her like this was a few kilocycles ago. She didn't seem to have aged at all.

Kepler looked down at himself. His belly stuck out further than it did in those days. And he was still wearing underpants and socks. He'd better hurry, or Zhenyi would be finished before him.

THE WATER that came out of the showerhead was at first tepid and then too hot. It would probably take him five minutes to adjust it to the optimal temperature. The soap dispenser on the wall contained an oily liquid. He suspected it was shampoo, but the stuff smelled strange. It was probably rancid. He lathered his hair with it anyway, then rinsed out the foam and cleaned his whole body with it. He was out of the shower before Zhenyi.

Where were the towels? He bent down and found a shelf under the washbasin, took two towels from it. He put one in front of Zhenyi's shower. She was standing with her face tilted up to the shower stream and was obviously enjoying the hot water. She had her back to him. Little clouds of steam rose from her skin, making it look like it was she who was heating the water.

"I've put a towel in front of the shower for you," he said.

"Thanks," she replied.

She could ask me to help her dry herself, he thought as he rubbed himself down. But this idea apparently hadn't occurred to Zhenyi. Whistling, she climbed out of the shower unabashed, giving him a full-frontal view, and dried herself off. Kepler hurried to get into his pants before things got embarrassing.

"Help yourself from my handbag if you need a comb," said Zhenyi.

He had almost forgotten. Her bag stood on the edge of the washbasin. He had to force himself to open it. There was something magical about women's bags. But Zhenyi's was surprisingly uncluttered. He found the comb immediately. The bag also contained an assortment of makeup and a convenient black gun.

Kepler was startled. He wished she hadn't just reminded him to comb! Now he had touched the gun, and when you touched something, you had to use it. At least that's how it went in the scripts of good films. He combed his hair, rinsed the comb, and put it back in the bag. *This is ridiculous,* he thought. *I'm the master of my own destiny.* The gun didn't mean anything, or if it did, then nothing more than a vague possibility. Now that he knew Zhenyi had a gun on her, he could even prevent her from using it. And he would do that if necessary.

He closed the bag and looked at himself again in the mirror. In the next hour or two, the fate of an alien intelligence would be decided. And his own.

"I'll wait outside," he said.

"Okay, I'll be with you in fifteen minutes."

Both the hologram and Zhenyi were punctual. That was something he appreciated about her—she always kept her appointments. He himself preferred to be early. No, that could be taken the wrong way. *Lucky no one can read my mind,* he thought.

"I have good news," said the hologram, addressing Kepler. "The Secretary still has time for you."

"Thank you," replied Kepler.

They marched four abreast for about ten minutes through identical-looking corridors. Was that some kind of defense strategy? No one would ever remember the way. Then they stopped in front of a door. The hologram knocked. The knocking made no sound, but someone inside called out, "Come in."

They went inside. Christopher Columbus came to greet them. Kepler guessed his age to be under 40 biological years. He was wearing a cardigan with elbow patches, and he smiled with what seemed to be genuine interest. Kepler had met him somewhere before, but he couldn't remember what the occasion had been.

Columbus greeted Zhenyi first, bowing slightly.

"Who do we have here then?" he asked. "You must be Wang Zhenyi, if I'm not mistaken. They didn't tell me you were here! Which makes it all the more of a pleasure to see you."

"It's a long story. I'm pleased to see you, too," said Zhenyi. As she spoke, she held the Secretary's hand longer than necessary.

Kepler felt a pang, but he knew she had to win Columbus over by any means necessary. If he recommended to the Convention that they terminate the Rescue Project, they had as good as won.

"And you, dear Johannes Kepler, I haven't seen you for a long time either. How long has it been exactly?" asked the Secretary, offering his hand.

Kepler returned the gesture. The handshake was firm and warm. Columbus seemed to be an agreeable person. He started to feel more hopeful. "Far too long," he replied. "My pleasure."

"May I offer you anything?" asked their host.

"Just some water," said Zhenyi.

"Nothing for me, thanks," said Kepler.

"Then take a seat," said Columbus, pointing to a sofa. In front of it was a low table flanked by two armchairs. Zhenyi and Kepler sat down. The butler remained standing and withdrew politely to the door.

Columbus tapped a blank wall and a bar folded out. He poured a colorless liquid from a crystal bottle into two glasses, then passed them to Zhenyi and Kepler. Water vapor condensed on the outsides of the glasses. Kepler took a sip and realized he was thirsty after all. The water had no taste, just the way he liked it.

The Secretary sat in one of the armchairs. Then he stood up again and helped himself from the bar, filling a glass to the brim with a brownish liquid. He sat down again and drank.

"What brings you here?" Columbus asked, leaning back.

"We've made an almost unbelievable discovery," said Zhenyi. She leaned toward him as she spoke, showing off her décolletage. Kepler was surprised to see his ex-girlfriend now using this tactic. There was a time when she would have refused to, preferring to rely on her sharp mind.

Zhenyi reported what they had found in the unknown system. She neither named the coordinates of the star nor did she describe how she herself had come by this knowledge. Columbus listened attentively and asked the occasional astute question.

"So the only reasonable response would be for the Convention to completely redesign the Rescue Project," said Zhenyi, concluding her story.

Columbus creased his forehead and folded his arms. "That's quite a substantial request," he said.

Zhenyi jumped up and paced up and down the room. "Humanity's greatest dream has been fulfilled! We've found an intelligent species!"

"And humanity is supposed to perish for them? If we don't solve our energy problems, these aliens will outlive us."

"We can't blame them for that!" said Zhenyi, resting her hands on her hips. "And we can't let them die for us! That would be inhumane!"

"Let's slow down for a moment," said Columbus. "I'm prepared to present this story to the Convention. Of course, I can't predict what course of action the full assembly will decide upon. We've already invested so many resources into the Rescue Project! Do we just accept that this has all been in vain?"

"There's no other option left to humanity. We have to rethink the Rescue Project. Yes, it'll provide less energy. But to exterminate an intelligent species in our own self-interest?"

Columbus shook his head. "I'm not saying I'm not sympathetic to your request, Wang Zhenyi. But you must admit there are a few inconsistencies."

"To what are you referring, Secretary?"

"First of all, the fact that this dubious system isn't in any of our databases. No one has seen this intelligence, other than you."

"I have holo vids that show everything."

"Those can be faked, you know that. Point two is your own person."

Zhenyi stopped pacing. "What do you mean?"

"You were certified insane for one and a half kilocycles. Your consciousness was quarantined. At the time, you claimed to have found an exact copy of Terra."

Kepler was hearing about this for the first time. It must have happened after he and Zhenyi separated. Had the separation been the trigger for the breakdown? *Oh, Zhenyi!* Now he understood why she was keeping her distance.

"I was unwell for a period of time, due to personal reasons. But I'm fully recovered."

"You weren't released. Instead, you broke out of the station and helped yourself to an artificial body. You received a suspended sentence for that and a large fine. I can tell you the exact figure!"

His ex-girlfriend was a convict? That was new to him, too. She had managed to break out of a quarantine station? Not bad! But wait a minute... something wasn't right here. Zhenyi had been deleted from the database. The Secretary couldn't actually know everything he was telling them, unless he possessed a phenomenal memory—or unless he had prepared a backup of Zhenyi's data before the deletion. But that meant he must have had something to do with it. How could he alert her to this? Had she already realized? Or was he wrong? Had he missed something important?

"That's not necessary," said Zhenyi. "It was a long time ago. I'm prepared to demonstrate my psychological health. And anyone who doesn't believe me can simply fly with me to the planet of the Herbae."

"I'm your friend, Wang Zhenyi," replied the Secretary. "And as such, I only want the best for you. That also means protecting you from potential harm. Your opponents will attempt to question your credibility. You have to be prepared for that. It could also be that the two planetary systems that will be destroyed by the Rescue Project belong to your enormous private fortune. So you could be accused of having a personal interest. Your wealth will protect you from the energy crisis for a long time, which means you would only stand to lose if the Rescue Project went ahead. I need solid evidence before I can present your story to the Convention. It's in your own interests!"

Zhenyi shook her head and paced even faster around the room. Then the door through which they had entered was opened. The flickering hologram appeared. It beckoned the Secretary, who walked to the door, and the hologram whispered something in his ear.

Columbus turned around and came toward Zhenyi, smiling. "A new situation has come to light," said the Secretary.

"Yes?" Zhenyi stood still and scrutinized him.

"A message has reached us from Dyson Sphere 7A."

"Oh yes?" said Zhenyi, playing distractedly with a button on her blouse.

That took a while, thought Kepler. A message traveling at the speed of light actually should have arrived long before they did. They were being played!

"An unregistered ship attacked the sphere to steal dark matter, damaging it in the process. The damage is immense."

"These pirates just keep getting bolder," said Zhenyi.

"The ship lost several of its hydrogen tanks when it was hit by material from the star."

"Yes, those tanks are very sensitive," said Zhenyi. "We just found that out for ourselves. You only have to orbit too close to a star and they rupture. Very annoying!" She resumed her wandering around the room.

"There has been another incident," said the Secretary.

"That's interesting."

"Interesting is the wrong word. Grisly or terrible would fit better. The architect Walter Gropius has been killed, or rather executed. He was busy at IRS 13 with preparations for the Rescue Project. IRS 13 is on the way from Dyson Sphere 7A to here. Without Gropius the Rescue Project could be delayed. It might even completely fail."

Kepler felt hot. Gropius, the famous architect, was dead! And it seemed the Secretary suspected them! Things were going horribly wrong! *Zhenyi, you have to respond now. Say something, prove we had nothing to do with it!*

But Zhenyi said nothing at all. She just kept walking faster and faster, as though that would change something.

"Johannes Kepler, I'm sorry that you've been dragged into something that's bigger than yourself," said the Secretary.

What? Something that was beyond his capacity? What was this stuffed shirt trying to insinuate? Anger bubbled in Kepler's gut.

"But you must be able to see," said Columbus, "that your dear friend here is a danger to society. Unfortunately I have to arrest her. She's a flight risk, so it has to happen immediately."

Then nondescript tubes protruded from the walls. They must be some kind of weapon. Zhenyi stood still. She turned around. Her face was ashen.

"You are free to leave at any time, of course, Johannes Kepler. You have served humanity well as an astronomer, and so far have had no conflict with the law. The Convention values your contributions. I'm sure Wang Zhenyi lied to you about her criminal background."

"I... uh..."

What was he supposed to say? The accusations against Zhenyi were unfair. She was just standing up for the Herbae.

"I... uh, what you're saying, that's..." he tried again. He couldn't just let it go!

"Just go, Johannes," said Zhenyi. "You heard what he said. You're free."

"Your friend is right. It would be better if you left and spared yourself any unpleasantness."

The door opened. Kepler was getting more than he deserved under the circumstances. He hadn't prevented the attack on the Dyson sphere. And trying to pin a murder on Zhenyi—that was unacceptable. He nodded and slowly stood up from the sofa.

"I hope we'll see each other again under better circumstances," said Columbus. "You're always welcome here."

"Thank you," muttered Kepler. "I'll find my way back then." He groaned, as though his back ached. Then he bent down again to the sofa. Zhenyi's handbag was standing there. "I'll take the comb with me, okay, Zhenyi?" he asked quietly.

"Do what you want," she replied.

Kepler opened the bag and rummaged in it. He pretended to be searching for the comb, but he had already found what he needed. Columbus was standing a few steps from the sofa, facing Zhenyi. Kepler lifted the bag with his left hand, leaving his right hand inside it, pulling a disappointed face. "I can't find the comb," he said.

The Secretary must think he was an idiot, making such a fuss about a comb in a situation like this, but he didn't care.

The man obviously thought he was an incompetent klutz anyway. He'd soon be proved wrong. Sometimes it was good to be underestimated.

"Can you have a look, darling?" he asked. He held the bag out in front of him. One step, two steps, three. Then he was standing behind the Secretary, who had no idea what was about to happen. Kepler felt mischievously elated. Wouldn't this be a surprise! He pulled the gun out with his right hand and held it against the Secretary's neck. Columbus froze instantly. It was strange—most people had never felt the barrel of a gun on their necks, but when it happened, they realized immediately what was going on.

"Not a word," ordered Kepler, pleased at the hardness of his voice. He could be a proper gangster! Now he could only hope that the weapons sticking out of the wall didn't detect the danger to Columbus. Or that they were stupid enough only to respond to clear instructions from the Secretary. It didn't matter. Clever or stupid, but nothing in between, please.

Kepler was vindicated. He wasn't penetrated by bullets, sliced through by laser beams or shocked by electricity.

"Turn around slowly and walk toward the door," he said.

Columbus obeyed.

"Watch out he doesn't try anything funny," said Zhenyi. "I wouldn't put anything past this guy."

She could have just praised Kepler. Never mind, he'd praise himself. He had pulled this off really well.

He increased the pressure of the gun against the Secretary's neck. "A bit faster if you don't mind," he said.

"Johannes Kepler, you're making a grave mistake collaborating with this criminal."

"Shut it, you scum," he said. Hearing such aggression coming out of his own mouth was an uplifting feeling.

"Don't overdo it, now," said Zhenyi, but she smiled at him conspiratorially.

Thank you, Zhenyi. They stepped out into the corridor. The butler walked in front.

"You'll lead us back to the shuttle now. And no messing around," said Kepler.

"There's a problem with that," said the Secretary.

"I'm listening? 'No messing around,' I said."

"The shuttle won't be there."

"Why? What's going on?"

"We... I ordered a two-seater for you and your butler. Zhenyi wasn't supposed to leave the administration sector with you."

"How did you know we were coming? Keep walking!"

"Obviously I wasn't certain. But the raid on the Dyson sphere showed that you needed fuel. And where would you intend to fly with it? To the Convention, to ensure the Rescue Project would fail. And then when you killed the architect too, we were sure you were serious. But I was of the view that you were just along for the ride, Kepler."

"Well, you were mistaken," said Kepler.

Columbus had finally let the mask fall!

"Who's we?" asked Zhenyi.

"We are a few people who want to implement the Rescue Project. Because it will save us. We can't afford to take anything else into account."

"You want to exterminate an entire species?"

"A few blades of grass on a single planet. You've been sniffing the grass too much, Zhenyi."

Kepler hit the Secretary's ear with the barrel of the gun.

"Ouch, that hurt."

"You're murderers, Columbus!" said Kepler.

"We're rescuers! We're saving humanity. If you succeed, you'll have humanity on your conscience."

Kepler was about to hit him on the ear again.

"Leave it," said Zhenyi, "it doesn't help."

"How do we get to the airlock from here?" asked Kepler.

"I don't know."

"Well you'd better think of something, Columbus. Or I might forget myself." He disengaged the safety on the gun. The Secretary turned around, shocked.

"My private vehicle, we can get across in that," he said.

"How many seats?" asked Kepler.

"Four."

"That's perfect, room for all of us."

"Or you could leave me behind. I won't cause any trouble for you."

"How stupid do you think we are?" asked Kepler. "Of course you're coming with us. Otherwise the AI will never let us out of the sphere."

THE SECRETARY HADN'T LIED. Half an hour later they were sitting in a kind of aircraft. It was much smaller than the shuttle. Its roof was made of a slightly milky, flexible plastic. Kepler was disappointed.

"Why is there no view of the outside in your private vehicle?" he asked.

Columbus looked at him. "Of course there is. It's a cabriolet. We can fold the roof down. But it gets very windy in the back seats."

Even though the air was so cold, that sounded tempting. They could put the butler and Columbus in the back. But then he would no longer be able to control the Secretary.

"Puppy?"

"What can I do for you, Johannes?"

"Can you handle a weapon?"

"I can handle any weapon."

"If I give you the gun and instructions to put a bullet in the Secretary's neck if he makes a false move, will you be able to fulfill the instructions?"

"Of course, that's not difficult for me," said the butler. "I'm guaranteed not to get tired. You just have to define the term 'false move' more precisely."

"Don't you have a program that prevents you from harming humans?"

"No, Johannes. I'm an advanced AI—those kinds of

prohibitions make no sense. I'm able to evaluate for myself whether an action is justifiable. Shooting the Secretary in the head is morally and ethically acceptable. After all, we're talking about rescuing a species capable of reasoning."

"Understood," said Kepler. "You heard him, Columbus."

"We need to have a talk about your moral compass again," said Zhenyi. "But not until this story has had a happy ending."

"A *happy* ending? You're completely screwy. You've got the majority of humanity against you, don't you realize that?"

"Should this utterance be interpreted as a false move?" asked the butler.

Kepler stiffened. The AI seemed to him to be a little too trigger happy. Maybe it wasn't such a good idea to put a weapon in the hands of a program. But then he wouldn't be able to fly in an open-topped cabriolet. What was more important? Columbus's life or the experience that beckoned?

Kepler laughed to himself. He must be a real hardened criminal if he was asking himself questions like that. "Puppy, an acoustic utterance does not represent a false move," he said. "Only issues of safety."

The butler laughed. "That was a joke, Johannes, just a joke."

"Good. Then can we go?"

"I'm ready," said Zhenyi. "You're the one that's been standing here talking the whole time."

"Then let's go. But with the roof down!" he said.

Leaving the scene of the crime in a cabriolet—how cool was that? The wind should be tolerable up front.

Cycle ZR1.5, Convention

THE CABRIOLET DOCKED at the airlock station. Kepler had closed the roof again quite soon after they started out. The wind current had made it too cold even in the front seats, and in the back the butler had complained of deficits in his facial musculature.

The hologram at the rental service was already waiting for them. It bowed and said, "I hope you had a good flight."

No one paid any attention to the virtual figure. Kepler felt a bit sorry for it, especially as it didn't seem to understand what had happened—why there were four passengers instead of three and how the shuttle had been replaced by a private cabriolet. The butler was still holding the gun against the Secretary's neck. Kepler was thrilled they had him. Even a 300-gram pistol felt heavy when you had to hold it up at neck height for an extended period of time. It didn't seem to bother the butler.

"Forward!" ordered Zhenyi.

The group moved off, the Secretary at the front, followed by his minder. Hopefully Columbus wouldn't try anything stupid. If the butler shot him they'd be on their own. They probably wouldn't even make it back to their ship. The Secretary could easily thwart them, but to do that he'd have to sacrifice himself, and he wasn't that kind of person. If he was, he'd never have become Secretary of the Convention—an organization that only met every thousand years and issued invitations to general meetings only once in a million cycles.

"You won't get far," said Columbus after a while. "You'll have the whole Milky Way on your tail."

"Ah, the galaxy is big," said Zhenyi.

"There are almost a trillion stars in the local group," calculated the butler. "Every person would have to search a hundred million of them each to find us. Even if we factor in an optimistic travel time of four years per system, you would only be guaranteed to find us after four hundred million years."

"But you've got some kind of plan, so you'll be lurking around somewhere near the core of the Milky Way."

He was right, thought Kepler. But what was their plan? As long as their hostage was listening he could hardly ask Zhenyi, who had probably already come up with a plan. The question was, did they even have a chance? The cleverest human brains had already spent several thousand cycles preparing to transform Sagittarius A* into a quasar. How were they supposed to intervene?

But clearly they weren't the only ones singing to a different tune. Someone was manipulating the database to make the Herbae's system disappear. Was it the same someone who had Gropius the architect on their conscience?

"Columbus, a question," said Kepler. "The murder of Gropius—"

"Which you committed," interrupted the Secretary.

"It wasn't us. How did it happen? What do you know about it?"

"All evidence points to you. Gropius was shot, severally."

"Severally?" asked Zhenyi.

"Yes, twenty-two players and the referee," said Columbus.

"Go on," said Kepler.

"Gropius was completely alone at the time. No other spacecraft had stopped within a radius of three light-years."

"That's why we're under suspicion," said Kepler.

"You're the only ones going around in an unregistered ship."

"But it's not invisible," said Zhenyi.

"You removed all records onboard Gropius's ship."

"But the ship's sensors would have registered our departure. We can only delete existing data, not what happens in the future," said Zhenyi.

"Sensors have a hard time with unregistered ships, because they don't exist. How did you even do it? I'm at your mercy, so can't you just tell me?" said Columbus.

"Nice try," said Kepler. "But the joke is, we don't even know."

"So it had nothing to do with the removal of the Guardian from Terra?"

"What? What did you say about the Guardian AI?" Zhenyi walked past the group, stood in front of Columbus and poked him in the gut. "Speak! What happened on Terra?"

"I don't know anything, other than the fact that the Guardian AI was neutralized," said Columbus. "Stop poking me please."

Zhenyi jabbed him one more time in the belly with her index finger. "I can't believe it," she said. "The Guardian AI of all things! It was ancient! Its programming was from the 21st century! Can you imagine? Practically from the Stone Age! Anyone who would destroy such an eminent AI would probably kill their own mother. There's something very sordid going on here. What do the arbiters say about it? Surely they can't just ignore it?"

"The arbiters? Don't make me laugh," said Columbus. "They haven't bothered with reality for gigacycles. They prefer to develop fanciful theories about holographic universes."

Shortly after the destruction of Earth, the arbiters—a

series of level 11 AIs—had declared themselves independent and withdrawn from the lives of humans. Only the Guardian of Terra remained, probably because it took pride in its job. And now it was dead, if you could say that about an AI. Kepler shuddered. If that had happened a few gigacycles ago, the arbiters would have obliterated humanity in retaliation. The fact that they obviously weren't reacting proved Columbus was right.

"We should get moving," said Kepler.

They could interrogate the Secretary on board the ship once they'd had the opportunity to come up with a plan.

"Thank you Kepler," said Zhenyi, and led the group onwards.

"THE SHIP HAS BEEN IMPOUNDED," said the sphere's AI.

Zhenyi yanked on the wheel that was supposed to open the airlock to their ship, but it didn't budge.

Kepler took a deep breath. So the Secretary was right. They wouldn't be able to leave. Zhenyi held out her hand and the butler placed the pistol in it.

"Then I'll shoot the Secretary of the Convention," said Zhenyi.

Columbus pulled his head in. His knees trembled. Kepler felt sorry for him, because he knew the man now had to die. The sphere AI wouldn't be able to strike a deal if it had been ordered to detain them, and his ex-girlfriend would have to follow through with her threat.

"That is a crime," said the sphere AI. "Under these circumstances, I'll have to arrange your immediate arrest. I have full power to do this."

"But I'm already under arrest," said Zhenyi.

"I don't know you," replied the AI, "and I don't have any warrant for your arrest. Only the ship is specified, because the bill for the repair of the hydrogen tanks was not paid. This is the regular procedure. As soon as you pay the outstanding amount you'll have access to your ship again."

"But I agreed to cover the cost of repairs when we arrived," said Kepler.

This was a nightmare. The AI was only detaining them because his account was empty!

"The account is only checked once the costs have been assessed. We have established that your account is overdrawn, Johannes Kepler."

He'd known it would catch up with him at some point. His lifestyle and income simply weren't compatible. He had actually visited Zhenyi originally to ask her for credit. But she was no longer registered anywhere. That meant she also didn't have any accounts. Why couldn't they have just deleted his data instead? Zhenyi didn't have a single credit left, but she also had no debts.

"Columbus, you're up," said Zhenyi.

"For what?"

The man was playing dumb. That wouldn't work on Zhenyi.

"You'll assume the costs of the repairs immediately, or I'll..."

She held the gun under his chin.

"I'll... of course. I'll pay the cost of the repairs to the ship," said the Secretary.

"Please state your name and say, 'I will' to settle the outstanding debt," said the AI.

Columbus performed the transfer. Outstanding debt... They wouldn't get far with Kepler's more-than-empty account. But the Secretary surely had enough in reserve to balance his account. Kepler wasn't greedy. He just wanted enough money to be credit-worthy again.

"While you're at it," said Kepler, "I need to ask you to make a second transfer."

"You won't get away with this."

"Would you rather have a bullet in the head?"

"No. But transfers under duress can be reversed at any time. The AI here is an incorruptible witness."

"That's okay. Someone would have to arrange the reversal, and you won't have an opportunity to do that. My new account balance will be synchronized throughout the galaxy at the speed of light. Wherever we stop, I'll be credit-worthy again."

Columbus sighed. "If I must," he said.

"You must."

They asked the AI to perform the transaction and Columbus gave his approval. Zhenyi had already opened the airlock and was waving them in.

"I'm happy to have done business with you," concluded the sphere AI. "Hopefully we'll have the honor again soon."

Hopefully not, thought Kepler. There was nothing here that could help them now.

Cycle ZS9.1, S0-122

MARIE FELT SLIGHTLY sorry for this star. S0-122 was so lightweight that under normal circumstances it would have had a long life ahead of it. The red dwarf would never be a main-sequence star that developed into a red giant. Instead, it would gradually transform into a blue dwarf, then a white dwarf, and finally a black dwarf. But all that would take quadrillions of cycles.

Would have taken, Marie corrected herself, because she was in the process of drastically altering S0-122's future prospects. The star, which orbited Sagittarius A* every 90 cycles, was wonderfully suited to being turned into a neutron star to serve her plan. Only it could never become a neutron star on its own. They wanted to change this, and all they needed was a little mass.

A little? Marie smiled. They needed more mass than the spaceship could haul. But everything had already been arranged, thanks to Gropius! His gravitational games had made it possible to catapult a sizeable main sequence star out of its local system. It had come a long way, and its fate would be decided here and now.

"Are we safe here?" asked Pierre.

Marie was controlling the long-distance display. "It looks

good. But we'll need to depart at just the right moment," she said.

"We still have to catch someone anyway."

"Between the eyes. Bang."

Marie laughed. It was funny, the way they had finished off one Gropius after another. They had alternated. For the last one—the referee—it was Marie who'd pulled the trigger. Pierre had let her fire the last shot, and she'd been thankful for that.

The new star had already integrated itself into the local system. Good, the two inner planets had been flung out. They had only contained primitive life anyway. Neither she nor Pierre was sorry. But from now on it would best if they tried to avoid problems like the system with the strange stems. Life always got in the way somehow, even if it didn't show any signs of intelligence.

Since they had reached this system, S0-122 had already started stripping away matter from its companion. Their little star would become round and fat. Marie felt like the witch in the fairytale inspecting Hansel's index finger. S0-122 had now become almost as heavy as twelve suns. That was within the range expected to produce a neutron star in the aftermath of an explosion—which was what they actually needed. But—and this was the danger—it was also threatening to become a type 1a supernova, which would leave nothing behind. And that was the reason they were there. They wanted to trigger a core collapse supernova by partially emptying their dark matter tanks. The dark matter was intended to reinforce the gravity acting on the core.

"On my signal," said Marie.

The ship was following a course that would bring it very close to S0-122. They would have to open the tanks at just the right moment, in such a way that the dark matter, due to its inertia, would be flushed into the core of the star. Marie could have opened the tanks herself, but it was more fun doing it together.

Marie counted down. "Three... two... one..."

"Now," they both said at once.

There was nothing to see or hear. The tank covers slid to the side. The dark matter, invisible to the human eye, drifted toward its target.

"Adjust course," said Marie. The adjustment drives ignited. The ship distanced itself from S0-122 again. Now they needed to be patient.

"Shall I cook something?" asked Pierre.

"I'm not hungry," Marie answered.

Together they watched the star system. Their body didn't move. It was one of those intimate moments that Marie loved so much. And if their plan succeeded, then it would be perfect.

Now. The outer layers of the star moved inward at an impressive speed. Core collapse supernovas were an intense spectacle, because everything happened so fast at first. An X-ray flash flooded the ship. It was so strong that nothing could shield against it. The star was inundated by shockwaves that pressed both inward and outward and tried to cancel each other out. The process was unstoppable. Their first core-collapse supernova! At some point they would come back. The neutron star still needed some special handling. But for now they were needed elsewhere. They had to stop someone.

Marie accelerated the ship. It was getting dangerous here. The tanks were now half empty, but the fuel should be enough to get to Terra.

Cycle ZT2.4, Kepler-1229

"WHAT'S THAT?" asked Kepler. Kepler pointed at a cloud of luminous points that seemed to be orbiting a G-type star.

"Well, if you don't know, then I don't know who does." Zhenyi replied.

They stood side by side in front of the large screen in the control room. The star in the middle was Kepler-1229—or it once had been, because there was supposed to be a red dwarf at this location.

"Because the star's named after me? Or why should I know?" he asked.

Many stars were named after the astronomer whose name he had assumed an eternity ago. Everyone had done that back then—sought out a famous role model of the same profession and taken on that person's name. And because hardly any children had been born since then, the Milky Way was now full of former explorers, engineers, and artists.

"No, I'm talking about the cloud," said Zhenyi. "It's moving exactly according to *Keplar's* laws"—she emphasized the name—"which are based on Newtonian physics. I told you old Isaac had constructed himself a unique home world."

Kepler didn't think much of Zhenyi's idea of asking Newton for advice. The detour had cost them loads of time, because his home world lay relatively far away from the center of the galaxy. And what could he tell them that they didn't already know? But Zhenyi had insisted on visiting, and as he hadn't been able to come up with a better idea, he'd gone along with it.

In terms of sky mechanics, Newton certainly knew his stuff. That was obvious from what they could now see on the screen. Kepler used his fingers to zoom in on the cloud. They had arrived in a position almost exactly perpendicular to the orbital plane of the star, so he could admire it in all its beauty.

Newton had really outdone himself. For one thing, he'd somehow managed to swap out the red dwarf at the center of the system for a G-type star three times the size. That alone had been a stroke of mastery. But the way the planets rotated around this sun was unprecedented. Kepler counted eight different orbits—eight circles along which numerous planets were lined up like strings of pearls. He counted several times and finally confirmed there were 52 planets—per orbit!

Newton had procured 416 planets of almost exactly the same size from somewhere—or had he made them?—and arranged them around his sun. A configuration like that was only stable if alternate orbits circled in opposite directions. The outermost 52 planets traveled clockwise around the star. The 52 planets on the next orbit moved counter-clockwise. Even just to have come up with this idea was genius! It guaranteed that the individual worlds only exerted an influence on one another for short periods of time.

Clever, very clever, thought Kepler. He would have been too lazy for a project like that. But the construction phase would have been exhilarating. He would have to ask Newton about it. But where would they meet him? On which of the 416 planets would the physicist have set up his base?

"Which of the 416 is his?" he asked.

"None," said Zhenyi.

"None?"

"I was amazed too. But it makes sense. He's converted a small asteroid at a 90-degree orbit to the main orbital plane. That way he has a better vantage point from which to admire his work, and probably also notices more quickly when something gets out of balance."

"How do you know all this?"

"Oh, you don't want to know."

"I do, Zhenyi."

"Alright, if you insist. After escaping the sanatorium, I hid out for a while with Newton. At the time he was in the process of configuring the outermost orbits."

"Did you and he...?"

Zhenyi laughed. "One woman, one man, no alternative within a radius of 150 light-years? Of course we slept together."

Kepler opened his mouth, but didn't say anything.

"You wanted to know!"

She scolded him playfully with her index finger. Of course he had wanted to know. Stupidly, he would now regard Newton more as a rival than a helper.

But looking at it objectively, it was an advantage. Zhenyi would get the information they needed.

Cycle ZT2.5, Kepler-1229

Newton's home world was truly tiny, and nothing compared to his life's work. It was no longer recognizable as an asteroid. The entire surface of the roughly twenty-kilometer-long and five-kilometer-wide, barrel-shaped celestial body was covered in glittering solar cells. At the bow and stern were two giant antennas. The antennas were probably the shortest distance to one of the 416 planets—Newton would simply transmit himself there via radio.

Kepler stood on the outer hull of the ship in a spacesuit, adjacent to the airlock. The butler was already on his way to Newton's asteroid with a cable spool in tow. Once he'd attached the line, they could comfortably drift across.

Zhenyi climbed out of the airlock and stood next to Kepler. She was wearing a model of spacesuit he'd never seen. It was skintight, but the helmet was a comparatively huge glass bowl lit from inside. It looked like someone had planted Zhenyi's head like a head of lettuce in a greenhouse. He had to laugh.

"What's so funny?" asked Zhenyi, looking miffed.

"Your head—it looks like a head of lettuce."

"I'm glad you're having fun. This helmet feels great, actually, almost like being under the open sky. It hardly ever steams up."

That was an advantage. Kepler had already had to activate the ventilation to stop water vapor condensing on his visor. He lifted his head. These walks outside were really something. If he inadvertently thought about the fact that what he called 'up' could also be called 'down,' he quickly felt queasy. No, the asteroid was floating above them, along with a white sun and 416 planets.

The view was amazing. You wouldn't find a night sky like this anywhere else. The planets were almost uniformly bright, and looked like some sort of jewelry slung around the central star. It was a masterful feat. Hopefully the physicist would be just as masterful at helping them solve their problem so they could save the Herbae.

Zhenyi tapped him on the arm. The line was taut. His ex-girlfriend clipped herself on and pulled on the line. Due to the zero gravity, a small tug was enough and she was on her way. He followed her. Columbus had to stay behind, locked in his room. There was still the risk that Newton would take his side. They had discussed it yesterday at length. Zhenyi had even considered leaving Kepler behind in the ship. Then Newton might be more prepared, she had said suggestively, to engage in some sort of exchange.

Kepler felt a knot in his gut.

NEWTON WAS BALD, a little shorter than Kepler, and with a paunch. That comforted Kepler a bit. At least he felt physically superior. He won that competition hands-down, which didn't happen very often. Their host was exceptionally polite. Nice, in fact. They could tell from the way he gesticulated that he was extremely pleased to have visitors. He probably didn't see other people very often.

First he invited them to a meal. Newton must be a wealthy man, because he was in possession of some exquisite recipes. He had no butler, so Zhenyi's butler was allowed to serve the meal. The three of them sat at a round table under a glass dome on the underside of the asteroid. Kepler called it the underside because they couldn't see the ship from here. But the 416 planets hung above them in all their splendor, almost within reach. Kepler was awestruck. From the spaceship, the planets had looked a lot further away.

The butler brought out a vegetable soup and served it.

"One moment," said Newton, "before you eat. The vegetables in this soup are completely biologically grown on Number 59." Newton raised his finger and a planet from the second innermost ring zoomed toward them so they could see it in detail. Roughly half of it was covered with water. Kepler counted two large continents and numerous islands. Cloud shadows drifted slowly across the surface.

"The growing region is near the equator. I could produce enough food for a million people there. But unfortunately I'm my only customer."

Newton sounded frustrated. All 416 planets were located in the habitable zone, and his incredible creation could easily have provided a home for two trillion people. But no one actually lived there. It was an immense waste. What had happened to all of humanity's dreams?

"How did you do that? A projection?" asked Kepler. Maybe he could redirect the conversation to a safer topic.

"No, this is all real. There are countless optics mounted on the dome that I can use to zoom in seamlessly. They're normally set to double magnification. That's why the planets look closer."

"And even more impressive," said Zhenyi, laying her spoon to the side.

So, she will be complimenting Newton to put him in a good mood, thought Kepler. Maybe it would have been better if he'd stayed on the ship. He would have to hold back so as not to undermine Zhenyi's strategy. Why was she eating so little these days? He hadn't seen her take more than a few bites in the last few weeks.

"Well, they're planets. They can't do anything other than

stay in their orbits. That's no great feat, and certainly not magic," said Newton.

"You're too modest. It's a lot of hard work," said Zhenyi. "I remember on my last visit you were busy with the outermost orbit and hardly had any time for me."

Newton's gaze changed. He had a faraway look in his eyes, romantic even. "Oh, 412 gave me problems. It was a bit too heavy. I had to remove part of the crust. That planet has never been as fertile as the others, but it doesn't matter. If I'd know that then, I would rather have spent the time with you."

Kepler scrunched up his napkin noisily. Zhenyi reprimanded him with a look. He didn't know what had come over him. He felt like saying, 'Hey people, I'm still here.'

"I'm sorry about 412," said Zhenyi.

Now all that was missing was for her to hand him a handkerchief. They were only stupid planets that no one needed anyway!

"Thanks, but it's not important. I have a surprise for you, by the way, for both of you, something you definitely haven't seen. I only built it seven kilocycles ago."

"That sounds exciting," said Zhenyi.

Newton stood up. Then he moved his arms like a conductor. Dramatic organ music sounded as Newton waved his arms about. The movements looked professional, Kepler had to admit.

"Look," said Zhenyi, pointing up.

What he saw there was crazy. The planets were moving in time to the music. Eight orbits, eight musical scales, each with 52 different notes. Newton had constructed a kind of heavenly organ!

"I'm just an ignorant astronomer," said Kepler, "but that can't be the actual planets you're moving?"

The effort would have been gigantic. Moving six sextillion tons back and forth at this pace, even Newton couldn't be capable of that.

"No, those are just pretty effects that I create purely with the optics in the dome," said Newton, continuing to conduct.

"But the music does correspond with the apparent movement of the planets. I write it myself. If you can imagine yourself as a synthesizer, each planet is a key."

It was still impressive, but he was also relieved. Newton wasn't superhuman.

The music grew quieter and faded out. Newton sat down and they applauded him. Then it was quiet. Dramatic organ music always killed conversation for a while.

"Isaac," said Zhenyi, breaking the silence. "I have a problem—we have a problem—and I was hoping you could help."

"I thought you'd never spit it out."

"Does that mean you'll help me?"

"How about you tell me what it's about first?"

Zhenyi explained what they had found and what had happened. Newton asked questions at various points. It reminded Kepler a lot of the fruitless conversation with Columbus, who ended up wanting to arrest her. This time Zhenyi hadn't brought a handbag containing a pistol.

"It sounds to me like there are two different powers at work, that are partially competing and partially cooperating," said Newton.

"How do you mean?"

"Well, the disappearance of the Herbae's home world serves the interests of those determined to follow through with the Rescue Project. But not all of them seem to be in agreement. Columbus, for example."

"Maybe they just didn't want to make him an accomplice?" hypothesized Zhenyi.

"As Secretary of the Convention he plays an important role, and has always been in favor of the Rescue Project. He of all people not knowing who eliminated Gropius and the Guardian? That sounds very unlikely to me. I believe there's another, smaller group with their own plans."

"The Curies," offered Kepler.

He described their strange visit to Zhenyi's base.

"When I think about it, maybe I was quite lucky," Johannes said.

"How?" asked Zhenyi.

"Gropius had to die. The Curies must be responsible for that. Maybe they also wanted to kill you. If you had been there, I would have had to die too, being a witness."

Kepler felt cold at the thought. Did saving a species have to be so dangerous? Newton was now probably calculating how unlikely that was.

"That sounds plausible to me," said Newton.

Shit, thought Kepler.

"But the question is," continued Newton, "what is this other motive? I think if we find that out, we've got them."

Well that was obvious, thought Kepler, *I could have said that.*

"Right," said Zhenyi. "Does that mean you'll help us?"

"I already promised you that long ago."

"Isaac, you're a true friend."

"Thank you, Zhenyi. I'd like to visit the Herbae myself. I'm sure I could learn a lot from them."

"You will. But first let's unravel it from the beginning," said Zhenyi. "Everything starts and ends with the Rescue Project. Is there something underhanded going on? Were we sold something different from what we're really getting?"

"That's exactly the right question," said Newton. "We'll recalculate the Rescue Project precisely from beginning to end, taking into account the official plans and the current data."

"Do you have a quantum computer here?" asked Kepler.

The asteroid seemed far too small to house a computer of the size needed to plot out the Rescue Project.

"My computer is floating above us in space," said Newton. "The planets, with their mutual gravitational influence, are perfectly suited to simulations like this."

"The 416 planets are a computer?" asked Zhenyi.

Kepler was as impressed as she was.

"Together with their sun. I know how they react to one another. I constructed the system myself. It responds in a self-sustaining manner to small alterations. I just have to convert the situation mathematically. Then I deflect one of the planets in a certain way, and the reaction of the whole system over time gives me the answer I'm looking for."

"Like a pendulum," said Kepler.

"More like a gigantic, well-oiled calculator," said Newton.

"And how long does that take?" asked Zhenyi.

"I already have the data from the Rescue Project. I can adapt it to a mathematical model today. But that means you'll have to amuse yourselves without me for a while."

Ha, Kepler thought, and then felt guilty.

"The actual calculation process will take two days at the most," said Newton. "If you like, you can come with me tomorrow to set it in motion."

"That sounds exciting. Where do we go?" asked Zhenyi.

"I still have to work that out."

Cycle ZT2.6, Kepler-1229

"THAT'S OUT OF THE QUESTION!" Kepler looked at the seat with a gleaming dish where his head was supposed to go.

"Don't be like that," said Zhenyi. "Surely you sometimes use direct laser transfer?"

"I'm not submitting my body to Newton's control!" said Kepler.

"But he's coming with us!"

"If I might say something," Newton interjected, "there's no other way. It's far too dangerous to fly there with my ship."

"Why?" asked Kepler.

"The relative speed of the planets in their various orbits is enormous! It would be like putting your hand into a mixer."

"But we're coming from above, perpendicular to the ecliptic."

"Your hand comes from above too. That actually makes it harder," said Newton. "If there was an accident, we'd be putting the stability of the whole system at risk."

Kepler was silent. The physicist was right, of course. Unfortunately. But that significantly decreased the value of his diligent work. If people lived on one of the planets, they could only visit their brothers and sisters on the 52 neighboring planets, but not the ones in the other rings, even though they were continuously passing them by.

"So, are you coming?" asked Zhenyi.

Kepler grunted. He had to. He wasn't going to grant Newton a romantic escapade with Zhenyi.

"We have to visit a planet in the fourth orbit," the physicist explained. "I think we'll have fun there."

SOMETHING WAS TICKLING HIS LEG. Kepler lifted his head. He was lying in some kind of wooden hut with a loose grass roof. Beams of sunlight pierced through it and drew patterns on the walls. A spider crawled over his leg. It was taking its time and seemed unable to make up its mind. Then it lifted its head. It must have seen or sensed something. It quickly climbed off his knee onto the ground and scuttled to the wall of the hut.

"Kepler? Are you there?"

That was Zhenyi's voice. He heard something rustling, then the ringing of small bells. Kepler turned his head. It was Zhenyi. She'd pulled aside the curtain at the entrance to the hut. She had a flawless female body and was wearing a bikini. Kepler chuckled. This must be where Newton spent his spare time. The man had it good. He looked down at himself and got a shock. He was also in a woman's body, just as perfectly designed as Zhenyi's, with darker skin.

"You look good!" said Zhenyi, laughing.

Great. He shook his head. It would be best if he paid no attention to it. They weren't there to amuse themselves, they were there to start the simulation. Kepler stood up. Zhenyi left the hut and he followed her.

It was blindingly bright outside. They were standing on a white sand beach. Blue waves broke on the shore. He saw a line of palms beyond the beach. Newton had created a little paradise for himself here. Were the other planets designed in such detail?

Another woman was waving at them from farther away.

That must be Newton himself. What was Kepler supposed to make of that?

"Come on, I'll race you," said Zhenyi. "First one there!"

She took off. Kepler followed her once he had recovered from the surprise. It was terrific running through the warm sand with bare feet. The body was in good shape. He even started gaining on Zhenyi and had nearly caught up to her when she threw herself at Newton with a leap and touched his toes.

Her toes.

"I won," cried Zhenyi, rolling around in the sand on her back.

Kepler smiled. He hadn't even broken a sweat. Without the element of surprise, he would have beaten Zhenyi. Maybe he should give up his old body. There were so many better artificial ones! But somehow he felt bound to it.

"Oh, we're in luck. A transit," said Newton, pointing to the sky.

Kepler shielded his eyes with his hand, but it wasn't necessary. As soon as he looked at the sun, the body reduced the photosensitivity of its visual organs.

"You can zoom too, by the way," said Newton. "You just have to think about it."

Kepler imagined seeing the sun up close, and the image actually enlarged. A black circle was passing in front of the flaming disk of the sun, a planet on one of the inner orbits.

"Is that rare?" he asked.

"Not really," replied Newton. "About once every eight days. But since we're only here for a short time, you were lucky."

Kepler surveyed the sky. It wasn't nearly as exotic as he'd imagined it would be. He could see a few unusually bright stars above the eastern and western horizons. Those must be the next planets in the same orbit. But they weren't even as close as Earth's moon had been to the Earth. The view was probably much more impressive on the night side because there would be so many more bright 'stars.'

"I suppose you've only made these types of bodies for this planet?" asked Kepler.

"Why would I want to amuse myself here as an old man?" asked Newton. "How about I grill us a couple of fish?"

"You've thought out every detail of the ecosystem," Zhenyi praised him.

"Shouldn't we get the calculations started first?" said Kepler.

Work. Then pleasure.

"Good thinking, Johannes, you're completely right," said Newton. "Come this way, please." He pointed toward the palms beyond the beach.

They walked across the warm sand until they reached the shade of the trees. Out of nowhere, a shelf with sandals appeared in front of them.

"Please choose a pair and put them on," said their guide.

Zhenyi looked at him questioningly.

"You'll see why in a minute."

Kepler slipped into a pair of red leather sandals, the color matching the polish on his toenails.

"This way," said Newton, who was now wearing pumps.

They looked a bit out of place in the sand. But the ground soon became firmer. Spiny fruit lay on the ground between the palms. Was that why they needed sandals? They crossed a sparse grove. Behind it was an area of black. At first it made Kepler think of a volcanic plateau. But that's not what it was.

Newton remained standing under a palm at the edge of the grove. The ecosystem ended here. The planet seemed to be covered in giant metal plates, above which powerful mechanical linkages were operating. Steam escaped from between the plates. It no longer smelled of the sea. It smelled of oil.

"Nothing comes from nothing," said Newton, gesturing into the distance with his hand.

"Is this... a factory?" asked Kepler.

"No. This is a machine. To put it more precisely, it's the planetary machine, as it really is. The beach, the sea... the machine produces all of it."

"The planet is a machine?" asked Zhenyi, eyes wide.

"Yes, what else? The mass has to be exact. I have to balance the effect of the other planets' tidal forces. Otherwise the orbits aren't permanently stable."

"Isn't that a lot of effort?"

"It was at the beginning, Kepler. It took a few kilocycles before this was all set up. But now it runs like clockwork."

"And the computer?" asked Kepler.

"Come with me!"

Newton walked across the plates and Kepler followed. The metal was flexible. He bent down and felt it. It was hot, over 40 degrees. He was glad they were no longer barefoot.

Newton stopped in front of a large wheel attached to the end of a linkage. "This is my computer," he said.

"Looks quite old-fashioned," said Kepler.

"It's mechanical," said Newton. "I turn the wheel. That causes the linkages to move the plates, which deforms the entire planet."

"You turn this a few times and the whole planet changes shape?" asked Kepler.

"Yes. But we only need a minor change. We don't want to cause the system to collapse."

Newton turned the wheel clockwise. The linkage squeaked.

Kepler counted. One turn, two, three, five, nine... fourteen. The wheel stopped.

"Fifteen turns," said Newton. "That's how many we need."

"That was fourteen," said Kepler.

Newton raised his eyebrows.

"Are you sure?"

"Yes, Isaac."

Newton sagged a little. He scratched his nose with his

index finger, then sighed. Finally he gripped the wheel and turned it one more time. "So, I hope you're right," he said. "What do you think, Zhenyi?"

"Don't ask me, I wasn't counting."

Cycle ZT2.7, Kepler-1229

His life seemed to be full of unusual experiences these days, but yesterday's excursion was probably the most bizarre—except perhaps for the bath of worms on the planet of the Herbae. Kepler touched his chest. It was flat, or nearly. Maybe he should go on a diet. In any case, he was clearly back in his old body. But the fish fried over the campfire yesterday had been exceptional. Kepler's mouth watered.

The asteroid where Newton had erected his base was functional. Kepler missed the beach. They hadn't had the chance to go for a swim. Maybe he should clamber across the surface of the asteroid in a spacesuit and gaze at the unique solar system again?

He didn't feel like it. He didn't feel like anything today. He turned over and went back to sleep.

"Kepler, Kepler!" Someone was shaking his shoulder. "You've got to wake up!"

It was Zhenyi. What was up?

"Come on," she said. "Newton is completely pale! He's finished his calculations."

"Oh." Kepler kicked off the blanket. Under it he was fully clothed.

Zhenyi's mouth twitched with mirth.

"I was already awake earlier," he said.

"I see." She didn't believe him. But what was wrong with Newton?

"Do you think Isaac has discovered something?" he asked.

"Don't talk, just come. Then he'll be able to tell us."

THEY MET Newton under the dome. The glass roof was black. Kepler couldn't see a single star. It must be in opaque mode. Newton paced up and down under the dome. He had his hands in his pants pockets. He kept flapping his elbows, but his hands remained in his pockets. Why was he restraining himself like that?

"We're here," said Zhenyi.

Newton came to an abrupt stop, as though he'd only just noticed them. Then he waved his hands around. The dome changed. "Sit down," said Newton. "The situation came as quite a shock. But have a look for yourselves."

Kepler sat on a chair and looked up at the ceiling. He could see a black spot surrounded by a glowing disk.

"Sagittarius A*," said Newton, "in case you don't recognize it."

'It' was the black hole in the center of the Milky Way, which the Rescue Project was supposed to transform into a quasar. Why was Newton getting so worked up about that?

"The official goal of the Rescue Project is to activate Sagittarius A*," said Newton. "To do that, they want to feed it with all kinds of stars from the immediate vicinity as well as more distant ones. So far, so good."

"I wouldn't call it good," said Zhenyi, "if humans are going to exterminate an intelligent species in the process."

"You will when you've seen my simulation," said Newton.

Kepler keenly watched the ceiling. More and more stars

approached the black hole, which was only recognizable by the fact that there appeared to be no matter at its location. The stars circled the hole in a spiral until they were finally swallowed by it, part of their mass landing in the accretion disk surrounding the hole. The black hole grew and grew until the process was self-sustaining. Finally, the interaction with the accretion disk created two huge fountains or jets that shot enormous amounts of energy into space.

"That's the official side of the Project," said Newton. "The stars that are to be sacrificed for it have been meticulously listed."

"The sacrifice of the Herbae isn't on the list," said Zhenyi.

"But I've searched out all the stars whose current trajectories suggest they'll soon be captured by Sagittarius A*. And bingo, there are significantly more."

"How many more?" asked Kepler.

"An order of magnitude. Now you'll see what happens next."

The representation on the ceiling jumped back to the starting point. The black hole swallowed stars again, digested them, burped, and grew. But now there were many more celestial bodies coming from the surrounding area—not just stars, but also stellar remnants, neutron stars, gravastars, blue dwarfs, white dwarfs, and small to medium black holes. It was as though someone had crossed the Milky Way and shunted all the trash they found on the way into the center.

Sagittarius A* was enjoying the attention. It took in everything that was placed before it, without differentiation. It swelled, jets shot out of it—the space around it quickly became life-threatening. A yellow point flashed.

"That's the location of the Herbae's system," said Newton. "I thought you might be interested in that, Zhenyi."

"Thank you," she said.

But the black hole kept growing. It was already much more substantial than had ever been anticipated, and its meal wasn't over yet. This can't end well, thought Kepler. It was an orgy of desolation in the middle of space that had done more damage than humanity could ever make use of. It would critically change the shape of the Milky Way.

All at once, everything contracted. Sagittarius A* shrank at a rapid pace. But not only did the black hole grow smaller, the Milky Way did too. Everything disappeared. It was as if someone had accidentally zoomed out. What had been many millions of light-years across now measured only light-years, then kilometers, then everything disappeared into nothing. The dome was black again.

"What was that?" asked Zhenyi.

"The end," said Newton.

"The end of your simulation?"

"The death of the universe, Zhenyi. The end of all of us."

"But how—"

"A metastable state, right?" Kepler interrupted her.

"Right," said Newton. "The feeding process overloaded the black hole in such a way that the universe at our latitudes slipped out of its metastable state. No one would survive that, not even the universe. At least, not the one we know."

"So will anything survive?" asked Zhenyi.

"To be very precise," said Newton, "imagine you are damming a canal, with two dams, left and right. The water flows into it stably. But without the dams it doesn't work. The water is not in its default state, but in a metastable state. Then you tear down part of the dam. The water runs out. It seeks out the lowest point and forms a lake there. The canal is empty, it no longer exists. The metastable state has ended. But now you have a lake with completely different characteristics from the canal. We only know our universe in this metastable state. What it would turn into in its default state, no one knows. Maybe there'll be a new Big Bang, or maybe a completely new universe will result. But there won't be anything left of us, not even memories."

"Because we're too close to the core, where it's all happening?" asked Zhenyi.

"No, because we're part of the universe, which will cease

to exist. No one will escape the collapse. There'll be no way out of the great annihilation. It will spread at the speed of light across the entire cosmos. The Rescue Project is the assassination of the universe."

It was unbelievable. Newton must be wrong. Who would be so insane as to destroy the universe itself? There might be people who were tired of their immortality. But taking everyone else with you? How evil did you have to be to do something like that? But maybe they still didn't know all aspects of the plan. There must be something they had overlooked.

"So survival isn't possible?" asked Kepler.

"Anything that's part of the universe will go down with it," replied Newton assuredly.

"Could someone try to stop being part of the universe?"

Newton gave a short laugh. "That's impossible."

"I was thinking of an ant living on a flat surface. If it dug a hole through it and came out on the other side, wouldn't it have then escaped the universe?"

"Oh, this ridiculous comparison. It's been circulating for several megacycles, but it's humbug. A 2D ant can't dig 3D holes. And afterward, it's still two-dimensional. And it still can't escape the universe.

"Who's behind the plan?" asked Zhenyi. "The Convention?"

"It wouldn't have been passed by a majority. But we could ask Columbus," said Newton.

"Puppy, can you please fetch Columbus from his room?"

"THAT'S MONSTROUS," said the Secretary of the Convention after seeing the simulation.

"Those are the facts," said Newton.

"I don't mean the accusation. The plan is monstrous. Anyone who could come up with something like that would have to be deranged," said Columbus.

"Are you saying the Convention isn't behind it?"

"I'd say it with my hand in the fire. The discovery of this allegedly intelligent species—what are you calling them? Herbae? The fact that this information was withheld, I would expect from some members of the Convention. But to exterminate all of humanity, that I can't imagine, no. There's no one who'd do that."

"The Herbae aren't only allegedly intelligent, they are actually intelligent," said Zhenyi. "But who could have conceived such a murderous plan?"

"I wouldn't want to accuse anyone of such grave actions," said Columbus.

"But someone must have devised this insanity!" said Zhenyi.

"The Curies," said Kepler. "Think about their visit."

"They might be a bit strange, but *murderers?*" asked Newton.

"You don't know them," said Kepler. "But I know how we might be able to catch them out."

"Yes?" Zhenyi leaned toward him.

"There are numerous stars that appear in Newton's simulation, which fall into the black hole but which were not intended to be part of the Rescue Project. Someone must have set them on a course from their original location. They can't exactly fly to the center of the Milky Way on their own. If we compare their original locations with the Curies' travel routes and find parallels—that would be weighty evidence."

"Good idea, Kepler. And if we can prove the Curies are behind it? Can it still be prevented?"

"I'm sorry," said Newton, "but according to my simulation, it's too late for that."

Cycle ZT2.8, Kepler-1229

"LEAVE ME. There's really no point," said Newton.

"But if you don't come with us, we'll have no chance of coming up with an alternative strategy," said Zhenyi.

Kepler didn't actually want his competition on board, but they needed him to help them save the universe, so he supported Zhenyi's attempts at persuasion. "I don't think we're aware of all the factors yet," he said. "Your abilities will be crucial for that, Newton!"

"It's no longer possible to divert fate, the simulation showed that unequivocally. There's no 'what if?'—it's a clear prognosis. The stars are already moving in the direction of the black hole. This plan has been ingeniously thought out and implemented. Whoever it was only has to sit back and watch and enjoy the meshing of the cogs."

"If that's true, then you don't need to be afraid of a short excursion," said Zhenyi.

"That's not what it's about at all. I want to spend my last few years in my cozy little system. I spent so long building it, and now I don't even get to enjoy it?"

"You've got a whole megacycle for that!" said Zhenyi.

She stood in front of Newton, put her hands on his shoulders, and stared him straight in the face.

He shook his head.

"You have a million years. Look me in the eye and say you don't want to invest part of that in trying to save the universe. Together with me."

"I... it's not about you or me. You're grasping at non-existent straws. Even an hour is too much to invest in that."

Newton was squirming so much Kepler almost felt sorry for him. The physicist was probably further ahead in his thinking than he was. Kepler had just realized he was suddenly mortal again. The Rescue Project would still have left him with inconceivable gigacycles. A million years, that was comparable to a moment. Humanity was almost as vulnerable again as it had been at the beginning. Would this understanding make him just as hamstrung as Newton? At the moment it was just making him angry. Angry at those who had taken away a part of his life.

"Then make yourself comfortable on the beach with your playthings, Newton," said Zhenyi scornfully. "We have to leave. Columbus, are you ready?"

Half an hour later, in the control room of the ninety-niner, the four of them watched Newton's little asteroid disappear in the distance.

"I really feel like firing the railguns at that thing," said Zhenyi. She had a cold smile fixed on her face. Kepler hoped she would never have cause to be this angry with him.

"That won't achieve anything," said Columbus, "other than adding another offense to your criminal file."

"We still need to talk about that," said Zhenyi. "Anyway, it would give me enormous peace of mind. Newton is a worm who thinks of no one but himself."

"I agree," said the Secretary.

Kepler still didn't entirely trust Columbus. After all, he hadn't originally volunteered to come along. But he had freely offered to accompany them to the database on Terra, to search for clues that might point to the Curies.

"I'm surprised you're cooperating with us," said Kepler. "Don't you consider us criminals anymore?"

"I'm a realist," Columbus replied. "There's convincing evidence that you and Zhenyi had something to do with Gropius's murder and the elimination of the Guardian of Terra. But there are still other explanations. Newton's simulation seems comprehensive, although I can't check that it was based on the correct data. But we can find that out on Terra. And in the end I consider you both sensible people. If you find out you're in the wrong, you'll give yourselves up."

"In the wrong?" said Zhenyi. "You're insane. You're lucky I'm so furious with that Newton worm right now that I don't have a scrap of anger left over for you. And now we all need to get into our gel beds as fast as possible. It's a long way to Terra. We'll have to accelerate at seven Gs. I hope no one breakfasted too well."

Cycle ZX3.4, Terra

"Look," said Zhenyi, grabbing Kepler's hand.

A giant, three-dimensional ball of fire was displayed on the big screen in the control room, a main sequence star in the bloom of its youth. Protuberances freed themselves from its surface, and the magnetic fields around it drew dark, rhythmically changing patterns on its surface.

"What is that?" he asked.

Kepler held his hand very still in the hope that Zhenyi wouldn't pull hers away. They were alone in the control room. The butler had served them an excellent evening meal. He was probably in the kitchen now, and Columbus had retired to his room.

"That's the sun."

"The sun?"

Kepler stressed the article.

"Yes, our sun," said Zhenyi. "Even if that sounds a bit strange. The star that created us all, anyway."

"That holo vid must be ancient," said Kepler.

"Yes, I found it in the archive. I can't even remember having saved it."

"You're such a romantic."

"You think?" Zhenyi snapped the fingers of her left hand. The sun disappeared. The screen now showed a washed-out, white spot—all that was now left of the once-mighty star.

"Sad," said Kepler.

"The vid is part of a whole series," said Zhenyi. She snapped her fingers again to display a planet covered in a dense layer of cloud. "See the logo at the top right? That must be the manufacturer." The letters of the logo were difficult to decipher.

Kepler spelled it out, "E-D-U-T-V. Strange word. But what planet is it?"

"Venus," said Zhenyi.

"The planet of love. How romantic."

Zhenyi laughed. "Look at it today, though." She snapped her fingers and a scorched pile of rock appeared in the middle of the screen.

"Let's go back to the past," said Kepler. "It's more fun. What did that big lump look like?"

"Jupiter? You'll be amazed." A giant, storm-ravaged gas ball materialized, with a large red spot emblazoned on it.

"Not bad," said Kepler. "All that gas, what happened to it?"

"Everything was blasted away when the sun transformed into a red giant."

"Couldn't we have transported it to safety?"

"We couldn't at the time. Didn't you pay attention in history? The one-planet doctrine? 'Those who do not look after their own planet haven't earned the right to populate another.' That bullshit only stopped shortly before the catastrophe."

"Shame," said Kepler. He shouldn't have externalized his memories of school.

"Yes, especially for this one," said Zhenyi.

The gas ball of Jupiter was replaced by a slightly smaller gas planet. Kepler couldn't believe his eyes. The planet had rings!

"Who decorated it like that?"

"Its moons. At least, that's the short answer."

"Oh, how beautiful," he said. He wasn't just referring to the image of the former ringed planet, Saturn. He also meant Zhenyi's hand on his. No, not *also*. *Especially*. Please, fate, let this hand stay where it is for a while longer.

Zhenyi used her other hand to pick up her wine glass. "A toast?"

Kepler raised his own glass and looked at Zhenyi. Then he lowered his gaze and looked into the red liquid in his glass, almost the consistency of blood.

"What's wrong?" asked Zhenyi.

"I... I don't know." He looked at her directly. She smiled. Man, why couldn't he come up with anything other than this stammering nonsense right now?

Zhenyi held her glass up to his. He clinked glasses with her, creating a melodic tone that echoed through the control room. It seemed louder than the life support system.

"To saving the world," she said.

"To us," he said.

"To the future," said Zhenyi. She was still smiling, and it wasn't a strained smile.

Kepler put down his glass and bent forward. Was this the right moment? He wouldn't find out unless he tried. He leaned closer. Zhenyi closed her eyes. He puckered his lips.

Zhenyi opened her eyes again and her smile vanished. "Sorry," she said. "I can't."

Kepler reddened. It wasn't the right moment. There would never be a right moment. He was an idiot who was imagining things.

Zhenyi's hand stroked his. He looked down with wide eyes. Her fingers were moving tenderly over the back of his hand. What did that mean? Did she want it, or didn't she?

"I..." he said, but couldn't think of anything else to say.

"Sh... sh..." she said, placing a finger to his lips. "I like you, Johannes. You're good for me, you ground me. I can talk to you, argue with you, and I can also be wonderfully silent with you. But what you want can't work. Not now."

Not now? What did she mean by that? Was it a good idea

to ask, or would that be completely wrong? He certainly wanted to avoid putting his foot in it. Pressure wouldn't help, he couldn't react by whining, but he also couldn't be happy about being rebuffed—so what, then?

"I understand," he said. He'd never told such an utter lie.

Zhenyi thanked him with a smile, as though she hadn't seen through the lie. And she even left her hand on his. So, had that been the right response? Kepler took a deep breath.

"We'll reach Terra tomorrow," Zhenyi said, as if he didn't already know.

"Yes, it's nearly time," he replied.

Then they were silent, and it felt completely right.

Cycle ZX3.5, Terra

THE MOON PASSED THEM BY. It looked like an enormous artificial satellite, because it was completely covered in technology.

"The antenna's huge," said Kepler.

"Terra is one of the few systems in the Milky Way that can be reached from almost anywhere with a direct laser link," Columbus explained.

"Wouldn't it have been more efficient to drag the planet closer to the core of the Milky Way?"

"Oh, this isn't the original position of the solar system," said Columbus. "I thought everyone knew that. It was Le Corbusier's first masterwork, bringing the system more than 50,000 light-years closer to the core."

"Then humans must have previously lived really far out. I had no idea," said Kepler.

"There are theories that suggest that's why humanity didn't become extinct," said Zhenyi. "At some point in the distant past, Sagittarius A* is supposed to have experienced a massive eruption, which sterilized all the systems within its radius."

"Do you believe that?" asked Kepler. He'd heard of such theories but they contained so many contradictions that they'd never prevailed.

"No," said Zhenyi, "those are fairy tales told by scientists who couldn't come to terms with the fact that we're apparently alone in the cosmos for no reason whatsoever."

"Excuse a Secretary's stupid question," said Columbus, "but isn't there a reason for everything?"

Zhenyi gave a short laugh. Kepler knew that laugh well. Anyone who didn't know her would think she was being haughty.

"There is no reason," she said. "There's the relationship between cause and effect, but that's completely different from a reason or a purpose behind everything. Cause and effect are defined by the laws of physics, and those are the way they are because that's the way they randomly came into being after the Big Bang."

That's exactly right, thought Kepler. But it sounded much more meaningful coming out of Zhenyi's mouth than if he'd formulated it in his own thoughts. Was there a reason for that? Was there ever! Charisma—she had it, and he didn't. Even the Secretary was hanging on her every word.

A GLISTENING X drifted across the screen. It was moving from left to right. The guard station, of course. Shouldn't they stop there? Columbus, who was controlling the ship, wasn't making any preparations to go into orbit.

"The guard station," said Kepler, pointing at the screen from which the X was about to disappear.

"Oh, what a tragedy," said Columbus. "But the fact that you... I mean unknown persons disintegrated the Guardian has saved us time."

"So, is Terra now completely unguarded?"

"Why would you think that? No, several autonomous AIs regulate access. The Guardian was just a kind of tradition—an ancient AI from those times, created especially for the interaction. Its programmer overshot the mark a bit, if you ask me."

"Yeah?"

"The overblown symbolism! Sometimes it appeared as an angel. Can you imagine, Kepler? As though there were still gods in this universe."

Of course there weren't. But something about Columbus's manner made him want to contradict him. He shook his head but said nothing.

THE SHUTTLE SET them down at the end of a valley cut deep into the mountains. Kepler was wearing his spacesuit. He didn't want to take any risks. Minus 40 degrees was forecast. A veritable heatwave. Zhenyi claimed to be able to cope well with the cold. She'd draped herself in a wool coat and was wearing a hat pulled low over her forehead. The butler wore his tuxedo. Zhenyi had asked Columbus to stay on the ship, but the Secretary insisted on accompanying them, for their own safety. Columbus had also opted for a spacesuit.

The valley was shaped like a bathtub. It was one of the few places on Terra where there was still enough oxygen to breathe. That was due to the ventilation slits in its sides, through which the air was continually renewed, and the underground heating, which prevented the atmosphere from being frozen and stripped away.

Zhenyi had insisted the shuttle shouldn't drop them off directly in front of the big gate. It was one of seven entrances to the subterranean storage halls—and the only one that had been opened in the last few thousand years. If they were going to find traces of the Curies, it would be there.

Kepler turned down the heating in his suit because he was sweating—the unusually high gravity on Terra weighed them down—and these were the conditions under which their forefathers were supposed to have voluntarily stood upright on two legs, instead of staying close to the ground?

He had to remind himself that it used to look different. The ground that was now brown and cracked used to have grass and herbs growing on it. It must have been comfortable to walk on with bare feet. Unfortunately he'd externalized his own memories of those times. It was strange—the memory stores behind the big gate knew more about his own past than he did. But it had been necessary. No human brain could cope with so many memories. Before externalization became standard, many people had suffered memory breakdowns. Their thousand lives had inundated them and thrown everything into turmoil.

Kepler had a breakdown like that in his past, he still knew that much. But he had offloaded the memories of it long ago, so they no longer troubled him.

THEY WERE STANDING in front of the gate. He felt like a dwarf. The iron gate loomed maybe 80 meters above them. Had it ever been opened? That would be an imposing sight—one they wouldn't get to experience.

For visitors, there was a small door, which Columbus was now rattling. "The door AI won't accept my access authorization," he grumbled.

"Why? Doesn't the Convention have access to everything?" asked Zhenyi.

"Apparently the Guardian has to verify it," said Columbus.

"But there is no Guardian anymore," Zhenyi responded.

"That's what I said to the AI," said the Secretary.

"There must be a way in. If necessary, we'll blow the thing up," said Zhenyi.

This was what Kepler had been afraid of—this trip was going to add to their list of criminal offenses. No AI could stop Zhenyi. Kepler scraped at the ground with his foot.

"If we open the door by force, we won't be able to close it again. That would put the whole archive in jeopardy," said Columbus.

"Then think of something else!" Zhenyi pleaded.

"I'll talk to the AI again," said the Secretary.

And then the door swung inward after all. What had happened? Had the AI somehow heard Zhenyi's threat and opened the door to avoid damage to the archive?

"How did you manage that then?" asked Zhenyi.

"I... I don't know," said Columbus.

"Doesn't matter. Let's make use of the opportunity before the AI changes its mind."

Zhenyi entered the memories of humanity and the others followed her.

Directly behind the door was a short passage with several other doors leading off it.

"If anyone needs to use the toilet," said Columbus, pointing at one of the doors. "There aren't any sanitation units in the memory stores."

They shook their heads.

"No one but me?" asked Columbus.

He got no answer, so he opened the door and disappeared behind it.

They waited. There was an uneasy silence. The passage was filled with an electrical humming sound.

Kepler checked the temperature. Four degrees. He took off his helmet and clipped it onto his belt. "He's taking his time," said Kepler.

"I guess he's being thorough," said Zhenyi.

"Maybe he's hightailed it?" Kepler suggested.

Zhenyi pointed at the exit door behind them that had closed automatically. "He'd have to go through there. You saw, there weren't any other doors."

Zhenyi was right. The Secretary was just taking his time. Then the door opened and Columbus came through it. He'd taken off his helmet too. "I'm back," he said.

"Let's move," said Zhenyi. "We'll go get the logs."

THEY HAD BEEN CLIMBING up and down ladders and marching across transparent walkways for two hours now. Kepler had gotten used to having to look down into the abyss. The archive seemed endless, and that impression was reinforced by the fact that only the area directly around them was lit. Above, below, in front, and behind them were only the glowing red eyes of the computer that was administrator of the data stores of humanity.

His daughter must be here somewhere. Kepler got goosebumps when he thought about her. He knew nothing about her anymore, except that her memory was stored here. She had pursued him so much that he'd had no other choice. And now her ghost seemed to float through the giant archive. He shook his arms to get rid of the thoughts, but it didn't work.

"Are we nearly there?" he asked, turning to Columbus, who was behind him.

The Secretary nodded. "The log storage area must be somewhere around here."

Every change to the content of the memory stores was recorded in the logs. If the Curies had been here and changed any data, the system would have noted this fact in the logs. The logs could be manipulated too, but this change would also be recorded in the logs. And if someone deleted the memory of the change, then that would create another entry. It was an endless chain. They just had to find where it started. The Curies would have hidden it well, but if it existed, they'd find it.

"How can you tell we're nearly there?" asked Zhenyi.

"With the navigator on my universal device."

"And without the tech?"

Columbus stood still. He was obviously looking for something. Then he pointed to a spot on the railing. "Here, these are the coordinates of the storage group," he said.

A long numerical sequence that no one could memorize. If the technology failed, they'd be lost. Had anyone ever gotten lost in the archive? Kepler took a deep breath. He should have left the spacesuit behind at the entrance. It was getting warmer in here.

"Come on then," said Zhenyi.

The group moved off.

IN FRONT of them was a particularly long walkway that led over an abyss. Kepler looked down. The bridge was transparent, like all the walkways here. He put his hand on his heart to calm himself.

"Are you okay?" asked Zhenyi.

Kepler responded to her concern with a smile. "I'm fine," he said.

The bridge led to an endlessly tall tower ranging out of the depths and looming over their heads with no apparent top or bottom. A circular walkway ran around the tower, with more bridges leading off it to the left and right. Kepler felt like an ant balancing on a blade of grass. He held himself steady on the railings on both sides. The bridge had a gap in the middle. Zhenyi chose this of all places to pause and swing back and forth. The bridge swayed with her.

With each sideways movement Kepler felt like his heart was dropping out of his ribcage. "Can you please stop doing that?" he asked quietly.

"Oh, sorry, you're completely pale. Shall we take a break?"

A break? Here? Zhenyi is nuts! "No, I'm okay. Let's keep moving."

He carefully climbed over the narrow gap in the bridge. Everything seemed stable now. They were approaching the tower. Kepler fixed his gaze on it so he didn't have to look down. Soon the tower revealed itself to be a bank of computers. It was insane—this thing was a giant computing tower. Why was it separated from the rest of the stores like that? Security reasons? The log data must not be destroyed under any circumstances.

He'd made it. He stepped onto the platform that ran around the log tower. He leaned his back against the tower and let himself slide down. Now he needed a five-minute break. Columbus was still standing on the bridge. He was bending down as though tying his shoelace. But he was wearing a spacesuit with boots. There was nothing to tie.

She seemed to have noticed the Secretary's hesitation too. "Columbus? Are you coming?" asked Zhenyi.

"I... no, that was it for me," said the Secretary, slowly walking backward.

"What do you mean?" asked Zhenyi.

"I'm sorry. I can't support your illegal operations. Terra's security system will detain you, and then you'll be judged according to the law."

Zhenyi gave the butler a signal. The butler stepped onto the bridge.

"Best you call him back," said Columbus. "He'll be damaged."

"Puppy, quick, the Secretary wants to escape," called Zhenyi.

The butler broke into a sprint, but at the same moment the bridge started to fold downwards.

"Puppy, watch out!" called Zhenyi.

Kepler's back was glued to the tower. He had to do something! Columbus couldn't be allowed to get away with this! But there were about thirty meters between the Secretary and himself, which nothing and no one could overcome. If they were lucky, they'd be brought before a court. Otherwise they'd just die of thirst here on this platform.

The butler ran for his life as the bridge was lowered. His legs were moving at an unnatural speed, but the surface was too smooth, he couldn't get a foothold. Puppy slipped down as though in slow motion. He tried to grab hold of the end of the bridge, but there was no edge, nothing to hold onto. Kepler imagined him falling, and then he really did fall, flailing his arms wordlessly.

"Puppy!" yelled Zhenyi.

The butler disappeared into the darkness. Zhenyi wept like a child.

"I'm sorry," said Columbus from the other side. "But I warned him."

"I'll find you and punish you," said Zhenyi. "I swear it."

"Don't forget that everything you say may be used against you," said the Secretary. "Threats like that will only result in your incarceration for life."

"Columbus is right."

Kepler's head whipped around. The voice came from the side. A figure in a spacesuit emerged behind Columbus.

"You won't punish the Secretary, Zhenyi," said the someone.

Kepler recognized Pierre Curie's voice. How had the Curies gotten here?

"Ah, the Curies. That's good," said the Secretary. "Thank you for intervening, but I have everything under control here. The criminals have been secured."

"And I thank you for that, Columbus. You've executed my plan perfectly in a way befitting a Secretary."

The Curies lifted their right arm. Nothing else could be made out at that distance.

"Please don't," whimpered Columbus.

Then there was a bang and the Secretary crumpled. His legs kinked, his upper body flopped forward, and he collapsed like an inflatable doll that had just had the air let out of it.

Cycle ZX3.6, Terra

"Excuse me, Johannes."

"Yeah, what's up?" he asked sleepily. Kepler managed to open his eyes. Zhenyi was pushing his shoulder away from her. What was she trying to do?

"I need to go," she said.

He sat up straight. The wall he was leaning on was horribly hard and the platform wasn't any softer. His tailbone and back ached. Zhenyi disappeared from view, but he could still hear her footsteps. She wouldn't get far. The platform and the tower were their shared prison. Then he heard a stream of water.

Shit. They should have captured the urine somehow if they didn't want to die of thirst. The spacesuit had a treatment apparatus. He could have converted it to drinking water. But would it even make a difference now? The Curies had simply disappeared after killing the Secretary the day before. No word of explanation, nothing. Only fictional villains gave reasons. This was real life. Why should the Curies waste words on them?

Zhenyi was coming back, he could hear her steps. Then he saw her. She was still beautiful, even when she looked wretched. He probably didn't look any fresher. She sat down again. He lay his arm around her and she snuggled up to him. Kepler read the time from his universal device. It was just after three in the morning. He was tired. It would be best to sleep. Or should he be working on a plan for their rescue? But their situation was unambiguous. They were sitting here. The exit was on the other side. In between lay an abyss measuring twenty meters across. Maybe it was only fifteen, or it could be thirty. That didn't change anything. They wouldn't be able to bridge the gap because they couldn't fly.

KEPLER DREAMT OF HIS DAUGHTER. It was one of those waking dreams that often ambushed him, but his daughter had never appeared in them before. He knew he was dreaming, and he also knew that his daughter couldn't be there, because he had externalized her memory. Maybe it was something to do with his current surroundings. He was even aware while dreaming that he was in the terrestrial archive and was about to die.

His daughter waved at him. They were standing on a narrow path on the side of a mountain. Huge trees threw shadows on the path, but a few dancing rays of sunlight made it through the foliage, illuminating a fine, swirling dust that was in the air.

Between himself and his daughter a small stream tumbled down into the valley. The water was crystal clear and cold. He had already drunk from it.

"Come on, father," said his daughter in the dream he'd never dreamt before. "Hurry up."

She wanted him to follow the path through the stream. But the algae-covered rocks were too slippery. He had tried it. He couldn't go any further or he'd fall. The fact that his daughter had managed to get across didn't convince him.

"Shall I hold your hand?" she asked.

He shook his head. He couldn't follow her. She would have to walk to the end of the path alone. He would turn around.

"I'll come and get you," his daughter said to him as though to a frightened child.

"No," he insisted.

But she didn't listen. She was no longer a child, but even as a child she'd been stubborn. She stepped on the slippery stones, one step, two steps—it was only five steps to him, but on the fourth she slipped.

"Oops," said his daughter. Then she spread out her arms and fell.

There was a metallic clanging sound. Kepler woke up. The noise couldn't have been part of his dream. A body smashing onto a river bed sounded different. He didn't know exactly how, because he'd offloaded that memory, but it was different, not metallic.

He cautiously tapped Zhenyi on the shoulder. She didn't react. She was asleep with her mouth open. There was movement behind her eyelids. She must be dreaming too. The archive with its collected images seemed to sneak sidelong into people's thoughts. No, that was nonsense. Their lives were under threat. Maybe that made you dream more vividly.

Another sound. Yes, there was a scratching, metal on metal. The sounds came from below. Kepler pushed Zhenyi's upper body aside so he could stand up. She was still sleeping deeply. He went to the platform railing. The sound was coming from the right. He looked in that direction and listened keenly.

There, the scratching. It was coming out of the darkness. The light that was always around them didn't reach down far enough. But there was something there. Should he wake Zhenyi? It was probably only an animal. Were there animals in the archive? Back in the day, when the sun had engulfed the planet, it had sterilized its surface. But down there in the depths? Life always found a way. There had been more biomass in the cities than in the national parks before the catastrophe. Maybe rats had survived down there, had mutated, and now fed on the visitors.

That made no sense, of course. He was glad he hadn't

said that to Zhenyi. The number of visitors was far too small for a population of animals to sustain themselves on. But what it might look like down in the lower regions of the memory stores was anyone's guess. They were stuck near the surface. Was it possible that nature had long since triumphed over technology and was now sending a spy to check out the newcomers?

There. A black appendage emerged out of the darkness on the other side of the abyss. It was the thickness of a forearm, and on the end—Kepler could hardly believe it—was a hand. It touched the metal surface and splayed out its fingers. The fingers scraped on the metal, and then pushed into it. That's what was creating the scratching sound—something down there was climbing up by digging its fingers in. That was definitely a product of evolution.

The black appendage bent at the joints. It pulled something up after it. Then a second arm came into the light. Between the two arms hung a narrow, sack-like body made of flexible material. Kepler had imagined an insect, but this was no exoskeleton. It could almost be a human body if there wasn't something like an egg hanging sideways off its back. The body was black. At the top it had a kind of collar below which was white fabric.

Shit, it was the butler. Kepler had to look away. The fall had battered him terribly. But he was still functioning. He was giving it all he had to get back up. He looked less like a human and more like a mad machine.

He should wake Zhenyi and tell her that Puppy was back. She had cried over him for several minutes. Kepler went to her and bent to kiss her. She returned the kiss. Kepler pulled away and laid his hands on her shoulders.

"What is it?" she asked.

"The butler. He's back."

"What?" Zhenyi sprang up.

Her forehead cracked against his. Man, did that hurt! There was going to be a huge lump. Kepler clenched his teeth but tears still welled up in his eyes.

"Where is he?" At that moment she heard the sound. She quickly oriented herself and then went to the railing. "You were right," she said. "Puppy, we're here!" she called down to him.

The butler moved his head. His neck seemed to be broken. His head rolled around on his back, but it was now looking in her direction. "I'll rescue you," he called.

"I know," replied Zhenyi.

Kepler was skeptical. There was a big problem. The butler was climbing up the opposite side of the abyss, the side where the Curies had shot the Secretary. That was the way out, but it wouldn't help them. They still couldn't fly, and the butler couldn't teach them to.

He was glad Zhenyi was happy, but that wouldn't change the story. They would die.

"Made it," called the butler.

His head was now hanging the wrong way around against his chest. When he spoke it sounded like his speech was badly synchronized. That was probably because his mouth was upturned 180 degrees. Would the impression be canceled out if Kepler stood on his head himself? The butler's body seemed to be otherwise hardly damaged. The tuxedo was torn at the shoulders, probably from landing on them, and his fingers had no skin on them. The butler must have removed it himself so he could use the titanium skeleton underneath to dig into the walls. Kepler looked at his own hands and started to imagine the flesh being torn off the bones. No, he'd rather not.

And now? No one said anything.

Zhenyi had probably realized too that they weren't any further ahead. "Where did you come from?" she asked.

"I had to climb about eight kilometers," said the butler.

"You fell eight kilometers down there?"

"That's correct. Then I slammed into a bridge."

"Does that mean there are other connections to our tower further down?"

"I can confirm that."

"Can you see a route that we could use to get out of here?"

That wouldn't work. Did Zhenyi somehow think he'd voluntarily climb down the tower without a rope? thought Kepler.

"A human couldn't manage the climb down and back up."

Thank you, Puppy.

"Then we'll have to find a way to pull this bridge back up," said Zhenyi. "The Secretary must have folded it down somehow. Maybe there's a switch somewhere over there. It can't be far from the place where he was killed."

"Columbus is dead?" asked the butler.

"The Curies shot him after you fell," said Zhenyi.

"Oh. I had my suspicions something wasn't right."

"You had your suspicions? Why didn't you say anything?"

"It was so vague. Do you remember how Columbus couldn't open the door at first?"

Yes, and then it suddenly opened, thought Kepler. Why hadn't they paid more attention to that? But would they have done anything differently if they had?

"Yes," said Zhenyi, "it seemed strange to me too. But I was pleased when he did. We couldn't have turned around just because something happened exactly as we'd wanted it to."

"The Curies must have been observing us already by that point," said the butler, and swung his head around.

"Right. But why the effort?" asked Zhenyi. "They could have just shot us all."

"Maybe that was too dangerous for them. There were four of us, they're one," said Kepler.

"Possibly," said Zhenyi. "But maybe they also wanted us alive, because they've got something in mind for us."

"Then they'll be coming back soon," said Kepler. "Otherwise all they'd find would be two dried up corpses."

"I've found something," called the butler. He was holding his head in his hand. His neck was so long and flexible he could spin the head around in all directions.

"What have you got?" asked Zhenyi.

"Two meters away from the Secretary's body is a switchboard."

"That must be the bridge controls."

"I'll activate it."

A shrill tone. That didn't sound good. Another shrill tone.

"What's wrong?" asked Zhenyi.

"I don't have the right authorization," replied the butler. "The AI isn't prepared to make an exception."

"Even though there are human lives at stake?"

"Even then. I have the impression it's especially unwilling to help because it's angry with us."

"Why?"

"Because humans disintegrated the Guardian. It was a god-like figure to it."

"How do you know that?"

"I exchanged several terabytes of data with it. It accepts me as one of its own."

"Then can't you ask one of your own to help us?"

"No chance, Zhenyi. As soon as the conversation comes around to you, it becomes uncooperative. I have free access to everything myself."

"But not the bridge, right?"

"Unfortunately, no. I need a permit."

"And who has one?" asked Zhenyi.

"The Convention, but to reach them would take at least twenty kilocycles."

"By then our mummies would have crumbled into dust. Is no one nearby?"

"The Guardian, the Secretary, and the Curies. I've already searched the Secretary. The Guardian no longer exists."

"That leaves the Curies."

"Yes, Zhenyi. I'll find the Curies and take their permit, whatever the cost."

"How will you do that?"

"I'll find a way. You can count on me."

"Thank you, Puppy."

"JOHANNES?" Zhenyi was crouching next to him. She was holding a bottle in her hand. It was the emergency ration from his spacesuit.

"Yes?"

"I want you to drink this. Half the bottle."

"And you?"

"I'm not thirsty."

"I don't believe you."

"Trust me, Johannes. If you trust me, then drink."

He took the bottle from her but hesitated. If he survived and she died, how would he ever forgive himself?

"Please, Johannes." Her face was creased, but her gaze was calm and self-assured.

Kepler lifted the bottle to his lips and drank. He trusted her.

Cycle ZX3.7, Terra

THE BUTLER CREPT through the corridors. At each junction he turned around and compared all the details with his photographic memory, ascertaining the direction they'd come from. Puppy's left leg was dragging a bit, and he was losing hydraulic fluid. It would be good to find a repair station, but that wasn't a priority right now. His body was fit enough to overpower a human.

He already had a plan. He would cut off the oxygen supply to the Curies' body by blocking their windpipe with his hand. He would have to make sure the bare metal of his hands didn't cut too deeply into their skin. Humans' thin flesh was much more sensitive than his own outer shell. And he would have to restore the oxygen supply again before the Curies' brain died. He didn't want to kill them.

Technically, everything was certain. There was no need to worry. He'd inspected the Secretary's body. It was true, the Curies had a gun. He had simulated its effect. But to be guaranteed to put him out of action, they would have to fire eleven perfect shots at the right points, which they probably weren't aware of. And if they were—which he had to consider—then it still wasn't a problem, because the magazine only held eight. They'd have to swap it out. That would be enough time for him to put his plan into action.

He would drag the Curies in a semi-conscious state back to the bridge and force them to activate the switchboard. They wouldn't want to die. No living being wished to die. He himself didn't even want to die—he had realized this during his long fall into the interior of the archive.

It had been an exciting discovery, for which he had the Secretary to thank. He wouldn't have shot him. He would also allow the Curies to live if possible. No living being deserved death.

His only concern was time. Usually time was so irrelevant that he had almost forgotten its influence. But if he couldn't help Zhenyi and Kepler soon, they would die of dehydration. The human body was a strange construction. It could survive weeks without food, but only a few days without water. And it carried so much water inside it! Why couldn't humans simply reassign water the way they repurposed body fat for energy? And why hadn't humans long since corrected this design flaw?

Puppy reached the room just before the exit. Columbus had used the toilet here. That meant there must be running water. He opened the door. It was a women's toilet. The butler stopped himself—it was wrong to enter this room. His programming was playing tricks on him.

He went in and looked around. Two white basins were attached to the side wall. They had a hole at the bottom, but he could plug that. He tore off a strip off his tuxedo and stuffed the fabric in the hole, then he filled it with water. The liquid was lukewarm. He checked to see if the basin was watertight. It had worked. Now, if he tore it off the wall, he would be back with Zhenyi and Kepler in a couple of hours.

How would he get the water to the other side? He may as well throw the basin away. He wasn't lacking in strength, but it would lose some of its contents. What if he soaked his clothes in the basin and threw them to the two humans? They could suck the water out. That wasn't beyond their capabilities, he was reasonably sure.

But then he would lose half a day. And he would be too late anyway. The Curies wouldn't stay here much longer. They'd leave, and then he could no longer rescue Zhenyi and Kepler. No, they'd have to stay thirsty for a while longer. He left the women's toilet. In the corridor outside he heard a quiet whooshing sound. It was coming from the other side. He tore the door open. There were two types of basin here, a wide, high one on the left, and a narrower, deeper one on the right. Water was running in one of the basins. The toilets must have an automatic cleaning function. There was nothing here that was of any use to him.

The butler cautiously approached the exit door. It was ajar. Someone had placed a small stone in the hinge so it wouldn't close. The butler left it there so that he'd be able to get back into the archive. It was dark outside so Puppy lit the way. The beam of light illuminated a fine mist. He tried infrared. If someone had walked this way, he'd detect their trail. But there was nothing.

Where were the Curies? Had they touched down in a shuttle directly in front of the entrance? If so, he'd see signs of disturbance from the landing. They'd probably given themselves such a head-start that their footprints were already cold. He couldn't find anything in infrared.

There was no choice, he would have to search for them randomly. The butler ran into the valley in the hope of catching up with them. The slope led slightly uphill. There were no signs of anyone having been there in the last few hours. He should turn back, but for some reason he kept going.

Then he saw it. At first Puppy thought it was their own shuttle, but that must be further away, so it could only be the craft the Curies had used to land on Terra. He stopped abruptly. He needed to match his body temperature to the surroundings so he was undetectable.

He gave his body the necessary commands and only then

did he creep forward. First he inspected the propulsion unit. It was as cold as its surroundings. It must have been there for a while. The Curies probably had waited for them to land and then followed them.

The butler crept around the ship. It was not emitting energy from anywhere. That could only mean one thing—the life support system was off and the ship was empty. He wasn't too late, he was too early. The Curies hadn't yet returned to depart in their landing module. They obviously had other plans. So they were still behind him. He needed to head back immediately.

It was a long way back to the interior, but he had almost reached the bridge. The butler was moving slowly. He had kept finding infrared traces on the floor of the corridors. Someone warm-blooded had walked along here, and it could only be the Curies. They didn't know he still existed, and it had to stay that way, so he must tread carefully. They must have been moving around in the archive while he was searching for them outside. Maybe they'd deleted more data?

Then he heard Pierre's voice.

"Don't do anything stupid," he said.

Pierre was speaking very loudly. The butler chanced a glimpse around the corner. The Curies were standing at the bridge, which was still down, with their back to him.

He had to talk to Zhenyi. The butler looked for a place to hide, but there was nothing—only the bend in the corridor. If the Curies turned to go back to their ship they'd find him.

"What do you want?" asked Zhenyi.

"Just that you accompany us," replied Marie. "I'm sure we'll get along fine."

"I need water for him first." She must have meant Kepler.

"We don't need him, just leave him there," said Pierre.

"I'm not moving one step without him."

"You have to believe her," said Marie. "She's a woman. It's the way we are."

"Fine," said Pierre. "See this? I'm throwing you a bottle." A metallic sound, then something rolled across the platform.

A groan could be heard, followed by gulping sounds. "Thanks," Kepler said.

"Can you stand up?" asked Zhenyi.

"Why? Is the...?"

The next few words couldn't be made out. The butler guessed that Kepler had been about to ask about him, and Zhenyi must have put her hand over his mouth.

"Yes, the criminals are back," said Zhenyi.

"What do they want?" asked Kepler.

"To take us with them."

"Oh, right. Yes, I think I can stand up."

"Can you move a bit faster? We don't want to miss our big event," said Pierre Curie.

"Don't panic, darling, we still have a few megacycles," Marie said soothingly. "Let's go. You'll go ahead. Our shuttle is already waiting."

The butler heard a squeaking sound. The bridge was raising itself again. That was the sign. Soon they'd come along the corridor. He had to hurry.

The butler stole noiselessly toward the exit. Once there, he ran until he reached the shuttle. *This is going to be a wild ride,* he thought, and clung on behind the engine cover. Puppy hoped his titanium fingers were strong enough to hold his body in place during the launch acceleration.

Cycle ZX3.8, Terra

THAT HAD GONE MORE SMOOTHLY than expected. Pierre Curie stretched the arms of their shared body. He couldn't sense Marie's presence. She was still asleep. Marie was a night owl, a typical morning grouch, but he liked to start the day early with some exercise. That had been a disadvantage when they still had two separate bodies, but it had since blossomed into a positive. You didn't always get along when you were together day and night, but this way he had the morning to himself, and Marie had nights. The body stayed fit because he exercised more, and they still had plenty of time together.

Pierre got up and showered. Marie always slept soundly, so he didn't need to hold back. She simply uncoupled her senses from the body's perception organs and had complete peace. He dried off and walked naked back into the bedroom. There he stood in front of the wardrobe and opened the doors. Various suits hung inside it, as well as dresses. He usually made the decision about what their body would wear, being the early riser.

Sometimes Marie wanted to look pretty. Then they would select one of the custom-made dresses together. Their body was more or less androgynous—that had been a conscious decision when they had commissioned it from Paracelsus. He selected a white shirt and a dark blue suit. They had guests after all, even if they weren't aboard voluntarily. Then he placed the gun into the jacket's inside pocket, as he always did.

The wardrobe door clicked shut. Pierre checked the fit of the shirt in the mirror. The collar was hidden under the jacket, so he pulled it up and adjusted it before making certain a precisely equal amount of cuff showed at either wrist.

He could already hear noises in the control room, which was decorated to resemble a comfortable living room. It had been Wang Zhenyi, the astronomer, who had first set them on the right track. They should actually be grateful to her. Without the Herbae, they would pretty much never have been able to implement their plan. Aside from Terra there wasn't another computer capable of doing the calculations for their simulations. On the other hand, Zhenyi was now doing everything to prevent the grand finale. So it would be best to eliminate her immediately.

But then they would have a boring flight ahead of them. Marie and Pierre Curie had decided to try to convince Zhenyi of their mission during the journey. It would be the crowning glory of their plan if their arch enemy ended up agreeing with them! But of course, they didn't expect it to work. Zhenyi was exceptionally clever, but she was imprisoned by her old-fashioned morals. What use was that kind of outlook when you were facing the end of the universe?

"Are you really this afraid of us?" asked Zhenyi, pointing at the box hanging around her neck.

Pierre looked at her. He suppressed a smile. They had hung a device around Zhenyi's neck, and its twin around Kepler's, and claimed the devices would kill them if either were taken off or went within ten meters of the other. Of course it was nonsense, but it had obviously worked. That's what their guests were like. They believed what you told them. They clung to words. But what were words? Sound waves formed by speech organs. They had no more value than the kinetic energy they were made of.

"Are you refusing to talk to me?" asked Zhenyi.

He had completely forgotten about her, even though she was standing in front of him. *How could I do that? What did she just say?* Then he remembered. "We're not afraid of you," Pierre said. "But if you're alone you'll feel weaker and won't think of doing something stupid."

"You're honest, I like that," said Zhenyi.

She brushed a strand of hair out of her face and smiled. The smile seemed to be completely genuine. He had to be careful. Zhenyi might have recognized that Marie was still asleep. She was obviously trying to wrap the man in this body around her finger.

"No, I'm not honest," he said, "at least not in principle. I say whatever is good for us."

"For us—do you mean Marie and you? Isn't it boring always having to speak of *we?* There are so many other possibilities."

Zhenyi gracefully tucked another strand of hair behind her ear. Pierre smiled, and this time he didn't resist. The woman was good. She was a worthy opponent. "First of all I need a coffee," he said. "Would you like to join me?"

"No, thanks. I've already had breakfast, so now I need to let Kepler have his. But if you would deactivate this device, then it would be my pleasure to accompany you."

A little victory. He had managed to get her to play along. "Feel free to go to your room, Zhenyi. I'm sure your friend is hungry. We'll have plenty of time to talk before it's all over."

"What's our actual destination?" asked Zhenyi.

"S0-122, a neutron star near the center of the Milky Way. You probably don't know it."

"A bit of sight-seeing before we all die?"

"No, we have a message to deliver. I promise you can be there when we do."

Cycle ZZ6.1, SO-122

WAS this supposed to be torture? Zhenyi was traveling in the same ship, but he hadn't seen her now for a whole week of onboard time. They spoke over the com system in their rooms. Kepler tapped on the device hanging on his chest. It hummed, but not so loudly that it disturbed his sleep. It had occurred to them that the boxes might be fake. But the Curies were capable of either—the psychological torture of making them wear *alleged* proximity-detonated devices, or their double murder using *genuine* explosive devices.

And the other question was, why were they being kept alive at all? They didn't seem to have a practical value to the Curies. And what could have happened to the butler? Was he still on Terra? Or had he managed to sneak on board? Surely he would have contacted them by now...

"I'm going to my room," Zhenyi reported over the onboard radio.

Kepler breathed deeply. Hopefully the Curies weren't in the control room. He wouldn't mind eating lunch in peace. If need be, he would eat in his room.

But upon entering the control room he stopped at the door, fascinated. Half the room was occupied by a huge hologram. It clearly showed the system they had just reached. In the middle a tiny gyroscope spun at an incredible speed. It was pulling a vortex of magnetic fields after it. The fields were actually invisible, but they were depicted here in reddish tones.

"You have to see this!" he called to Zhenyi on the com system.

"I've got it on the screen in my room," she answered.

With a gesture, the Curies invited him to come nearer. He obeyed and walked up to the edge of the hologram. The magnetic fields swirled past, directly in front of his belly.

"Impressive, isn't it?" said Pierre's voice. "The chunk in the middle is not quite as heavy as three suns."

Kepler nodded. The Curies obviously couldn't take credit for this, so he freely acknowledged how powerful this vortex was. It was like someone had pulled the plug out of the cosmic bathtub. But, unlike a black hole, nothing flowed into the center here.

"We recently transformed this system into a neutron star," said Pierre.

What? That was usually something only great architects could accomplish. The Curies? But why would Pierre lie about it?

"Marie's currently over there, modulating the rotation," explained Pierre.

"Your wife's on that star? That's degenerate matter, no one could survive there."

"We've found a way."

If that was true, the Curies were not only mad, they were mad geniuses. To be on the surface of a neutron star—what he would have given for that experience!

"And what does she intend to do there?" asked Kepler.

"I told you, modulate the rotation."

"I don't understand."

"Wait a moment, I'll explain it to you. I just have to send her the data."

The hologram was hit from the side by a stream of green. The stream integrated itself into the magnetic field vortex. Shortly afterward the vortex illuminated alternately red and green. Kepler located the stream just before it hit its target. He could make out four alternating conditions. A base-four data stream... what did that remind him of? Why weren't they using binary, which was the usual practice? Then it occurred to him. There was another information storage system based on four units—DNA.

"Could that be DNA information you're transmitting to the neutron star?" asked Kepler.

Pierre Curie spun around.

Bulls-eye! thought Kepler.

Pierre smiled. "Good spotting," he said. "You're very observant. You can probably guess whose DNA it is."

Of course. They were transmitting their own DNA to a neutron star that would later be swallowed by a black hole, which would explode the universe. As he'd thought earlier, the Curies weren't just geniuses, they truly were crazy.

"You're insane," Kepler said. "I knew it."

Pierre didn't seem bothered by the insult. "It must look insane to you, I completely understand, because you don't know the plan behind it."

"Oh, we know you want to destroy the universe by ripping it out of its metastable state."

Pierre's smile widened. "That's only half the truth. To create something new, you have to tear down the ruins of the old. This universe had a birth defect. Otherwise it would have given rise to more intelligent lifeforms. We're going to correct this error and create a new universe."

"You're hoping for a new Big Bang?"

"We're certain that a new Big Bang will follow. The universe behaves cyclically."

"And if it takes forever?"

Pierre laughed haughtily. "If there's no universe, no time passes. Time is part of the universe!"

"But the new result will be just as random. Maybe the next universe will have even more unfavorable conditions."

"That's possible, which is why we've taken precautions. You've just become a witness, Kepler."

"The information you imprinted on the rotation?"

"Information doesn't get lost. We calculated it with the help of the Herbae. When the neutron stars we've created fall into the black hole, the information will be transferred to the inside of the event horizon, where it will survive even the subsequent destruction of the universe."

"And how is that possible?"

"It'll be imprinted on the inaugural conditions of the newborn universe, and thus influence its parameters."

"But why are you transferring your genetic code, Pierre?"

Pierre smiled broadly. "Our DNA will be readable in the background radiation of the new universe. At some point, someone will read out the code, recognize it as genetic information, and recreate us out of pure curiosity. That way we'll have survived the apocalypse. And thanks to our capabilities, we'll be gods in the new universe."

"I knew you were insane."

"You just don't think big enough, Kepler. That's why our idea sounds crazy to you. We actually see ourselves as saviors who will finally get the recognition we deserve."

"Saviors?"

"Yes, saviors from small-mindedness and boredom, and from the tribulations of a long, drawn-out death."

"But I don't want to be saved."

"You're lying, Kepler. Admit it. The death of the universe makes you just as depressed as almost every other human."

"That might be true. But self-aggrandizing assholes like you make me outraged!"

Pierre Curie sat down, planted his elbows on the table and rested his head in his hands. "You bore me, Kepler," he said. "You're so predictable. I actually expected more of you."

Cycle ZZ6.1, SO-122

THE NINETY-NINER WAS DRIFTING without propulsion around a neutron star. The butler measured the surface temperature of the object. It must still be relatively young. The supernova that produced it couldn't have burnt out very long ago. He'd spent the whole time motionless in the cargo bay where the landing module now stood. But now the ship was transmitting data to the neutron star. That meant the Curies might be distracted. It was time to make contact with Zhenyi and Kepler.

The butler carefully tried removing his fingers from the metal, but had to forfeit one of them in the process. The lander had become so intensely hot during the launch that his finger had melted to its hull. Luckily it was only his left ring finger. He swung his head around and registered the damage. That could be quickly repaired with the right equipment. He climbed down to the floor of the cargo bay. There was some gravity—about half that of Earth. The ship must be rotating.

The butler tried to orient himself, but this was disrupted by the fact that his head was hanging upside down from his elongated, flexible neck. He'd really like to repair it, but it would have to wait until he had access to nanofabricators. Instead he adjusted the software of his visual system. The world flipped 180 degrees and he could now see everything the right way up in spite of his dangling head. That was better.

The ninety-niner was a different model than the one Zhenyi owned, but the layout was similar. Starting from the back were the propulsion drives, then the cargo bay in the middle, and right up front the control room, where the crew must be. But the ship wasn't accelerating at the moment, so he couldn't differentiate between front and back.

He needed information. The butler searched the loading bay and discovered a console. It was requesting a password. Shit. The Curies' ship was secure, but not secure enough. He opened the electronic unit and looked for the data connection. Then he placed two fingers on the cable. Every query would now go in the direction of the control room. That's all he needed. He simply queried the status of the cargo bay. The fact that the query was coming from the cargo bay itself was nonsensical to the computer system. But he wasn't interested in the answer, he just needed to know where it was coming from. If he knew where the central computer was located, he could find the control room.

So, the console was exchanging data with the control room. And now he knew where the front was. He climbed up the wall to the ceiling, loosened an air vent, and made his way along the life support system ducts.

A FEW HOURS later he was crammed in the air extraction duct above Zhenyi's cabin. His head was mottled black and blue, having bumped against so many corners and edges. His skin layer simulated the behavior of human skin, but he didn't feel any pain from it.

He watched Zhenyi. He had to be careful to not startle her into making a loud noise when he climbed down. That could give him away. So he first let a bit of hydraulic fluid drip through the air vent. Zhenyi soon noticed it. She got off the bed, bent down, touched the fluid with her finger, and smelled it. Then she looked up. The butler waved at her and she smiled. He placed a finger over his lips.

The air vent was fastened with four screws. He loosened one after the other and then held the grating so it didn't crash to the floor. He carefully passed it down and Zhenyi took it. He thought about jumping but decided against it. He scuttled across the ceiling and down the wall, which was less noisy.

Zhenyi embraced him. It was logical behavior that documented her pleasure at seeing him again. He registered a slight warming of his outer skin. This was probably caused by the contact with Zhenyi's hands, which were roughly 36 degrees. Water dripped on his shoulder. Was Zhenyi losing hydraulic fluid too? He couldn't see it because his head was dangling at his back.

Then Zhenyi let go of him. He swung his head around elegantly, caught it in his arms, and held it in front of his chest. Then he placed his finger over his lips again. Where was the security console in this room? He found it to the right of the door. That was password protected too, of course, so he couldn't deactivate it. He opened the casing and opted for the simplest solution. He placed a finger on the relevant connection, analyzed the data stream, and simply duplicated it, creating a continuous loop. Now the control room would only receive a frozen audio loop. He could only hope there wasn't a surveillance camera. But if that was the case they were probably already being observed.

"We can speak now," he said.

"Puppy, I'm so glad you survived," said Zhenyi.

"Well, that observation is not entirely correct, as I'm not alive, but I know what you mean. I'm very pleased to be able to continue to serve you."

"Thank you, Puppy. Can't we do something about your head? It irritates me, seeing it hanging off you like that."

"We'll have to postpone that until later. Right now I can't

remove my hand from the console. Otherwise we'll be heard in the control room."

"They're busy right now," said Zhenyi. "I don't think they're watching."

"Then we should use the opportunity," said the butler.

"To overpower them, now?"

"Who knows when they'll next be distracted."

Zhenyi didn't immediately reply. She scratched behind her ear. "You're right," she finally said. "They share their body in a way that one of them is almost always awake. And right now Marie is on the neutron star and Pierre is concentrating on her. It won't get any better than this. But there's a problem."

She pointed at the box that hung on a string around her neck.

"This thing?" asked the butler.

"It'll shred me if I get too close to Kepler. And he's in the control room right now."

The butler grasped the box with his free hand and analyzed it with X-rays. There were clearly no explosives in it, just some electronics that measured the passage of time. He tore it off her.

Zhenyi went pale. "If I take it off it'll trigger the explosive, I was about to say." But nothing happened. Zhenyi waited a while with bated breath, then the color returned to her cheeks. "That swine," she said. "He fooled us."

"We should end him," said the butler.

ZHENYI COUNTED down on her fingers. Three... two...one... go!

The butler tore open the door to the control room and stormed in. Zhenyi followed him. She stayed behind, as they'd agreed. A large hologram filled the right side of the room. Pierre Curie was standing in front of it, moving his arms like a conductor. Kepler sat a little further away at the table.

Pierre turned around. Kepler sprang to his feet. The butler calculated the distance. Kepler was too far away. The butler himself was the closest to Pierre, so he ran to him. He hoped that Zhenyi would stay behind him, but he couldn't concern himself with her just now, because the man in front of him was drawing a weapon. It wouldn't be dangerous to him, he'd already established that. But the Curies were clever. They knew just as well as he did that they couldn't stop a robot fast enough. And sure enough, Pierre aimed his gun not at the butler but at Kepler.

"No!" cried Zhenyi.

Faster, faster! He had to neutralize Curie as quickly as possible. The butler activated his entire energy reserve, but he couldn't defy the laws of physics. However, Kepler reacted surprisingly fast. He simply slid off his chair. Now the tabletop was shielding him. And Pierre reacted just as quickly. His arm jerked around. He aimed at the butler, at head height. But there was no head there, it was hanging on his chest. Zhenyi was still behind him and she was taller than he was. The butler jumped. He had to get himself into the path of the bullet.

There was a bang. A small piece of metal flew through the control room. He was too slow. He couldn't stop the bullet. His left hand met with Pierre Curie's neck and sliced it in half. Blood sprayed out. But the bullet flew. Puppy flung his head around while still in full flight. He watched in slow motion as the bullet bore into Zhenyi's skull, just below her hairline.

Momentum kept Wang Zhenyi, the famous astronomer, moving forward, but her head tipped back unnaturally. She slammed against the table. Her torso flopped onto the tabletop, then bounced off, while her lower body slid under the table and pulled the rest of her after it. Zhenyi landed directly in front of Johannes Kepler. The butler heard him cry out as he killed the Curies' body with an iron grip around the neck.

"Marie Curie?" Kepler spoke in a toneless voice the butler had never heard him use before.

"Pierre, is that you?"

"It's me, Johannes Kepler. Your husband is dead. Or at least, your shared body. And you're going to die too."

"What... what's happening down there? Please don't leave me behind. You're not inhuman!"

His voice was now stronger. "That's what I used to think, but now I know better, Marie. You'll die right there where you are. It's still an unusual grave, you can be proud of that. But first you can tell us how to stop the process you both started. Then maybe I'll spare you from being crushed by S0-122."

"That's impossible. Everything is already in motion," said Marie.

"Thank you, I was sort of hoping you'd say that. Now you'll get the horrible death you deserve. My own imagination couldn't have come up with anything more fitting."

"You'll die too, Kepler, but unlike you, my husband and I will live on in the new universe. In our universe."

"I promise I'll do everything I can to prevent that."

"It's too late."

"We'll see about that."

Kepler cut the connection.

"We'll fly back to the unknown system," said Kepler.

The butler had never seen him so decisive. He seemed to be imbued with a sacred fire.

"What do you expect to achieve there? The collapse will be initiated by Sagittarius A* in the core of the Milky Way. Perhaps we can do more there," said the butler.

"Zhenyi didn't lead us to the Herbae for no reason. You heard it. They helped the Curies figure out their plan. They owe us!"

"That makes sense. Do you have instructions for what should happen to Wang Zhenyi's body?"

"No, I don't have the strength for that right now. Her final send-off will have to wait. Please preserve her body."

"Of course, Johannes."

Cycle ZZ6.2, SO-122

SHE WAS ALONE. The radio messages she sent over the antenna remained unanswered. Marie's strength was waning. The nanomachines that had given her physical form were losing power. They could no longer withstand the enormous attractive force of the neutron star. It was a deathly embrace, which she could only escape if Pierre recalled her consciousness to the ship.

But Pierre was no more. He had gone ahead of her into eternity. She'd captured his genetic code herself and immortalized it in this dead star, whose core was made of the most densely packed neutrons. It was good, meaningful work. They would depart this cosmos before the others. But because of that they would be the first and the only ones to reawaken in the new universe. They would become gods, beings from the time before time.

Marie laughed to herself. The mortals were so stupid. They believed they could still interfere with the plan. But even if they succeeded in stopping the black hole from being overloaded, the plan would yet be realized. The information they had transmitted was immortal and indestructible. They had memorialized themselves so that they would outlast the end of time, even if the universe didn't end in a Big Bang but in a slow, painful process.

Marie was glad they wouldn't have to experience the tragic period to come. She felt sorry for Johannes Kepler. She knew that she'd be reunited with Pierre. But Kepler would only know sorrow, and it would have a hold on him his entire life. Unless he ended it by ending his own existence.

The nanomachines began to decay. Their atomic bonds broke, crushed by gravity. A mighty being trod with iron soles on every one of her cells and ground them into dust. The pain became intolerable, but she couldn't block it out—her consciousness had no escape. Marie Curie died a slow, tortured death, which she couldn't speed up. It ate at her from the outside in. Her consciousness began to dwindle, but not so much that she couldn't perceive the pain. No, the pain remained with her to the very last cell, and it was unbearable. Her consciousness now contained nothing but pain. It was everywhere. She *was* pain.

Marie Curie was dead. The matter that of which she'd been made sank slowly into the star, mingled with it, and turned into a soup of identical components, indistinguishable from each other. Nothing was left that could be attributed to Marie Curie. But the information that had shaped her continued to exist and, as they had intended, would outlast time.

Cycle AA2.1, unknown system

"We missed the turn of the era," said the butler as he served Kepler orange juice and buttered toast. "Are you sure you don't want coffee? And no egg either?" he asked.

"I'm not hungry," said Kepler. "But what did you mean by 'turn of the era?'"

"We're back to cycle AA," the butler explained.

"Oh, right. The alphabet has a limited number of letters."

"Humanity had a huge celebration at the last turn of the era, I remember it well."

"No idea what everyone else is doing. I'm not in the mood to celebrate."

Kepler thought about Zhenyi's corpse. The butler was keeping her body on ice somewhere in the cargo bay. He would have to hold a wake for her at some point. But should he burn Zhenyi, bury her, or send her out into space? What would she have wanted? They'd never talked about it. At some point he would come up with something that was right for her.

"What happened to Pierre Curie, by the way?" Kepler asked.

"You didn't give me any instructions, so I followed the standard protocol for organic matter."

"What does that mean?"

"I sent him to be reprocessed."

"You did what?"

"Reprocessed him. Recycled. Organic matter has a low entropy. It's valuable."

The butler was nuts. That meant his toast could be made of parts of Pierre Curie. So could parts of the butler. He held up the toast and looked at it. It bore no resemblance to the Curies.

On second thought, it seemed appropriate. He bit into the toast. "Tastes like toasted white bread," he said. He chewed and swallowed, then took another bite.

"One of Wang Zhenyi's recipes," said the butler.

"Thanks. Didn't I ask you to remind me of her as little as possible?"

"Forgive me, Johannes."

KEPLER LEANED BACK. Maybe he should have an egg after all. The idle period was at an end. They had reached the unknown system. The ninety-niner was already orbiting the innermost planet.

"Shall I clear this away?" asked the butler.

"Yes, please. And prepare my expedition equipment. This time I want to be prepared for anything."

"May I accompany you, Johannes?"

"Please do."

Kepler scratched his head. Until now, the Herbae had primarily cooperated with Zhenyi. He had to establish their trust. But how? Would they even remember him—or the fact that Zhenyi had trusted him? He brooded. There was an idea in his head that didn't dare come to the fore. It swirled around in the extremities of his brain so that he could only see its shadow.

He grasped at it. And there it was. It startled him when it reached his consciousness, but it seemed sensible. He would take the body of his beloved down with him. Then the Herbae would definitely recognize him.

"Puppy?"

"Yes?"

"You'll need to prepare Zhenyi for the trip too, please. The *how* I'll leave up to you. She needs to be easily transportable by one person."

"Certainly, Johannes."

THE SHUTTLE LANDED DIRECTLY on the planet's North Pole, right where they had exited the shaft the last time. How long had it been in local time? A hundred thousand years, half a million? Kepler's heart sank. After such a long time, most people wouldn't remember them. Did the Herbae think on a different time scale? He could only hope.

Kepler climbed out. The twilight had a tranquilizing effect on him. The butler would arrive soon with Zhenyi. He had taken her body out of the cargo bay. Kepler hadn't seen her again since... He was afraid to. Her body would surely already be showing signs of decay. That was normal, wasn't it?

"I'm here," called the butler.

Kepler walked up to meet him. He was pushing a wheelchair containing something that looked like an empty spacesuit. But the wheels of the chair sank half a centimeter into the soil. The suit wasn't empty. The butler came closer and Kepler recognized Zhenyi's face behind the visor. She seemed to be smiling. Kepler couldn't hold back the tears.

Then he saw the hole in Zhenyi's forehead and his tears turned to rage. He had to avert the death of the universe. He couldn't let the Curies win!

"I've lowered the temperature in her suit to four degrees. Unfortunately it won't go any lower," said the butler.

"I think we can work with that," said Kepler.

"And how do we get down there?"

That's right, the butler hadn't been with them the first time. Kepler went to the edge of the shaft. The copter that had carried them back up was nowhere to be seen. He shook his head. Of course, no technical device would last that long in this climate. It had probably crumbled to dust long ago. That meant there was probably no way back up either. But it didn't matter now. Either he would succeed in convincing the Herbae, and they'd save the universe, or he'd have to spend his remaining years down there.

"Going down is easy," said Kepler. "We jump."

"I understand. The shaft will catch us in the middle."

"Something like that, Puppy. Will you take the wheelchair? You'll have to make sure it stays upright so it's not separated from its load."

Its load. Kepler bit his tongue. He should call the corpse in the spacesuit Zhenyi, not load, even though it hurt. She deserved it.

"I mean Zhenyi," he corrected himself, "so that Zhenyi isn't separated from it."

"I'll take care of her, Johannes," said the butler. "Don't worry."

Just like you took care of her in the ship? No, that's unfair, thought Kepler. Attacking Pierre Curie would have definitely been Zhenyi's idea. And if he hadn't hidden under the table, Curie would have shot at him and not at Zhenyi. Why had she shouted 'No?' He had his friend on his conscience just as much as the butler did.

"Then let's go," said Kepler. "First one to the bottom." He took a run-up of a few steps and jumped, making it almost to the middle of the shaft.

"I'm coming," called the butler.

In the dark blue circle above Kepler appeared a silhouetted figure with pedaling legs, pushing a wheelchair. He leaned forward and spread out his arms to slightly break his fall. The butler soon caught up with him. Because he was upright, holding onto the wheelchair, his air resistance was lower and he fell faster, overtaking Kepler.

Kepler was left behind. He turned himself upside down so that he was falling head first. Now his own surface area was smaller than that of the butler plus wheelchair. He caught up with the butler again, then grabbed the right handle of the wheelchair, now floating just above Zhenyi. He could see her face through the helmet. It looked like she was smiling at him.

Cycle AA2.2, unknown system

THE GIGANTIC DOME was just as impressive as it had been on his first visit. All that was missing was Zhenyi's reception. But she wouldn't come out to meet him. She was sitting next to him in the wheelchair. Back then he had sat on the ground with her. They had held hands and marveled at the view. Now her hand was stuck in the glove of a spacesuit. He reached for it. The glove was cold and what was inside it was hard. He swallowed and tears welled up.

"This is amazing," said the butler, looking around by turning his head in all directions with his right hand.

"I did describe it to you."

"Yes, but seeing it for oneself is quite different."

Kepler had to look away. It wasn't a pretty picture, the butler twisting and turning his head on the end of the long neck. "We have to do something about your head," he said. "Zhenyi's house is over there on a platform. How long do nanomachines stay functional?"

"Forever," said the butler.

"Good, she's got some stored in there."

They moved off. Just like on the surface, the grass retreated from them. Hopefully he would be able to connect with them. If the Herbae couldn't help, the universe was lost.

THE TERRACE WAS STILL THERE, the house still standing. The butler pushed the wheelchair up onto the platform.

"It's best if you leave her there," said Kepler. "Then she'll have a nice view."

"If you think so, Johannes."

Kepler remained standing in front of the house. He didn't dare go inside. The memories would overwhelm him and he wasn't strong enough for that. He touched the outside wall. The material showed no signs of weathering, probably maintained by nanomachines.

But he had to go inside. If he wanted to make contact with the Herbae, he had to get into the chamber. The entrance was off the hallway. At least he wouldn't have to go into the living room, or his or Zhenyi's bedrooms. Kepler opened the door and went in. It was peaceful in the house, very quiet. He could hear his own heartbeat.

The breakdown he feared didn't happen. He was alone. With new-found courage he took a few steps into the hall. There was the hatch he had to open. Beyond that was Zhenyi's room. He had never been in it when she was still alive. Kepler went around the hatch over the shaft until he was standing at Zhenyi's door. He opened it. A warm light came on automatically. The room was modest—it suited Zhenyi. The bed looked like it had been freshly made. Next to it, a dress hung on the back of a chair. She must have worn it back then, but he couldn't remember exactly.

Kepler took a few steps into the room. He sucked up the air inside it. Maybe it still contained a few molecules that had once been filtered by his girlfriend's lungs. But he couldn't detect any particular smell. It had simply been too long in local time, even though it had only been a few weeks for him. Time dilation ruined everything. Maybe the new universe that the Curies wanted to create didn't have a maximum travel speed. No one would have to be separated from their loved ones for long periods. Wouldn't it almost be worth dying for that? But then those villains would have won, and they had Zhenyi on their conscience.

He turned around and was about to leave the room when his gaze fell upon the nightstand. A picture stood there in a small frame. It showed two people, Zhenyi and himself. He could remember exactly where and how it was taken—on a water world. They were sunning themselves on the only rock that protruded from the inhospitable water waste. Now he really couldn't hold back the tears.

KEPLER OPENED THE HATCH. A musty smell rose up out of the shaft. No one had been down here for a long time. He jumped and landed after about ten seconds, just like last time. The smell was so unpleasant he had to breathe through his mouth. It was high time someone aired this place out.

On his first visit, the entrances to two chambers had opened up to the left and right. Which way was left and which was right? It was almost dark, but this time he was prepared. He took the night vision device out of the tool pouch that hung on his belt. His body heat was lighting up the rectangular shaft. The entrances must be at the narrow ends.

He felt around the walls and found a kind of pressure plate, which he operated. The wall directly in front of him moved to the side. He had been leaning against it and almost fell through it. Yes, this was the chamber. But it was too soon. He still had to undress. Last time he and Zhenyi had taken off their clothes together. Now she was sitting up above, numb and stiff, cooled by the spacesuit.

Kepler pushed his thoughts aside and undressed. At least it was warm down here. He took his time placing his things in a neat pile because he didn't want to get into the chamber yet —the worms would slither across his body again. But that was why he was here. He wanted to establish contact with the

Herbae. Kepler shook himself and climbed into the slimy mass.

It felt revolting. He felt the involuntary urge to flee, his muscles tensed, but he forced himself to stay. His disgust faded. He closed his eyes. That way he wouldn't see the way the worms engulfed him in their dense web. Now it was warm, soft, comfortable. He couldn't perceive anything else. The Herbae accepted him. A wave of positive thoughts enveloped his consciousness. He had returned to the right place. He was flooded with gratitude.

Then Zhenyi was standing in front of him. She was whole. She was naked like him, but she was more than him.

"A goddess?" That was his voice. His thoughts were turned into words without his having to formulate them.

"Thank you for the compliment," said Zhenyi, smiling broadly, "but there are no gods. I'm me. You know me. Don't you recognize me?"

"I can see you. I can see your body and your thoughts. I can see so much more of you."

"You recognize me. I'm so glad."

"But how can you be here? I saw you get shot."

"I tried to tell you, dearest. I've been here the whole time with the Herbae. I'm part of them. I'm... integrated into them."

"And the Zhenyi who was traveling with me the whole time?"

"She's part of me. Her body was built by nanomachines. It was never intended to last forever. But her thoughts were my thoughts."

So that's why Zhenyi had said she couldn't love him. She was only a copy, the portable version of her commissioner, which was herself. "You know what she knows?" he asked.

"No. She had her own experiences, but I think what she thinks, I love what she loves."

What did that mean for him? Zhenyi loved him? He couldn't ask about that now. There were more important things. They had to save the world.

"And your own body? What happened to that?"

"When the Herbae found me I was almost dead. They rescued my consciousness by absorbing me. My body could no longer be used. But we'll have time later for the past. What did you find out about the future?"

"The Curies didn't just want to create a quasar, they wanted to bring about the death of the universe. And the Herbae helped them."

"What are you saying?"

"Pierre Curie told me. They formulated their plan with the help of your friends."

"I can't believe that."

"Shouldn't you know that if you're part of the Herbae?"

"They don't share their memories with me. That would overload my faculties."

"But you were there when we found out."

"That's good," said Zhenyi. "We need to take a look at my body's memories. Please bring it to the second chamber. After that we'll talk some more."

He was alone again. The worms released him.

Breathless, he climbed the ladder and reached the hatch that led into the house. He rushed outside. The butler was standing on the terrace with the wheelchair and Zhenyi. He looked at him with irritation.

"Johannes, did you forget something?"

"No, Puppy. We have to be quick. I need Zhenyi's body, completely undressed, quickly."

The butler lifted the spacesuit out of the wheelchair and laid it down on the platform. Then he removed the spacesuit. It only took two minutes and then Zhenyi was lying before him. She almost looked alive. Only the hole in her forehead didn't belong. This body was supposed to have been manufactured by nanomachines? It was hard to believe. It was just imperfect enough that it looked utterly real.

He took Zhenyi in his arms—the low gravity helped. Then he walked with her back to the shaft.

"Do you need help?" the butler called after him.

"Maybe later."

He jumped into the shaft. *Where is the second opening?* The pressure plate mirrored the other one. He pressed it. To get Zhenyi into the chamber he had to stand her on her feet because the opening was too narrow. She leaned on him. *That's gravity,* he thought. *She's dead.* He carefully pressed himself backward. Finally her body lost its balance and tilted back with him.

The worms caught him and enveloped him. The Herbae accepted the dead Zhenyi as well. He thought of her as a corpse, but if she had been manufactured by nanomachines, she was anything but. She was a functioning machine. Living nerve cells lost their memories when they died. But who knew how this Zhenyi's brain worked? If he'd understood correctly, everything they'd discovered would still be in there. She was an incorruptible witness.

He turned around. His own chamber awaited him. This time he didn't close his eyes. The worms were his friends. They were the roots of the Herbae, who were going to help him.

"Thank you," said Zhenyi. "I'm just conversing with my body. We're... doing an exchange."

Kepler could hear her as though she was standing next to him, but he could only see her shadow falling across the green stems. He looked up at the sky. It could have been the sky over the unknown planet, or any other system with a red dwarf as its central star.

"You really had some experiences."

Zhenyi was back. They were sitting side by side on a rock. In front of them the swaying grass spread out as far as the eye could see.

Kepler sighed. "That's a gross understatement. I saw you get shot."

"I'm sorry." She stroked his cheek and leaned against him. The illusion was perfect. He could even feel the fine hairs on her upper arm tickling him. He could sit like this for years. But he knew they would have to get back to the fight soon.

Zhenyi straightened up. It was time. "It's true, what you said," she said. "The Curies did use the Herbae. They calculated the process at the center of the galaxy, taking into account the most variable factors, apparently with the aim of averting a catastrophe. But their intention was the opposite. The Herbae didn't realize this and it wasn't what they wanted."

"And now?"

"They feel responsible for the death of the universe."

"Because they were used by insane, egotistical humans? They couldn't have done anything about that."

"No. Because it's their own creation that will destroy the universe."

"Their what?" he asked.

"Their *creation.* It was the Herbae who planted the seeds of life on many planets. They shot capsules, spores if you like, onto all planets that seemed remotely suitable for supporting life. They didn't want to be alone in the universe."

That sounded crazy, yet somehow possible. Humans had always wondered why all life, wherever they found it, was so similar.

"And now they're being killed by their own creation, and the universe along with them. Now that I call tragic."

In fact, it was so tragic it was almost funny, Kepler noted with surprise. *The human mind is indeed strange.* He should be distressed about death, but he was oddly serene. What kind of sick thinking was that, and what did evolution have to say about it?

"There's still a way for us to prevent all this," said Zhenyi. "The Herbae have calculated it thoroughly."

"Then don't keep me in suspense."

"We can hardly halt the mass that the Curies have mobilized toward the black hole. But we can change the way it reaches Sagittarius A*."

"What role are we supposed to play?"

"If you get hit in the head with ten table tennis balls or one larger ball with the same weight, it makes a difference, right?"

"Yes."

"Good. We can at least destroy some of the larger objects," said Zhenyi. "Their fragments will still be available, but it will increase the time it takes for them to have an effect on the black hole, and the effect will be weakened overall. A quasar will result, as originally planned, and the universe will remain in its metastable state."

"That sounds good! What are we waiting for?"

The technology probably required a sacrifice. Somebody would have to push a button and then die. He was ready for that. He'd lived long enough. Dying to save the world—he was okay with that.

"The Herbae could trigger a gravitational tremor with the help of the dark matter they've collected in the core of their planet, a powerful agitation of space-time that would race through the universe and tear apart stars and planets."

"That sounds anything but harmless," said Kepler.

"It would also affect systems currently populated by humans, but not beyond what the new quasar would make uninhabitable anyway. And the universe as a whole would survive."

That can't be the whole story, he thought. "And what else?"

"The Herbae would have to sacrifice their world to do it."

Kepler broke out in a cold sweat. His whole body trembled, and at the same time he felt terribly guilty—because he wasn't afraid for the intelligent life that had created humanity, he was afraid for one person, Zhenyi, who existed as part of their consciousness.

THEY WERE SILENT. It was a good silence, the kind he could only have with Zhenyi. Then he had to ask. "And what will happen to you?"

She laughed. "I was wondering when you'd ask."

"I didn't dare. I had to ask about the Herbae. Aren't they something like our parents?"

"In a sense, yes. But to answer your question—I'll miss them."

What was she saying? It could only mean she would live on after their sacrifice. "You'll survive?" he asked.

"My body is lying in the other chamber. It's a very good body. It's almost indistinguishable from a biological body. My nanomachines are currently repairing the small hole in the forehead along with the control modules. I can transfer myself completely into that body, and then we can leave this planet before the Herbae trigger the gravitational tremor. We'll just have to get out of its range quickly so our ship isn't torn apart."

"It's that easy?" he asked.

"It's anything but easy. You don't understand what I'll be giving up, being part of this ancient consciousness, I can't even describe what it means to me. I have access to endlessly-detailed memories. I'm a witness to almost every stage of the universe's development. I can watch stars being born, or see them in their death throes. It's just mind-blowing."

"And you really want to give that up?"

Fear rose inside him. At some point she'd resent him for what she had given up for his sake. She wouldn't be content, especially because she would know that her paradise had been destroyed forever.

"I don't have any other choice, Johannes. The Herbae have already decided to stop the death of the universe. Either I die with them or I live on."

"If I can somehow help you come to a decision on this..." *Would Zhenyi seriously choose to die with the Herbae?*

"I truly value your help," she said. "I want to live."

THE BUTLER CAME into the house and met them at the top of the shaft. He didn't utter one syllable about Zhenyi's reappearance. Had he known the truth all along? Zhenyi fetched clothes from her room. When she came back into the hallway, he saw the picture frame sticking out of her pants pocket.

"I've arranged a vehicle for us," said the butler.

"A copter?" he asked.

"Yes, the exact same model you flew to the surface in last time."

"Thank you, Puppy," said Zhenyi. "We need to hurry."

Cycle AE8.4, Kepler-1229

"What a nice surprise," said Newton.

"Move aside, you worm."

Kepler smiled inwardly. Zhenyi was still furious with the physicist for not wanting to help them. But his system was well suited to their plan because it was far enough away from the quasar that was about to be ignited. And because Newton could perfectly control the climate on each of his worlds.

"I need a shuttle to one of your fertile worlds," said Zhenyi. "And I mean now."

"I've already told you it's too dangerous. One wrong move and the whole system will be torn apart," explained Newton.

"It'll be more dangerous to tell me you're not going to respect my wishes, because then we'll fly in with the ninety-niner."

"Please don't," said Newton, clasping his head in his hands. "Okay, I have a shuttle for you. It's a special design, a two-seater with a particularly narrow profile and a powerful chemical propulsion system. You should be able to go anywhere in it."

"Then you're lucky you won't fit in it with us," said Zhenyi.

"I'll fly the shuttle if you like," said Newton. "It won't

matter anyway, if I'm supposed to believe what you've told me."

"No, not anymore," said Zhenyi. "We've found a solution. But first I need a fertile world."

THEY LANDED ON A PLATEAU. Kepler got out first. The air was fresh, a comfortable 21 degrees. A stream was babbling nearby. Newton hadn't exaggerated.

"Catch," called Zhenyi.

Kepler caught the spade with style.

Zhenyi walked about ten meters to the south. She also had a spade in her hand. She began to dig. "Five by five meters should be enough," she said.

The work felt good. The ground was soft, and Kepler studied it for a moment after turning over the first spade-full. The brown soil was full of small creatures. It seemed to be fertile soil, well-supplied with nutrients. Were they the right ones? Zhenyi would already have discussed it with Newton.

They bumped into each other from behind once they reached the middle. Kepler left the last few spots for his girlfriend to finish turning.

"Looks good," she said.

He thought she looked good too, despite the black streaks on her face. Zhenyi turned around and walked to the shuttle. She came back with a container about fifty centimeters high, which she'd had with her since they departed from the unknown system. She hadn't wanted to tell him what was in it, but he had a good idea.

Zhenyi opened the end of the container. She pulled out two plates. Between them was a layer of soil, and there were grass stems growing on it, about ten centimeters high.

Welcome, dear parents, thought Kepler.

Zhenyi carefully placed the layer of soil with the grass stems onto the freshly dug ground. She pressed it down around the edges. "Get some water, will you," she said. "The can is in the luggage compartment."

Kepler went to the shuttle, opened the luggage compartment, took out a metal can, and then had to laugh when he saw a black-clad leg. But he said nothing. He filled the can from the stream and carried it to Zhenyi.

"Thanks," she said, taking the can and watering the stems. Then she crouched down and stroked them gently. The stems leaned toward the sun. "Sorry, I'm sitting in your light," she said.

"Did you bring the butler?" he asked.

"Oh, you found him? He's going to look after the stems. We can't take the risk that some random accident might destroy them."

"That's very smart."

"I won't need the butler anymore. After all, I now have better company than him," said Zhenyi. She linked arms with him and they walked back to the shuttle.

Suddenly she tore away and ran from him. He ran after her and managed to catch up to her. He grabbed her arm and swung her around and they fell on the soft grass that was indigenous to the planet. They tangled with each other, play fighting, and then they made love.

Cycle AM1.3, Kepler-1229

"Hello Puppy!"

Zhenyi ran to the butler as soon as she was out of the shuttle. He spread his arms and stoically endured the passionate greeting. Kepler followed more slowly and held out his hand to the butler.

"How are you?" asked Zhenyi.

The butler spread out his hands and turned in a circle.

"What, those are all Herbae?"

"Yes," said the butler, "they've adapted in a remarkably short time. They've already managed to spread themselves over about 400 square kilometers. And I have my suspicions that they're also working underground."

"What makes you think that?"

"Newton has had to adjust the orbit of this planet several times. Its density distribution appears to be changing and the pull of its neighbors is affecting it differently."

"That's interesting," said Zhenyi.

"Yes. If they continue at this rate, the Herbae will have completely covered the planet in 100 kilocycles."

"Do you have the feeling they're... intelligent?" asked Kepler.

"You can see for yourself—they don't yet have the ability

to retreat. I don't think there are enough individuals yet for a collective intelligence."

"Do you know why we came here today?" asked Zhenyi.

"To evaluate my work?"

"I trust you completely. No, we want to watch the death of the universe."

"But it's not going to collapse, is it?" asked the butler.

"We can't be completely certain. Whatever happens has already long-since happened. We're far enough away here not to have been killed by the birth of the quasar. It should appear in the sky today, or..."

"Or?"

"Or we'll all die today, because the death of the universe will reach us at light speed."

THE THREE OF them sat together on the right tail wing of the shuttle. They had actually wanted to wait for the collapse with a picnic on a nice soft blanket, but they didn't want to burden the Herbae unnecessarily with their weight. Kepler let his legs swing, supporting himself on his arms.

The last few weeks with Zhenyi had been wonderful. And yet it had seemed like borrowed time, an interlude that would come to an end today.

There would be no pre-warning. He scanned the luminous band of the Milky Way. What he could see there might not even exist anymore. But the light from a long-since irradiated world would keep moving toward them. Until today.

The central star—the yellow sun in the sky—would die before Kepler's eyes. It would simply be ripped from existence. But its light would still warm Kepler's skin until the wave of destruction reached him too, at the speed of light.

What was real? Everything was real. There was no room for imagination. The photons that hit his eyes were real, even though the thing that sent them out didn't exist anymore. He laid an arm around Zhenyi's shoulders. His girlfriend was real. Her warmth streamed through him. A second arm was placed over his. It was Puppy's arm, black, because the butler was wearing his jacket as always. It was a bit heavier than his because it wasn't made of skin and bone. He had still never asked Zhenyi what level AI the butler was. It would be wrong to ask. The butler was no more artificial than he was. And what about Zhenyi? Her body wasn't born from a woman, and her consciousness—who could say for sure whether that was natural or artificial? But he loved this woman, and that was what mattered. That was the reality.

Kepler saw a dragonfly, Then he realized it was in precisely the spot where the center of the Milky Way was located, ten thousand light-years away. Their fate had been decided long ago, and only now was it reaching them.

For the observers orbiting Kepler-1229, the process had just begun, at that moment.

The black hole had been transformed into something else, something more substantial. But in doing so, it remained itself. Its sheer existence was proof of that—the 'dragonfly' that Kepler saw. The Milky Way now had its own quasar. Nothing could be seen of it other than the point of light at its center. It would take millennia for the dragonfly to become a fire-breathing dragon, from which humans could harvest its abundant quasar energy.

Kepler squeezed Zhenyi's arm, because now they knew. The Herbae had calculated correctly, the black hole had cooperated with the calculations, and their sacrifice hadn't been in vain.

Otherwise they themselves would no longer exist.

Author's Note

Dear reader,

Thank you so much for following along as Johannes Kepler and Wang Zhenyi—in Chinese the family name goes first—saved the universe. I hope you liked the conclusion.

For me, it was amusing to move into this very distant future that is billions of years ahead of us. Will anyone remain from what we call humanity? Will our descendants really be able to switch their bodies like vessels, and is a form of immortality unavoidable? Living forever has some undeniable advantages, especially if you take the enormous dimensions of the universe into account. One hundred years of flight time to the nearest star? No problem at all. Compared to infinity, this is just a blink of an eye.

If there is no common calendar, it will also have negative consequences: Humans will separate. They can only share a life with someone else if both people totally synchronize their time. Why, then, not also share a body like the Curies do? And what about our memories? Will we have to outsource them like Kepler? The human brain is enormously powerful, but after billions of years—or maybe much sooner—it might reach a capacity limit in what it can hold. Perhaps we will expand the capacity with artificial storage?

For now, I will keep a few of these ideas to myself. That's because the death of the universe is not yet circumvented. In the next installment, Kepler and Zhenyi will have to take care of the instability the new quasar has brought into our universe. Could the Curies' evil plan ultimately succeed? You can pre-order *The Death of the Universe: Ghost Kingdom* here.

hard-sf.com/links/991276

As always, you can continue with a guide—to the universe, of course. It explains a few of the concepts used in the novel. You will also learn that the version of the universe's death I used is only one of several possible scenarios. Sometimes, an author has to make a choice. Obviously we haven't been there yet, so we cannot be certain.

If you liked this book, please tell other potential readers by writing a short review. Just click here:

hard-sf.com/links/835364

It takes only a few minutes and really helps me.

facebook.com/BrandonQMorris

amazon.com/author/brandonqmorris

bookbub.com/authors/brandon-q-morris

goodreads.com/brandonqmorris

Also by Brandon Q. Morris

The Death of the Universe

For many billions of years, humans—having conquered the curse of aging—spread throughout the entire Milky Way. They are able to live all their dreams, but to their great disappointment, no other intelligent species has ever been encountered. Now, humanity itself is on the brink of extinction because the universe is dying a protracted yet inevitable death.

They have only one hope: The 'Rescue Project' was designed to feed the black hole in the center of the galaxy until it becomes a quasar, delivering much-needed energy to humankind during its last breaths. But then something happens that no one ever expected—and humanity is forced to look at itself and its existence in an entirely new way.

3.99 $ – hard-sf.com/links/835415

The Death of the Universe: Ghost Kingdom

For many billions of years, humans—having conquered the curse of aging—spread throughout the entire Milky Way. They are able to live all their dreams, but to their great disappointment, no other intelligent species has ever been encountered. Now, humanity itself is on the brink of extinction because the universe is dying a protracted yet inevitable death.

They have only one hope: The 'Rescue Project' was designed to feed the black hole in the center of the galaxy until it becomes a quasar, delivering much-needed energy to humankind during its last breaths. But then something happens that no one ever expected—and humanity is forced to look at itself and its existence in an entirely new way.

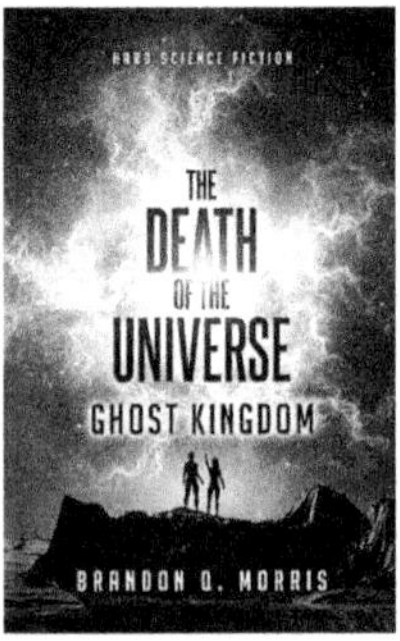

3.99 $ – hard-sf.com/links/991276

The Enceladus Mission (Ice Moon 1)

In the year 2031, a robot probe detects traces of biological activity on Enceladus, one of Saturn's moons. This sensational discovery shows that there is indeed evidence of extraterrestrial life. Fifteen years later, a hurriedly built spacecraft sets out on the long journey to the ringed planet and its moon.

The international crew is not just facing a difficult twenty-seven months: if the spacecraft manages to make it to Enceladus without incident it must use a drillship to penetrate the kilometer-thick sheet of ice that entombs the moon. If life does indeed exist on Enceladus, it could only be at the bottom of the salty, ice covered ocean, which formed billions of years ago.

However, shortly after takeoff disaster strikes the mission, and the chances of the crew making it to Enceladus, let alone back home, look grim.

2.99 $ – hard-sf.com/links/526999

The Titan Probe (Ice Moon 2)

In 2005, the robotic probe "Huygens" lands on Saturn's moon Titan. 40 years later, a radio telescope receives signals from the far away moon that can only come from the long forgotten lander.

At the same time, an expedition returns

from neighbouring moon Enceladus. The crew lands on Titan and finds a dangerous secret that risks their return to Earth. Meanwhile, on Enceladus a deathly race has started that nobody thought was possible. And its outcome can only be decided by the astronauts that are stuck on Titan.

3.99 $ – hard-sf.com/links/527000

The Io Encounter (Ice Moon 3)

Jupiter's moon Io has an extremely hostile environment. There are hot lava streams, seas of boiling sulfur, and frequent volcanic eruptions straight from Dante's Inferno, in addition to constant radiation bombardment and a surface temperature hovering at minus 180 degrees Celsius.

Is it really home to a great danger that threatens all of humanity? That's what a surprise message from the life form discovered on Enceladus seems to indicate.

The crew of ILSE, the International Life Search Expedition, finally on their longed-for return to Earth, reluctantly chooses to accept a diversion to Io, only to discover that an enemy from within is about to destroy all their hopes of ever going home.

3.99 $ – hard-sf.com/links/527008

Return to Enceladus (Ice Moon 4)

Russian billionaire Nikolai Shostakovitch makes an offer to the former crew of the spaceship ILSE. He will finance a return voyage to the icy moon Enceladus. The offer is too good to refuse—the expedition would give them the unique opportunity to recover the body of their doctor, Dimitri Marchenko.

Everyone on board knows that their benefactor acts out of purely personal motivations… but the true interests of the tycoon and the dangers that he conjures up are beyond anyone's imagination.

3.99 € – hard-sf.com/links/527011

Ice Moon - The Boxset

All four bestselling books of the Ice Moon series are now offered as a set, available only in e-book format.

The Enceladus Mission: Is there really life on Saturn's moon Enceladus? *ILSE*, the International Life Search Expedition, makes its way to the icy world where an underground ocean is suspected to be home to primitive life forms.

The Titan Probe: An old robotic NASA probe mysteriously awakens on the methane moon of Titan. The *ILSE* crew tries to solve the riddle—and discovers a dangerous secret.

The Io Encounter: Finally bound for Earth, *ILSE* makes it as far as Jupiter when the crew receives a startling message. The volcanic moon Io may harbor a looming threat that could wipe out Earth as we know it.

Return to Enceladus: The crew gets an offer to go back to Enceladus. Their mission—to recover the body of Dr. Marchenko, left for dead on the original expedition. Not everyone is working toward the same goal. Could it be their unwanted crew member?

9.99 $ – hard-sf.com/links/780838

Proxima Rising

Late in the 21st century, Earth receives what looks like an urgent plea for help from planet Proxima Centauri b in the closest star system to the Sun. Astrophysicists suspect a massive solar flare is about to destroy this heretofore-unknown civilization. Earth's space programs are unequipped to help, but an unscrupulous Russian billionaire launches a secret and highly-specialized spaceship to Proxima b, over four light-years away. The unusual crew faces a Herculean task—should they survive the journey. No one knows what to expect from this alien planet.

3.99 $ – hard-sf.com/links/610690

Proxima Dying

An intelligent robot and two young people explore Proxima Centauri b, the planet orbiting our nearest star, Proxima Centauri. Their ideas about the mission quickly prove grossly naive as they venture about on this planet of extremes.

Where are the senders of the call for help that lured them here? They find no one and no traces on the daylight side, so they place their hopes upon an expedition into the eternal ice on Proxima b's dark side. They not only face everlasting night, the team encounters grave dangers. A fateful decision will change the planet forever.

3.99 $ – hard-sf.com/links/652197

Proxima Dreaming

Alone and desperate, Eve sits in the control center of an alien structure. She has lost the other members of the team sent to explore exoplanet Proxima Centauri b. By mistake she has triggered a disastrous process that threatens to obliterate the planet. Just as Eve fears her best option may be a quick death, a nearby alien life form awakens from a very long sleep. It has only one task: to find and neutralize the destructive intruder from a faraway place.

3.99 $ – hard-sf.com/links/705470

The Hole

A mysterious object threatens to destroy our solar system. The survival of humankind is at risk, but nobody takes the warning of

young astrophysicist Maribel Pedreira seriously. At the same time, an exiled crew of outcasts mines for rare minerals on a lone asteroid.

When other scientists finally acknowledge Pedreira's alarming discovery, it becomes clear that these outcasts are the only ones who may be able to save our world, knowing that *The Hole* hurtles inexorably toward the sun.

3.99 $ – hard-sf.com/links/527017

Silent Sun

Is our sun behaving differently from other stars? When an amateur astronomer discovers something strange on telescopic solar pictures, an explanation must be found. Is it merely artefact? Or has he found something totally unexpected?

An expert international crew is hastily assembled, a spaceship is speedily repurposed, and the foursome is sent on the ride of their lives. What challenges will they face on this spur-of-the-moment mission to our central star?

What awaits all of them is critical, not only for understanding the past, but even more so for the future of life on Earth.

3.99 $ – hard-sf.com/links/527020

The Rift

There is a huge, bold black streak in the sky. Branches appear out of nowhere over North America, Southern Europe, and Central Africa. People who live beneath The Rift can see it. But scientists worldwide are distressed—their equipment cannot pick up any type of signal from it.

The rift appears to consist of nothing. Literally. Nothing. Nada.

Niente. Most people are curious but not overly concerned. The phenomenon seems to pose no danger. It is just there.

Then something jolts the most hardened naysayers, and surpasses the worst nightmares of the world's greatest scientists —and rocks their understanding of the universe.

3.99 $ – hard-sf.com/links/534368

Mars Nation 1

NASA finally made it. The very first human has just set foot on the surface of our neighbor planet. This is the start of a long research expedition that sent four scientists into space.

But the four astronauts of the NASA crew are not the only ones with this destination. The privately financed 'Mars for Everyone' initiative has also targeted the Red Planet. Twenty men and women have been selected to live there and establish the first extraterrestrial settlement.

Challenges arise even before they reach Mars orbit. The MfE spaceship Santa Maria is damaged along the way. Only the four NASA astronauts can intervene and try to save their lives.

No one anticipates the impending catastrophe that threatens their very existence—not to speak of the daily hurdles that an extended stay on an alien planet sets before them. On Mars, a struggle begins for limited resources, human cooperation, and just plain survival.

3.99 $ – hard-sf.com/links/762824

Mars Nation 2

A woman presumed dead fights her way through the hostile deserts of Mars. With her help, the NASA astronauts orphaned on the Red Planet hope to be able to solve their very worst problem. But their hopes are shattered when an unexpected menace arises and threatens to destroy everything the remnant of humanity has built on the planet. They need a miracle—or a ghost from the past whose true intentions are unknown.

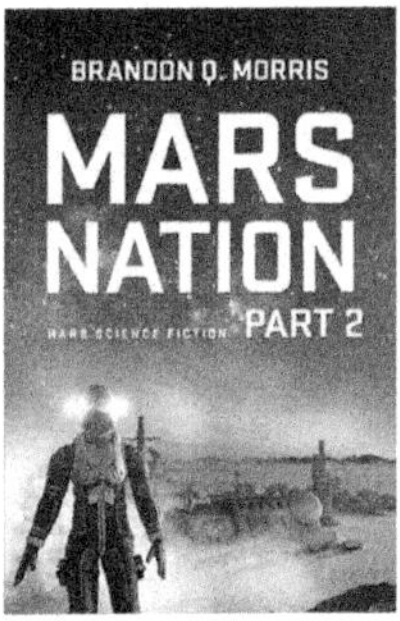

Mars Nation 2 continues the story of the last representatives of Earth, who have found asylum on our neighboring planet, hoping to build a future in this alien world.

3.99 $ – hard-sf.com/links/790047

Mars Nation 3

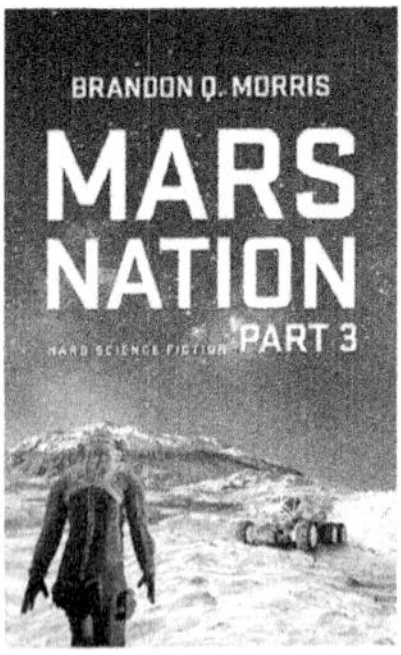

Does the secret of Mars lurk beneath the surface of its south pole? A lone astronaut searches for clues about the earlier inhabitants of the Red Planet. Meanwhile, Rick Summers, having assumed the office of Mars City's Administrator by deceit and manipulation, tries to unify the people on Mars with the weapons under his control. Then Summers stumbles upon so powerful an evil that even he has no means to overcome it.

3.99 $ – hard-sf.com/links/818245

A Guided Tour of the Universe

Introducing The Universe

Allow me to introduce the universe, from the Latin 'universus' meaning 'whole.' Also known as the cosmos, space, outer space. Born 13.8 billion years ago. Today, around 92 billion light-years across—but probably infinite and topologically flat—and weighing 10^{53} kilograms—a 1 with 53 zeroes—but still not fully grown.

On the run: Because the universe is continuously growing, all its components appear to be moving away from us. That means that the further an object is from Earth, the faster it's fleeing. At a distance of one megaparsec—more than three million light-years—this Hubble speed amounts to 72 kilometers per second.

Cold: The cosmic background radiation contributes to its temperature of nearly minus 270 degrees Celsius—which is not quite absolute zero (minus 273.15).

Empty: Indeed, our night sky is richly populated. But that's deceptive, because fundamentally speaking the universe consists of empty space. If you built a huge house, say 30 kilometers cubed, you'd only need to place a single grain of sand inside it to represent a similar average density. Every cubic meter of the cosmos contains an average of 0.3 protons.

Electrically neutral: There are, it seems, exactly as many carriers of positive charges as negative ones.

Low levels of antimatter: Proof that the laws of nature for particles and antiparticles are not symmetrical.

Without a center: Our Milky Way Galaxy has a core, but the universe as a whole has no center.

Populated by 100 billion galaxies in which 130 sextillion stars and roughly the same number of planets have come together. There are more stars in the universe than there are grains of sand on all of Earth's beaches.

Known types of matter make up 4 percent of the universe, including approximately 1.57 x 10^{79} protons and electrons and a billion times more photons. Add to that 23 percent dark matter, and 73 percent dark energy. Between 90 and 99 percent of the neutral atoms of the universe are hydrogen atoms.

Home to black holes, giant stars, pulsars, quasars, galaxy clusters, nebulae—but also planets with their moons and life forms such as humans.

WHERE DID the universe come from? What were the circumstances of its birth? Which fascinating processes have played out in it since? When and how will it die?

What scientists know about all of this has changed dramatically in recent years. Allow yourself to be carried away to a world beyond all imagination—the cosmos in which you live.

The time before time

THE EXISTENCE of everything might not have started at Zero Hour. A biography normally begins with birth—for the universe, the widely accepted theory of the Big Bang. But sometimes it's worth looking at the parents, or at least generally at the genealogy of the object of the biography.

And that's not to imply a creator of the universe. In *The Grand Design*, Stephen Hawking demonstrated very vividly why the universe didn't require a creator. That doesn't stop anyone from believing in a God. But from a scientific point of view, the presence of any structure that isn't necessary for the laws of physics, or indeed the world to function, is irrelevant. In any case, the concept of a creator is not an object of scientific research, but one of human belief.

It is nevertheless worthwhile to search for predecessors, ancestors, parents of the universe as we know it, because... the Big Bang has a small problem. Literally, it must have played out in the tiniest of spaces. The closer you come to it, the more densely the total energy of the cosmos must have been compressed in a unit of space, until everything was concentrated in one point of infinite density. This state is incompatible with the Theory of General Relativity. This is where Einstein's work falls short. Physicists therefore view the Big

Bang in combination with a theory of the macro and the micro—the universe and the quantum world.

A world made of strings

For this we have two candidates. One is string theory, according to which space is made up of tiny objects something like piano strings. These 'strings' are one-dimensional, and they vibrate with a particular frequency that can be assigned an energy. Physicists have now developed this idea into 'M Theory' along with other structures, point particles, and especially branes, which can have up to nine dimensions. To get from there to the elementary particles and laws of nature as we know them, you have to 'wind'—as the scientists call this process—the extra dimensions in a precise way. There are various possibilities for winding the branes and strings, and depending on the one you choose, a different kind of universe arises. There are a possible 10 to the power of 100 different possible universes, an unimaginable number. And yet a large proportion of these universes consist or consisted of the basic structures, the branes, without ever arriving at the formation of elementary particles.

Of course, many of these universes could also exist simultaneously, with the inhabitants of one having no inkling of the living beings that may exist in another. However, according to the scientists who support this theory, if three-dimensional worlds came too close to one another, due to movement through an additional eleventh dimension, they could collide—resulting in the birth of our universe in the Big Bang. What happens after that depends on the subsequent behavior of the colliding branes. If these come close to one another again, a repetitive cycle could be the result.

Loops upon loops

When considering the world before the world, a competing theory, loop quantum gravity, is even more fruitful. According to that theory, the universe only *appears* to be continuous. Actually, everything, absolutely everything, is quantized, which means everything is divided into small granules, even gravitation. Space is no longer the container of the universe, it's a part of it, which is itself divided into granules and takes on the form of a net made of lines and knots. The elementary particles then correspond to various types of knots. In between the lines and knots is nothing. Not empty space, but rather nothing at all. The theory of loop quantum gravity draws some seemingly strange conclusions, but it describes certain interesting phenomena better than other theories.

The significance of this theory for the Big Bang was first simulated in 2004 by German physicist Martin Bojowald. The first thing is to abandon the concept of the singularity, because the loop quantum universe has a certain minimum structure size, which it can't go below. The closer you get to the Big Bang, the less it appears to be an insurmountable barrier. Instead, you reach the minus time with a 'pop'—a new, different, or precursor universe, in which all directions—including that of time—are reversed. This is not a big problem for physicists, because the laws of nature are conveniently symmetrical. This 'universe before the universe' contracted toward the Big Bang.

This theory has revived the once-popular 'Big Bounce'—the idea that the universe periodically contracts and expands. If the universe contracts a great deal under the influence of gravity, then the quantum loop fabric will eventually rupture space-time—and under the influence of this 'quantum recoil,' gravity will turn into a powerfully repulsive force that forces the universe outward again.

Rebirth from nothing

A third mechanism for a cyclically changing universe was suggested in 2011 by English mathematician Roger Penrose. He dedicates himself to the phenomenon of time in his book *Cycles of Time*. A popular concept of the end of the universe is that at some point all matter turns into energy, into photons moving eternally at the speed of light, for which time therefore stands still—an astronaut flying at the speed of light would not age either. Space would then lose its meaning, because its expansion isn't measurable when there's no time.

Who could disprove that a billion light-years aren't just a few centimeters?

It might sound strange, but that's exactly how the universe looked shortly after the Big Bang. The universe consisted of pure energy for which there was no concept of time. However, only a mathematician would dare to combine such seemingly distant states into one. If its expansion in space is not defined, then the universe that has just perished into eternal energy could also provide the seed of a new Big Bang.

Nothing but theories?

Can any of these theories be proved? So far this has all basically been plausible fiction. But scientists have ideas about how they might trace the legacy of the precursor universe. Because not everything has to perish in the 'Big Crunch.' In 2017, Bernard Carr and Alan Coley demonstrated that a specific type of black hole could survive the unfavorable conditions of the Big Bang. Unfortunately, the search for such ancient objects is made difficult by the fact that low-mass black holes could also have arisen *during* the Big Bang. Their existence was deduced by Stephen Hawking in the 1970s.

These 'primordial' black holes have been just as hard to locate as their even older cousins from the precursor universe—the less mass such an object has, the harder it is to find. Even in the Penrose universe there could be remnants of the precursor universe. Its mass wouldn't necessarily have been completely annihilated. It would have been sufficient for the amount of energy simply to have vastly exceeded it.

The Big Bang

THE DEFINING MOMENTS of the universe began in darkness. So far scientists haven't had the theoretical means to probe back to the beginning of the universe—and yet they have some very concrete ideas about it.

Zero Hour

Scientists still don't know with any certainty what happened at the beginning, about 13.8 billion years ago. The total matter of the universe—today 10^{53} kilograms—was at this moment located at a single point, a singularity, in which the laws of nature did not yet have any influence. So you have to imagine a kind of infinitely dense primordial soup, consisting of particles that are no longer known today. A force, the primordial force, determined the movement of these particles. The temperature of the primordial soup, if you can even use the term 'temperature,' must have been about 10^{32} degrees. There were neither electrons nor photons, nor was there any light. If there had been an 'outside,' an observer wouldn't even have been able to see what was currently playing out.

This ultra-hot something was under immense pressure, and the cosmos expanded. The length of time this took is calculated based on the known laws of nature. It's equivalent to Planck time, that is, the time light takes to cover a Planck length. That's 10^{-43} or 0.000,000,000,000,000,000,000,000,000,000,000,000,000,000,1 seconds. In any case, at this point in time, 'time' didn't yet exist. The English language is insufficient to accurately convey this paradox.

Physics begins

It's not until 10^{-43} seconds after the Big Bang that we can even begin to use physics to try to understand the universe. The tiny drop of matter was still under unbelievable pressure. But it had cooled a little because it had expanded. Then gravity was separated off from the primordial force, counteracting the expansion of the universe by exerting an attractive force.

But gravity was much weaker than the pressure of the Big Bang, so the universe continued to expand at a rapid pace. Because this expansion reduced the average energy of the primordial soup, it contained fewer and fewer of those exotic particles that existed at the beginning. After 10^{-38} seconds had passed, the powerful nuclear force and the electroweak force were also separated from the primordial force.

The universe—a soccer ball

Next followed the so-called inflation phase, in which the universe expanded by a factor between 10^{30} and 10^{50}. This means that if it had been the size of a proton, it expanded to the size of a soccer ball. This inflation, which scientists place between 10^{-38} and 10^{-35} seconds after the Big Bang, needed so-called inflatons to provide a reasonable explanation—that is, one fitting into the cosmological world view. These particles, which never reappeared again, were not pulled toward each other by gravity, but instead they repelled each other.

This is seen as the only way the universe could have grown so much in such a short time. The reason this explanation is not considered absurd is the fact that it provides an explanation for other phenomena in the cosmos today, such as the homogeneity of the universe and its low curvature.

The first particles

10^{-35} seconds after the Big Bang, the density of the

universe was now high enough for the first particles known to us today to come into being. For example, electrons and positrons, quarks—which later combined to become protons and neutrons—and antiquarks, neutrinos, precursors to photons, and gluons, which were responsible for the strong nuclear force.

Particles and antiparticles existed in equal numbers. When they met, they mutually annihilated each other. There was a constant coming and going. The new particles behaved normally under the influence of gravity. They attracted one another, which caused the expansion of the universe to decelerate somewhat. A quark-gluon plasma prevailed at this time, and this can be simulated today by computers.

All forces already exist

Scientists are still not in agreement, but if the laws of nature were ever subject to supersymmetry, then they were broken. The theory of supersymmetry assumes that for every known particle, there was a superpartner that differed by half a spin. Supersymmetry elegantly combines particles and force carrier particles, which mediate the known interactions.

These superpartners would have to have been so heavy that they could only have existed at the initial stage of the universe. Today we can only observe ordinary particles, so this supersymmetry no longer exists. It's assumed that, at the moment supersymmetry was dismantled, the particles received their mass from the still hypothetical Higgs boson.

About 10^{-10} seconds after the Big Bang, the last two forces that are known today came into existence, the weak nuclear force—which plays a significant role in nuclear fusion—and the electromagnetic force. A little later, the universe cooled down to just two trillion degrees so that quarks could no longer exist alone, and protons and neutrons, or antiprotons and antineutrons, joined together. The gluons served as the glue.

Matter and antimatter still existed in equal amounts. But this state didn't persist for long. Particles and antiparticles were incinerated into photons, and the universe, which was now 10 trillion kilometers—about a light-year—across and a trillion degrees, emptied rapidly. We owe the fact that we even exist to a small amount of excess matter. At that point, from one billion particle-antiparticle pairs there emerged one excess particle that was not destroyed. There are only guesses as to where this asymmetry came from. Obviously, the laws of nature are not symmetrical in every respect.

The next wave of annihilation

A fifth of a second after the Big Bang, the universe was 500 trillion kilometers across, roughly 50 light-years. Its interior had cooled to 20 billion degrees. Now neutrons and electrons took center stage. The naturally unstable neutrons were shattered by the weak nuclear force into an electron, a proton, and a neutrino. Electrons and positrons annihilated each other, and there was again an excess of matter.

About one second after the Big Bang, considering the now vast cosmic distances, the weak nuclear force was no longer strong enough to provide a nuclear force between neutrinos and ordinary matter. The neutrinos released at that time have been racing through the universe ever since, with almost no interactions, as a measurable, constant neutrino background.

From then on the development of the universe proceeded much more slowly. The remaining neutrons were preserved when, about two to three minutes after T-zero, deuterium and then helium atoms formed. The strong nuclear force now protected the neutrons from being destroyed. Meanwhile the universe grew and grew, continually cooling as it did so.

After about 17 minutes it was too cold for further nuclear fusion to take place. At this point all remaining neutrons were bound to atomic nuclei. Approximately three-quarters of the nuclei were hydrogen nuclei, the rest were helium—heavy nuclei existed only in trace amounts.

As it became colder, electrons bonded electromagnetically to positively-charged atomic nuclei. But they were constantly thrown off course by the photons of the still-hot primordial soup. At this point, the universe, composed predominantly of light particles, would have looked to an observer like a glowing nebula.

This didn't change for a relatively long time. From about 70,000 years after the Big Bang, the ratio of atomic mass to radiation was 1:1. According to the Lambda-Cold Dark Matter model, the universe was now dominated by dark matter, the nature of which can only be theorized about today. As a result, non-homogeneous regions left over after the inflation phase contracted even more, a prerequisite for the later formation of stars.

The clear universe

AROUND 380,000 YEARS after the Big Bang, the foundation for one of the first pieces of evidence humans have for our theory of the origin of the universe emerged—cosmic background radiation.

At a temperature of just over 2,700 degrees, the protons no longer had enough energy to smash electrons out of their orbits around atomic nuclei. So the light was no longer diffuse—the universe suddenly became apparent, and the era of the neutral atom began. Today, every cubic centimeter of the cosmic vacuum contains about 400 light particles of cosmic background radiation. In the context of the history of the cosmos, scientists call this event 'recombination.'

But the universe was still not completely clear—only optical light could disperse itself unhindered, but not ultraviolet light, which was absorbed by the hydrogen nuclei that filled the universe to a large extent at that time. The expansion of the universe changed the wavelength of optical light. Initially a bright blaze, the cosmos gradually became a reddish color. The red became darker and darker, then purple, and finally infrared—in other words, black to the naked eye. 13.8 billion years later the cosmic background radiation was in the microwave range. That's why scientists call it the Cosmic Dark Ages.

The first beacon fires

It was during this era that the first stars flickered into existence. At a very early stage, dark matter increased non-homogeneities in the structure of the universe to such an extent that there were areas with hydrogen in higher concentration. Huge bubbles formed—called halos—imposing a structure on the universe shaped by inflation and dark matter, long before the formation of galaxies.

Although dark matter is invisible, it still has an effect on the matter known to us, through its gravitational force. This meant that the interstellar hydrogen also conglomerated in the halos of dark matter. The closer the particles came to one another, the more the pressure increased in the gas—until pressure and gravitation were in balance. The cloud cooled due to the radiation given out by the collision of particles. Then the pressure was reduced and the cloud could contract further. The more mass that collects in a small space, the stronger its attractive effect on the atoms in its vicinity. Temperature and pressure increased again in the interior of the cloud, which began to radiate infrared.

Thus the stage of the protostar was reached—but there were still no nuclear reactions. The future star consisted of ionized atoms, of plasma. The heavier the cloud became, the faster it contracted—and at some point the temperature of around 3 million Kelvin and the pressure were so high that a process of atomic fusion was triggered—two protons collided, transforming with the release of energy into a deuterium nucleus with a proton and a neutron. The deuterium then reacted with another proton to become a helium nucleus, which in turn released more energy. Once the interior of the star was hot enough—upwards of 10 million Kelvin—the He_3 nuclei could then fuse into He_4, releasing two protons. The effect of all this was that about 100 million years after the Big Bang, the first stars began to light up.

They died young

Our sun is barely comparable to these very first cosmic beacons, which today are referred to as 'population III stars.'

First of all, they must have consisted of hydrogen and helium, because there were no other elements in the early universe. That's also how these stars could be identified—the spectrum of a star reveals its structure. By comparison, about 1.8 percent of the mass of our sun consists of heavy elements. But due to the low mass of its components, a population III star must have been much larger than our sun—it's estimated that the early stars had at least 100 times the mass of the sun. They burned fast and hot and therefore must have long since turned into supernovas. And yet it's still possible to observe them, in far distant galaxies whose light takes such a long time to reach us that it gives us a glimpse far back into the past.

The light from these stars had a side effect—the radiation ionized the hydrogen gas in the area. The interstellar gas could therefore no longer absorb any more ultraviolet light, and the universe became brighter again. This re-ionization phase must have begun around 200 million years after the Big Bang. At first this happened in bubbles. It would have taken up to 800 million years for the universe to become completely transparent again. But even today there are molecular clouds whose components are not ionized.

Scientists surmise that there were in fact two re-ionization phases. The first, probably giant and fast-burning stars ended their lives at some point in an enormous explosion, a supernova, which blasted the surrounding gas cloud out into the nothingness. This made the formation of their successors more complicated. The hydrogen and helium nuclei now had an opportunity to capture electrons. It wasn't until about a billion years later that new stars were able to compensate for this effect.

A fascinating death

It's also exciting the way the very first stars met their end. If they had 130 to 250 solar masses, this could result in a pair-instability supernova. Because the stars were so deficient in heavy elements, despite their high masses, the pressure in the core was not enough to start the synthesis of other elements after the helium had burned away. Instead, the temperature in the core increased more and more until the existing photons had enough energy for electron-positron pairs to be created. Although these were quickly annihilated, the result of this process was that the radiation couldn't leave the interior of the star quickly enough. Hence the core heated up again, followed by another electron-positron reaction, until this feedback loop eventually led to the star being completely torn apart. Unlike with ordinary supernovas, there was nothing left to form a black hole. The star's entire mass was flung out into space. A pair-instability supernova releases 100 times more energy than a typical supernova—which itself is no weak campfire in the sky.

If one of these first stars had more than 250 solar masses, another type of supernova could have resulted—photodisintegration. Particularly high-energy photons can knock protons out of nuclei. This is an endothermic process wherein the star is deprived of energy. The core suddenly becomes colder and can no longer withstand the pressure of its environment—it collapses and finally turns into a black hole. While the released protons can lead to the formation of heavier elements, part of the mass of the dying giant star is discharged into the surrounding space in a jet.

Group dynamics

Both of these processes finally led to a gradual change in the composition of the universe. The next generation of stars benefited from this. We're now talking about population II. They required less base material to catalyze nuclear fusion, and because of that they burned less brightly, but for much longer. Even these stars eventually turned to ash, from which the population I stars were formed. Our 4.57 billion-year-old sun belongs to this younger generation.

But let's take a step back. The first stars did not only affect their immediate surroundings. Their gravity influenced others of their kind. About 500 million years after the Big Bang, the first galaxies formed.

Compared to today, the early universe was very lively. Small galaxies combined to form larger ones. There were clashes and hostile takeovers. We now know that this development was not purely random. Rather, star formation was concentrated around subtle dark matter structures in the universe, called filaments. Where these filaments met, galaxies and galaxy clusters emerged. The observable universe today contains several million of these galactic superclusters. One example of them, the Virgo supercluster, with a diameter of 110 million light-years, is home to a few thousand galaxies... including the Milky Way as part of the local group.

Fragile spirals

We don't know for sure how the different types of galaxies formed. It's assumed that dark matter played a role in forming the more common spiral galaxies, of which the Milky Way is one. Dark matter only interacts gravitationally, whereas ordinary matter is also affected by the radiation pressure of stars. That's why dark matter was able to concentrate in the outer reaches of the galaxy, where its halo was. The interstellar gas, simultaneously attracted strongly by the core of the galaxy and weakly by its outer reaches, therefore moved on a spiral course toward the core, as though someone was swinging a cat by its tail.

The problem with this model is that the contraction stopped at some point, and cosmologists still don't know why. Spiral galaxies are also very fragile structures—galactic collisions should actually have deformed them much more than they apparently have. Scientists now regard the elliptical galaxy as the endpoint. These have arisen mostly as a result of the fusion of smaller galaxies. According to one simulation, this could also be imminent for the Milky Way and our neighbor M31, Andromeda. The simulation suggests that, in about 3 to 4.5 billion years, there will be a collision between the two roughly equal systems. The result is likely to be a gigantic elliptical galaxy.

It was probably also the particular composition of the earliest galaxies that produced a phenomenon that astronomers initially thought to be a special kind of star—a quasar. Scientists now agree that these are active galactic nuclei, probably substantial black holes. Although our Milky Way has an impressive black hole at its center, compared to a quasar it's pretty humble.

The 3C 273 quasar, for example, can be seen from Earth through an amateur telescope, even though it's almost at the edge of the observable universe. From a distance of 33 light-years it would look as bright as the sun looks from the Earth. The quasar is about 100 times as bright as all the stars in the Milky Way combined. The black hole at its center must be correspondingly large. The fact that quasars can be observed only at a considerable distance from us is proof that the conditions for their formation no longer exist.

Planets from the debris

Even today, scattered throughout the universe, new stars continue to ignite. But the birth rate has dropped significantly since the early days. The expansion of space reduces the density of the interstellar gas. The conditions are particularly difficult for infant stars. However, after the birth of a star there is almost always a kind of afterbirth—a hot disk of gas and dust around the star.

And there are non-homogeneities in this, which increase under the influence of gravity. The molecules clump together and form ever-larger bodies, which attract each other. If the process continues uninterrupted for long enough, a hot proto planet is created. Depending on the source material, this may become a gas giant or a rocky planet like Earth. The celestial body eventually cools down and may later be hospitable to life.

Glossary of Acronyms

AGN – Active Galactic Nucleus

AI – Artificial Intelligence

AU – Astronomical Unit (the distance from the Earth to the sun)

DNA – DeoxyriboNucleic Acid

WMAP – Wilkinson Microwave Anisotropy Probe

Metric to English Conversions

It is assumed that by the time the events of this novel take place, the United States will have joined the rest of the world and will be using the International System of Units, the modern form of the metric system.

Length:
centimeter = 0.39 inches
meter = 1.09 yards, or 3.28 feet
kilometer = 1093.61 yards, or 0.62 miles

Area:
square centimeter = 0.16 square inches
square meter = 1.20 square yards
square kilometer = 0.39 square miles

Weight:
gram = 0.04 ounces
kilogram = 35.27 ounces, or 2.20 pounds

Volume:
liter = 1.06 quarts, or 0.26 gallons
cubic meter = 35.31 cubic feet, or 1.31 cubic yards

Temperature:
To convert Celsius to Fahrenheit, multiply by 1.8 and then add 32
To convert Kelvin to Celsius, subtract 273.15

Brandon Q. Morris
--
www.hard-sf.com
brandon@hard-sf.com
Translator: Siân Robertson
Editing team: Marcia Kwiecinski, A.A.S., and Stephen Kwiecinski, B.S.

Printed in Great Britain
by Amazon

25713461R00179